MY WILD IRISH
DRAGON

ASHLYN CHASE

D1025459

sourcebooks
casablanca

Published by Sourcebooks Casablanca, an imprint of Sourcebooks, Inc.
P.O. Box 4410, Naperville, Illinois 60567-4410
(630) 961-3900
Fax: (630) 961-2168
www.sourcebooks.com

Printed and bound in Canada.
MBP 10 9 8 7 6 5 4 3 2 1

To first responders everywhere.

Unlike my dragons, you're not fireproof,
and yet you put your lives on the line
every day, for complete strangers.

I am in awe of you.

Chapter 1

CHLOE ARISH SAT ON A HARD PLASTIC CHAIR OUTSIDE the fire chief's office, tapping her foot while she awaited her second interview for a job as a Boston firefighter. She had already passed the civil service exam and the candidate physical ability test. The written test and oral exam were more difficult for her than the physical stuff, but thanks to some coaching by her friend and fellow dragon/firefighter Drake Cameron, she had passed with flying colors.

Actually, the one thing she was most worried about was her fake birth certificate. Now that she was a naturalized U.S. citizen and had been a resident of Boston for over a year, she met the most basic requirements. But her life's history on paper was completely false, and this job came with background checks.

Fortunately, her Ulster cousins knew "a bloke" who could create a realistic forgery, picking a birthday that didn't indicate her real age, which was well over a thousand years old. She didn't look a day over twenty-three, so her phony birth certificate was made to match. Just for kicks, they picked July 4 as her birthday. America's birthday.

Just as she was checking her watch for the umpteenth time, the door opened and out strolled a six-foot Adonis. Dark hair, chiseled features, and olive skin.

He was followed by the chief, who clasped him in a man-hug, and they pounded each other on their backs.

"Give my best to your family," the chief said. "I'm sure we'll see each other soon."

"I will. And say hello to yours for me."

Oh, feck. They know each other. Chloe had heard that nepotism was a regular thing among firefighters.

The chief nodded to her. "I'll be with you shortly," he said and returned to his office.

The Greek god gazed at her with intense dark eyes. "So, you're here for an interview too?"

She straightened to her full five-foot-five stature. "I am."

"Let me guess. You're a secretary? Or what is it called now? Administrative assistant?"

Her eyes widened. *What a chauvinist pig!* Did she want to give him the satisfaction of an outraged reaction? Hell yes.

"I'm here to interview for the firefighter position. Not that it's any of your business."

He had the audacity to laugh. "A little thing like you?"

She seethed inwardly and longed to shift into her dragon form, to breathe a column of fire right into his face. Or not. That would be a crime—in more ways than one.

She tipped her chin up. "I passed the CPAT in record time."

"Really?" He said it as if he didn't believe her. "Record time, huh? I did too. I wonder who broke whose record?"

This arrogant fecker was getting to her. She had to tamp down her anger and quickly, before she started snorting smoke out of her nose. Revealing her paranormal status to humans was strictly forbidden. She had never done it, but she knew someone who had. Mother Nature herself had punished the offender. The goddess was *not* someone she wanted to piss off—and Gaia seemed to have a temper as quick as Chloe's.

Injure them with kindness was an American saying she was fond of. Or was it *Kill them with kindness*? She couldn't quite keep all the slang straight, but the meanings got through.

She smiled. "It looks like you may get the position. After all, they say it's *who* you know—not *what* you know." At least she hoped she'd quoted that one correctly.

His back stiffened and he frowned.

Yup. Got that one right.

Then he relaxed and smiled, as if he didn't care. "Or I could get it because of both. What do you have as an advantage—other than your sex?"

She gasped. "Excuse me? Are you accusing me of sleeping my way into the job?"

He coughed. "No, that's not what I meant. Not at all. I just meant that your sex is *female*. As in, your *gender*. There's only one woman in the whole department right now. They may want another one so they won't be accused of gender bias."

Oh, this ass is just digging himself in deeper and deeper.

"I don't need to use that to my advantage, but it's good to know." This time her smile probably looked somewhat evil as she pictured herself punching this guy in the gut. Messing with Chloe Arish was *not* a good idea.

The door opened and the chief said, "Come in, Miss Arish."

At last. It was her turn to prove she deserved and

wanted this job more than he did…probably more than *anyone* did. And her *sex* had nothing to do with it.

———

"So, you want to be a firefighter," the chief began as he took his comfortable-looking chair behind the desk.

"Yes, sir," she answered respectfully.

"Your scores are certainly impressive. You must be a lot stronger than you look."

You have no idea. Dragons were not only very strong, they were fireproof and healed quickly. She couldn't be better suited for the job.

"Tell me why you wish to join our band of *brothers*," he said. It almost sounded like he was trying to provoke a response.

She wouldn't rise to the bait. "Well, sir, there was a fire back in my hometown. Our small volunteer fire department took too long getting from their homes to the station, and then to the scene. I heard children crying. The garda—policeman wouldn't go in himself and wouldn't let me in. I could have helped. I'm fast and light on my feet. I could have made it to that bedroom before the whole place went up. One child died of smoke inhalation and the other was badly burned."

Leaning forward in his chair, the chief asked, "What about the parents?"

"They were at the pub, sir."

The chief waited, perhaps looking for some kind of judgmental reaction. She wouldn't voice her personal feelings about the adults involved in the incident. Her heart had broken when she'd seen those children.

She needed to change the subject before the lump in

her throat grew too large to speak around. "I've been helpin' me brother and his wife rebuild an old brownstone on Beacon Street for the past year, so this would be perfect timin'." *Get yourself together, Chloe.* She tended to lapse back into her Irish dialect when something upset her. "It was gratifying work, but it's done. I would like more than anything to do something even more satisfying, such as protecting the neighborhood I've grown so fond of."

Chief O'Brian's eyes lit up. "Did I detect an Irish accent?"

Feck. She had been working so hard to rid herself of the telltale accent, hoping she could pass for an American. "You did, sir. I was born in Ireland."

He grinned. "My grandparents hailed from County Clare. Where did you come from?"

She almost slipped again and said County Kerry...but thank goodness she caught herself in time. Her cousins had given her a birth certificate that said she was born in Belfast. The Ulster address grated, but she couldn't exactly be choosy.

"I was born outside Belfast, sir. But we spent a lot of time in County Clare when I was a child." Best not to share that her father's family were the kings of Ballyhoo, Ireland—farther to the south—and she'd grown up in a castle built into the cliffs. If he checked the history books, he *might* find her name dating back a thousand years, so she left it at that.

His expression became serious. "Belfast... That might actually help. In this job, we don't *only* respond to fires. You may see some gruesome things. Did you grow up knowing any survivors of the IRA bombings?"

She thought back to the Battle of Ballyhoo. Her father, the king, had had to slaughter his own brother and others involved in his attempted overthrow. They'd used boiling oil as well as crossbows, swords, and other weapons of the time. Such was the way of kingdoms and family feuds back then.

"I have seen many burn victims, dismembered bodies, and the like. It isn't pretty, but that's another reason I'm motivated to prevent such tragedies."

The chief leaned back in his chair, apparently impressed. He didn't say anything for several moments. And then, "Have you ever thought about becoming a nurse?"

Ah. There it was. That bias. But how should she answer that?

"Well, sir, by the time people come to the hospital, it's too late to *prevent* these tragedies. I'd really like to do all I can to stop the situations before anyone gets hurt."

He stared at her as if he had something specific in mind. "How are you at teaching?"

Shite. If not a nurse, he wants me to become a teacher. Can't women do anything else? She was just about to go off on a rant when he steepled his fingers and continued.

"I only bring it up because we're sometimes asked to present talks to elementary school kids. Most of the guys dread those things. You seem to like children."

"Ah." *Whew.* She was glad she'd managed to keep her famous temper under control. "I'd consider it an honor to teach fire prevention to such an impressionable population."

The chief smiled and seemed satisfied with her answer. Then he shifted uncomfortably in his chair.

When he was settled again, he stared at her. "There's only one position, and to be completely honest, I had thought the last candidate was a shoo-in. Now I'm not so sure."

How should I respond to that? Thank you? She opted not to respond at all. She really did feel she was the right *woman* for the job, but saying so might sound like she was playing the gender card.

"Hmmm…" The chief stroked his clean-shaven chin. "I'm going to have to give this some serious thought. Keep your cell phone on. I want to talk with someone and get back to you as soon as possible."

Hallelujah! She had a chance.

Chloe walked into the hall and was surprised to see the Greek god still standing there.

"Sorry, sweetheart. I hope you didn't have your heart set on the position."

He's still assuming I can't do the job. Well, I'll show both of them I can. She dipped low and grasped him under his delectable buttocks. Then she hoisted him over her shoulder and swung around to face the stunned chief.

"As you can see, lifting a grown man isn't a problem. In fact, I could carry him down the hall and deposit him on the sidewalk without breaking perspiration."

The chief burst out laughing, but her hostage let out a growl and said, "Put me down. Now!"

"Sure, *sweetheart.*"

As soon as she'd set him on his feet, she turned to leave. She didn't miss the furious look on his face nor the flash in his dark eyes that would have skewered her, if he'd had the power.

"I think you meant to say, 'without breaking a sweat,'"

the chief called after her. He chuckled and murmured, "Adorable," under his breath. Fortunately he returned to his office before any more could be said.

—⁓⁓—

Ryan Fierro stared after the retreating figure of an incredibly surprising woman. She'd embarrassed him in front of an old family friend, and if it got back to his large, legendary firefighting family, he'd never hear the end of it. Even with that, he couldn't help being impressed by the slender blonde.

She didn't look back as she rounded the corner. Behind him, the chief's door clicked shut.

Oh no. He wasn't about to leave Chief O'Brian with *that* as his final impression. He pounded on the door.

As if the chief had been expecting a reaction, he opened it right away. He didn't stand aside, however. Apparently they were to have their parting words right there in the hallway.

"You can't... I mean... I hope you won't consider her based on that little stunt she just pulled."

Chief O'Brian folded his arms. "Not at all."

Ryan let out a relieved breath—until the chief spoke again.

"I was already considering her."

What? "But my family... If I lose out to a girl..." He scrubbed his hand over his face. He didn't know how to finish that sentence. *They'd never respect me? Never forgive me?*

Sure, his mother would. She was a saint. Her face should be in psychology textbooks next to the words "unconditional love." His father and six brothers, however, were another story. Their Sunday dinner conversations were unmatched when it came to fire-fighting bravado.

The chief clasped his shoulder. "Look, Ryan, I have to consider every candidate who makes it this far. I'm sure you understand that. It's nothing personal."

"Nothing personal? It sounds as if you've already decided."

"Not at all."

The chief took a good look at Ryan's face, which must have been etched with worry lines. At last he lowered his voice and said, conspiratorially, "I'm going to speak to the commissioner. Perhaps we can find the funds to hire both of you."

So it all comes down to money. What a surprise…not.

There wasn't a damn thing Ryan could do about a budget. He doubted the chief could influence the com-missioner—or the mayor—into allotting more money, even for the pricey Back Bay neighborhood. They had recently lost two firefighters in the line of duty. He'd heard one had already been replaced, but he assumed *he* would be replacing the other one.

Ryan gazed at his feet and nodded. "I understand. Well, thank you for the opportunity."

"You're not out of the race yet, boy. Something could still come from the background checks, or any number of things. I want to be fair and thorough. Don't get dis-couraged if there's a bit of a wait."

"I won't, sir." The chief extended his hand and Ryan grasped it firmly. The handshake felt like a formal dismissal.

As the chief's door closed, Ryan thought that maybe

he should do a little background checking too. Just in case they missed something on the blonde.

———∞———

"How did it go?" Ryan's mother asked at the dinner table that night. "Do we have another firefighter in the family?"

His father laughed. "Of course we do! There's no way they could turn down our brightest son." He turned toward his wife and beamed. "It's a good thing the rest of them aren't here. Don't tell them I said he was the brightest."

"Of course I won't," she said. "All of our sons have their own strengths and talents, and we love them all equally."

"So, which one are you again?" his father asked jokingly.

Ryan felt his face heat. He tried to hide it by shoveling an extra-large bite of spaghetti into his mouth.

His mother folded her hands. "So, when do you start, dear?"

He shrugged and chewed slowly.

His father eyed him. "Something's not right. What aren't you telling us?"

They waited silently, until he couldn't pretend to chew anymore and swallowed.

"Uh, there are background checks to finish and I guess some financial stuff has come up. The chief said to be patient."

His father leaned back in his chair at the head of the table. "Ah. That's just a formality. You've never been in any trouble with the law. You're a U.S. citizen…"

As his father droned on about the reasons an applicant could be denied, Ryan had a brainstorm. The blonde had an accent. Granted, it was faint, but he'd heard it. And the way she'd butchered American slang… She wasn't from the USA. With any luck, she'd turn out to be an illegal alien.

"So, how many applicants did you beat out?" Mr. Fierro was asking.

Shit. Lying wouldn't do any good. The chief was his father's oldest friend and the blonde would come up in conversation at some point.

"I only saw one other…*person* when I went for the interview. There were about a dozen names on the roster, taking the CPAT, but we didn't all go on the same day. They said I broke the record that day, so I took that as a good sign."

His father looked at him askance. "You didn't do anything that would tip them off about our paranormal abilities, did you?"

Ryan stiffened his back, offended. "Of course not. I ran the course completely as a human. How can you think I'd do anything else?"

His father nodded slowly. "Just checking."

"You've always been so competitive," his mother added. "I don't blame your father for asking, even though we believe you know better."

As always, she was playing the diplomat. Still, it was time to change the subject.

"So, what's new with you, Mother? Have you beauti-fied the city lately—other than with your lovely face?"

His father rolled his eyes, but his mother gave him a loving grin and giggled.

"How sweet of you to ask. Yes, as a matter of fact, the gardening club found this barren traffic island in Mattapan near the T station. We thought we'd plant some daffodils there."

"Waste of time, if you ask me," his father grumped. "Nobody's gonna take care of them."

Gabriella Fierro laid her gentle hand on his arm. "That's why we decided on bulbs. They come with their own food supply and as long as they receive a little rain, they'll bloom easily year after year. They even multiply on their own."

"Yeah, like the rats," Antonio Fierro muttered.

"We can't all be lucky enough to live in the charming South End," she said and patted his arm. "In fact, this very street wasn't always beautiful."

His father nodded.

Ryan had heard that the neighborhood was once pretty run down, but it had gone through an urban renewal when his grandparents lived there. Other areas of the city were going through even more drastic revivals. Places that had been nearly slums were sporting brand-new high-rises with incredible views and even higher prices.

No one else in his family cared about the ocean views, maybe because they'd relocated from the Southwest. But Ryan loved boating and fishing. One day he hoped to be able to afford an apartment in one of the new waterfront buildings. Living with his parents was the only way he'd be able to save that kind of money.

"So, getting back to the job…" his father began.

Crap. Apparently the change of subject hadn't helped much.

"You said you saw one other candidate who made it as far as the second interview. Was it anyone we know?"

He sighed. "No. It was some woman I've never seen before." A woman hot enough to light his own personal fire.

His father's bushy brows rose. "A female? Ordinarily I'd say you have nothing to worry about, but with only one female firefighter in the whole city—well, you know how it looks."

His mother tilted her head. "No, dear. How does it look?"

He growled though his teeth. "Don't get all feminist with me, Gabriella. You know darn well a woman can't physically equal a man, but if it looks like the department might be accused of bias… If certain groups obsessed with equality find out another female firefighter candidate is applying, it could unfairly disqualify our son."

His mother batted her eyelashes. "Oh dear. I wonder if Gloria Steinem has heard about this yet."

"Mom. Dad. Don't worry about it. Seriously. I've got this."

His father's frown said it all. "You'd better."

Chapter 2

RYAN AND CHLOE EYED EACH OTHER AS THEY PACED the hall outside the chief's office.

Ryan spoke first. "I never expected to see you again."

She halted and jammed her hands on her hips. "What's that supposed to mean?" *Easy, Chloe.* Her sister Shannon's only advice when Chloe had told her about this guy was, "Ignore his shenanigans. A quarrel is like buttermilk. Once it's out of the churn, the more you shake it, the more sour it grows." Shannon might be right, but this guy pushed her buttons and it was hard not to react.

"I just meant when I got the call to come in and see Chief O'Brian, I thought it was to fill out paperwork and firm up a starting date for training."

She took a deep breath and tried to relax. "I thought that as well."

He strolled up to her and looked down, looming over her, as if he wanted to express dominance. "I hear an accent. Where are you from?"

Feckers. He'd better not think he has an advantage by being born a man in the USA. Chloe had spent the last year not only working hard with her brother to bring his brownstone back to its former elegance, but she'd also been watching and listening to the electricians and plumbers with Boston accents. When she wasn't doing anything physical, she watched HGTV and YouTube videos, trying to adopt American expressions.

She decided to fight fire with fire. Facing the haughty man, she said, "Where are *you* from? You have an accent too."

He leaned back and laughed. "Nice try, sweetheart. I was born right here in Boston. Now, you never answered my question. Where are you from?"

"I may not have been born here, but I love my adopted country. I worked hard to become a citizen." That much was true. She'd studied her heart out and passed the citizenship exam without getting one wrong answer. Her apartment managers, Sly and Morgaine, had dropped by and given her pop quizzes. They enjoyed helping fellow paranormals and had even created a clubhouse in one of the vacant apartments just for them. That was one of Chloe's main reasons for staying in Boston instead of returning to her lonely existence in rural Ireland.

He shrugged. Then, almost as an afterthought, he said, "I don't even know your name."

"And I don't know yours." So far she had refrained from pointing out that she wasn't his *sweetheart*, but it might be less irksome if he used her real name. She sighed and extended her hand. "I'm Chloe Arish."

"Ah! I knew it. You're Irish. Your last name even says so."

He hadn't clasped her hand yet, but she kept it extended. "It's pronounced *Ah*-rish. Spelled with an A, not an I. And you are?"

"Ryan Fierro." He finally clasped her hand in a firm, almost punishing, handshake.

She smiled. He'd have to squeeze a lot harder to make a dragon wince.

At last Chief O'Brian's door opened. "Come in," he said.

They glanced at each other, hesitating.

"Both of you," the chief added.

Ryan gestured with a sweep of his hand. "Ladies first."

Ignore, ignore, ignore, Chloe told herself. She smiled and strode in, taking a seat on one of the hard plastic chairs in front of the chief's desk. Apparently he didn't want anyone to get too comfortable, leading to extended visits. That was fine with her.

Ryan followed and took the other seat, adopting a relaxed pose.

When the chief was finally seated in the only comfortable chair, he folded his hands on his desk and leaned forward.

"This was a difficult decision. On one hand, Ryan is well-known to us and his test scores were excellent."

Shite. He has the job.

"On the other hand, Chloe's scores were equally good, and in the spirit of equality—"

Ryan groaned and rolled his eyes.

The chief stopped mid-speech and glared at him. Chloe's hope resurfaced. Even if she got the job based on her gender, she'd take it without hesitation.

"If you'll let me finish…"

"I apologize," Ryan said quickly. "Please continue."

Chief O'Brian took a deep breath and said, "I had to go to the commissioner and beg for extra funding. I pointed out that the Back Bay not only houses a wealthy population with high expectations, but our area includes the Boston Marathon's finish line, historical landmarks, plus lots of dorms and fraternities with careless students who think nothing of drinking and lighting cigarettes or candles. Anyway, I got the funding. We're taking you both."

Chloe let out a whoop and grinned. Meanwhile Ryan's eyes rounded and his mouth hung open.

I guess that was quite unexpected. "Thank you, sir," she said. "You won't be sorry."

"I'd better not be," the chief stated bluntly.

"It looks like we'll be working together, so..." Chloe said.

Ryan was tempted to say, "so what?" but he had to tread carefully. This chick was a threat. If one of them had to be transferred to another house, it would probably be him.

Chloe was replacing the only female firefighter in Back Bay. The previous one had gotten a promotion after an inferno in which two firefighters were lost. Because she had sifted through the debris until she found the wedding ring that one of the widows desperately wanted, she was considered a hero. Many thought only a woman would have persisted until she found the sentimental item.

Her promotion transferred her to another station where not only was an officer needed, but a hero to boost morale—or in this case, a heroine.

Ryan had a brother, uncle, or cousin in almost every firehouse in Boston, and he'd rather not be a probie in front of one of his family members. Every misstep would be reported at Sunday dinner or summer barbecues, and his family's skills were legendary. He didn't want to let them down.

He desperately wanted to be the hero in *his* station. And he was better suited than most. His family were phoenixes. They could take risks their mortal brotherhood couldn't. None of them would die in a fire—at least not permanently. It was also the reason his mother was so easygoing about her husband and all of her sons being firefighters.

He glanced over at the deceptively strong female walking down the corridor beside him. He hadn't spoken for a while, but he had no idea what to say. She glanced back at him. Finally she broke the silence.

"Is that a problem?"

Huh? Had she said something he was supposed to answer? "Is what a problem?"

"That we're to be working together?"

He frowned. "Why would it be?"

"I'm well aware that as a woman I may have to prove myself to the other firefighters." She smirked. "I wouldn't want to show you up."

He halted. When she realized he was no longer in step, she spun around to face him.

He folded his arms. "What makes you think you're going to show me up? Ah. I get it. You're insecure about being a woman and might overcompensate."

Her posture stiffened. "I am not."

He mirrored her earlier smirk. "I could understand it if you are, but relax. The guys in District 4 are used to having a female firefighter around."

Chloe matched his confident posture. "I hope you don't think I plan to take it easy or expect special treatment."

Oh no. She has a chip on her shoulder. Someone probably told her she doesn't have what it takes and she's out to prove him wrong. He assumed it was a guy. Probably a father or boyfriend who didn't want her in danger. And who would? She was perfect—when she wasn't being a little too feisty.

"Look. No one will expect you to be a hero—especially as a probie. So you can tell your husband or father to relax."

She tipped her head and studied him quizzically. "I have no husband or father."

"Are you saying there's no one to worry about you?" It sounded as if she were alone in the world. *Why do I care?* He was surprised at his own reaction, but maybe he shouldn't have been. Being protective was a natural tendency for him. Even as a kid, he'd stood up to bullies if he saw anyone being picked on. And during his tour in Afghanistan, he'd stuck his neck out for a fellow soldier more than once.

"I have siblings, but they don't worry about me because they know I can take care of meself. I—I mean, myself."

So she lapses into her accent when she's upset. A good thing to know. Ryan mentally filed that away along with other clues to this puzzling, fascinating woman.

It had been a year since Melanie had broken his heart. Everyone told him it was time to get back out there and find another girl. Only he didn't want a girl. He wanted a woman. Someone who had a life and goals of her own. This woman seemed to fit his wish list. She was strong and independent—and he could barely keep his libido under control when he was around her.

Suddenly it occurred to him that starting a relationship with her would probably mean a transfer. Hmmm... If only he could be sure *she* would be the one to go elsewhere. Not only did he want to make his family proud without hearing about his learning curve, but he wanted to do it at this particular firehouse—his father's former firehouse. Better yet, maybe they could keep dating on the down-low and he could continue to see her pretty face often.

But no matter what happened between them personally, she'd better not try to show him up on the job. He'd hate to accidentally show his supernatural side. He suspected that would put the kibosh on any kind of relationship. Especially a personal one. And that would be a damn shame since she was the first woman to tempt him in a long time.

Chloe had to admit—to herself only—that on the first day of academy training, she *might* be a bit nervous. Not just because it was something new and different, or *God forbid* there was any aspect of this job she couldn't do, but because she had to keep her strength believable and yet top-notch. It would be a bit of a balancing act.

Another balancing act would to be to resist the magnetic effect Ryan had on her. Their rivalry helped keep him at a distance, but she was afraid that gap was closing.

She'd noticed a few guys sitting in the back row of the small classroom, so she sat up front. Hopefully it would show she was anxious to learn.

The training took place on Moon Island in Boston Harbor. Probably a good, safe place to set fires. If the wind blew a spark, it would land in the ocean surrounding them. But Chloe remembered the old wooden bridge she drove over to get to the island. What if that went up in flames?

As if the thought of being stranded with Ryan had conjured the man himself, he strode into the room and seated himself right next to her. She glanced over at him, about to wish him a good morning, when he winked at her. *Argh.* So much for burying the ax…unless it was in his chauvinistic head.

"Rolling your eyes at me already?" he whispered. "I thought maybe we'd just gotten off on the wrong foot and could be friends from now on."

She heaved a sigh. There hadn't been any indication that he wanted her friendship. In fact, she'd have bet against it.

"We have eight weeks of firefighter training. More if you still need EMT certification." He reached out his hand as if he expected her to shake it. "I'd like to extend an olive branch," he said. "How about if I take you out for coffee after this?"

She tentatively clasped his hand. "I don't drink coffee, but thank you for the offer." This time he didn't squeeze the hell out of her hand as he shook it, so she supposed he might really be attempting to establish a friendship.

"What do you drink?"

Before she had a chance to say Guinness or tea, he chuckled. "I bet I know. You probably go for those health food juices. Wheatgrass and stuff."

She was about to deny it, but then a small, evil thought crossed her mind. *It might be fun to watch him drink a big frothy mug of grass.* "I like to stay healthy. Don't you?"

After a brief hesitation he said, "Of course. I know a place on Boylston Street where we can get something very healthy."

"Awesome," she said, mimicking an American expression that seemed to be popular.

"Wicked awesome," he said and grinned.

Just as she realized he might misconstrue this as a date, their instructor walked in. Best keep that question to herself until they could speak privately again. She didn't know the fire department's policy on dating coworkers, but she knew her own. She didn't date. Period. Why ask for heartbreak when she already knew her destiny? Like it or not, she would remain alone.

The instructor leaned against his desk and folded his arms. "I've been waiting for two more. Unfortunately they're late. I can't stand people being late and this isn't a good start for them. I'd rather not make the rest of you work overtime, though." He pushed off of his desk and began to pace. "I'm going to start without them."

Just then the door opened and two more guys rushed in. "Sorry," one of them mumbled. "We missed the exit off 93."

"You commuted together?" the trainer asked. "And *both* of you missed the exit?"

"Yeah. I guess we were talking about the job," the other one said. "We're friends who decided to do this together. You know…mutual support and everything."

"From now on you can use the carpool lane and get here early."

It looked like their instructor was a hard-ass. That suited Chloe just fine. *Bring it on.*

"Camaraderie is fine as long as the job comes first. Each one of you will need to develop a trusting relationship with your fellow firefighters. But more importantly, you'll need to follow orders from your superiors— without question."

And so their training began.

———∿∿∿———

After their first day, some of the guys appeared drained. There wasn't much physical exertion, but a lot of information had been thrown at them at once. Trying to take it all in could have been daunting. Not for Ryan. And unless she hid it well, Chloe wasn't tired either.

"So, about that health food restaurant…" she began.

Oh no. She isn't thinking of canceling, is she? He wouldn't give her a chance. He was looking forward to spending time with her. Sitting across from that beautiful face would give him an excuse to gaze at her—and he couldn't keep his stare from wandering to her anyway. "I can follow you back to the city and take you from wherever you park your car."

"I don't have a car."

Huh? "You don't? Then how did you get all the way out here on Moon Island? You'd be spending a fortune on cab fare."

One side of her mouth curled up in a sly smile, as if she were going to say something snarky, but instead she said, "I used a Zipcar."

"Oh." He'd heard about the program. It saved city dwellers from having to own their own vehicles, paying for insurance, and parking when they'd only use them a few times a year. "So, do you want to leave it here overnight and come in with me tomorrow, or did you want to drop it off in one of the designated spots and pick up another one tomorrow?"

"I'd rather not put you out. I'll drop it off at the Prudential Center garage and walk since you said the restaurant is on Boylston Street. What's the name of it?"

"How about if I meet you at the entrance to the garage. We can walk there together."

She shrugged. "Whatever floats your dinghy."

"The saying is, 'whatever floats your boat.'"

That sly smile lifted the side of her lip again. "I know."

He sighed. *Trying to date her isn't going to be easy.* Fortunately, he loved a challenge.

--- ⁓⁓⁓ ---

An hour later, Ryan was pacing outside the garage. What the hell could have happened to her? Traffic wasn't *that* bad on the Southeast Expressway.

He looked at his watch again. "Jesus," he muttered. What was taking her so long? As if it had just occurred to him, he stopped and balled his fists. *If she stood me up…*

That thought was replaced by, *Of course not. She has to see me tomorrow, and the next day, and the next.*

Now he was back to worrying. But why? She was a grown woman. One who'd made it abundantly clear she could take care of herself. So why did he have this niggling feeling he should take care of her?

It was annoying.

At last he spotted the bright-green compact car literally zipping down the ramp and into the underground garage.

When she emerged on the escalator, all thoughts evaporated. She was stunning, even wearing a serious expression—which he saw way too often. He'd love to make her laugh and see what her smile looked like. A real smile, not a smirk.

"Nice of you to show up," he said.

She held up one hand. "Don't start."

"Start what?"

"Bitching at me because I'm late."

"I don't bitch," he bitched. *Do you hear yourself, Fierro?* "So what happened? Are you okay?"

She let out a deep breath. "Yeah. Just frustrated. I had to stop for gas. The Zipcars need to be at least one-quarter full for the next person. Using the gas card was stupidly complicated."

"Let's walk. You'll probably feel better when we get some juice into you." He turned toward the street they had to cross and took off at a brisk pace. She came up beside him and matched his stride, something Melanie could never do. She was forever asking him to slow down. Crossing busy streets like Boylston with her was downright dangerous.

"*We* get juice into me? What are you going to do? Pour it down my throat?"

He chuckled. "Only if I have to."

She let out a snort. "I can feed meself."

"There's that Irish accent again." He wondered why she had come to this country.

"So, what brought you to America?"

When she didn't answer, he added, "Another potato famine?"

"Sheesh. You're nosy," she said.

A suspicious reaction if he'd ever heard one. He let her dwell on it. When they arrived at the restaurant, he held the door for her. There was only so much "equality" he could give her without feeling like a douchebag.

The place was packed. There was a small opening at the "standing room only" raised bar. "Why don't you grab that spot and I'll order."

"Why don't you grab it and I'll order? You'll take up

more space, and when I come back you can turn sideways and there *might* be room for both of us," she said.

She didn't wait for him to tell her what he wanted, she just walked off and joined the line. She didn't leave him much of a choice other than to jam himself into that one open spot and wait to see what she came back with.

Fortunately, the guy next to him finished his tall, orangey drink and left. Now Ryan had to try to hold the spot for Chloe. He reached toward his back pocket for a paper from class to plunk down on the bar next to him. As much as he'd like to stand close to Chloe, he didn't dare let her bump up against his arousal.

He grabbed *something*, but it wasn't the handout.

A woman's shriek hurt his ear. When he turned to see what had happened, she slapped him.

"How dare you?" the forty-something sophisticated-looking woman cried out.

"I'm sorry. It was an accident."

"Like hell," she said as she stormed off.

The place had gone silent and all eyes were on him... including Chloe's.

When she returned with their drinks, she plunked the swamp-green one in front of him and asked, "What was that about?"

He picked up the handout so she could set her orange-colored drink down. "Uh...I went for the papers in my back pocket to save your place and I guess I grabbed something else."

She reared back and laughed—hard. Yeah, he'd wanted to make her laugh and smile, but not by making an ass of himself.

—◦◦◦—

Chloe didn't usually laugh at the misfortune of others, but this time she couldn't help it. She'd wanted to slap Ryan's face a few times herself.

She'd bought him the wheatgrass drink he'd mentioned, hoping it tasted as bad as it looked, but now she almost felt sorry for him. He was having a very bad start to his evening.

He nodded to her drink. "What did you get?"

"Orange mango." She tried to look innocently at his gross green drink and said, "You mentioned wheatgrass before, so I *guessed* that's what you must like. There's a little carrot juice in it too."

He picked up the glass and examined it. "You could have asked."

She shrugged one shoulder. "I suppose…"

He sniffed it and wrapped his handsome lips around the straw. After sucking up a generous amount, his nose wrinkled a bit. But he gazed at her amused face, then smacked his lips and said, "Ahhh…" as he slapped the glass back down on the counter.

"So, I guess I got your order right?"

"The carrot kind of saves the rest of that disgusting crap."

She burst out laughing again.

He grinned. "You did that on purpose, didn't you?"

"Kind of," she admitted. "For all I knew it really was what you liked. There's no accounting for taste."

He held her gaze. "That's for damned sure." Then he surprised her by picking up the drink and taking another long pull on the straw.

"You don't have to drink it. I'll get you another."

"Oh no. Please don't. As probies, we might as well get used to this kind of treatment. It's going to happen a lot. Probably more to me than you."

She was sincerely puzzled. "What do you mean?"

"You know. The razzing we'll get just because we're probies."

Her eyes widened. "Are you saying the more experienced firefighters will be mean to us just because we're new?"

"It's an age-old tradition."

"Feck," she murmured under her breath. She thought she'd said it quietly enough so as not to be overheard in the noisy restaurant, but he laughed and his dark eyes twinkled at her.

"But I imagine they'll take it easy on you."

"Why? Just because I'm a female?"

He tipped up his chin. "Exactly."

"What if I don't want them to?"

He barked a laugh. "Why? Are you a glutton for punishment?"

"Not at all. I just don't want to be treated any differently. Anything a man can do, I can do too."

He raised his eyebrows. "You can pee standing up?"

Her back stiffened, and he quickly held up one hand. "Sorry. I was just giving you a taste of the kind of teasing you're apt to get."

"Don't worry. I can give as good as I get. I'll just infer that they probably pee sitting down."

He reared back and laughed, long and loud. "Yep. You'll fit in fine."

Then his thoughts darkened, and she must have noticed the change.

"What's wrong?"

He shook his head, but said nothing. What could he say? That she might fit in better than he would? Since both of them would be on probation, and it wasn't like the city to create a position for a new firefighter, he deduced that one of them could be transferred to another station as soon as something opened up.

"What?" she insisted.

When he ignored her a second time, she folded her arms. "I demand you tell me what you're thinking."

"You demand?" He snorted. "What are you? Some kind of princess?"

Her eyes rounded as if she were shocked for a moment, then she schooled her features. "Never mind. It's clear that you're afraid to tell me."

"Afraid? Hell no, princess. I'm not afraid of anything."

He was a phoenix. He had nothing to fear. He'd survived Afghanistan. Even if he did die, his parents would pour gasoline over his body, light him up, and he'd be reborn from the ashes. It had happened before.

"So, I was just wondering about your background…" he finally said.

He'd turn the focus back on her and keep her from asking too many questions.

A brief flicker of what could only be called *fear* crossed her face. *There. What was that?*

"I don't know what it is you want to know about me background. I mean, *my* background. I already told you I'm from Ireland."

"I thought you said you were from Ulster."

She waved away the comment like she was swatting

a fly. "Ulster, Erin, Northern Ireland, Ireland, it's all the same to you people."

"*You people?* What, Americans?"

She nodded and took a long sip of her mango drink.

"I thought *you* were an American."

"I am. I'm a naturalized citizen. That means I have the same rights as you. The only difference is, I know what they are." She smiled wickedly.

"What do you mean by that?"

"I had to study the Bill of Rights for my citizenship exam. Can you rattle off the entire Bill of Rights?"

She had him there. Americans who were born in the States often took those rights for granted and probably didn't know the third from the Tenth Amendment. Even though she was just pointing out a truth, it made him sad.

He tried to get back his swagger. "That's what the Internet is for."

Her sexy smirk appeared. "Oh, is that what it's for? I thought it was for porn, pictures of kittens, and shopping."

"Maybe for you."

She laughed, and he was reminded that she could take a joke as well as dish one out. Yeah, the guys would love her…

Chapter 3

CHLOE FOUND THE FOLLOWING DAY OF TRAINING easy and challenging at the same time. Unfortunately the most challenging part was Ryan's not-so-subtle pop quizzes about history—and not just America's history. He kept slipping in questions about her life before Boston.

Was he fishing? Knowing she had something to hide, she felt nervous.

When the day was finally over, she trotted to her Zipcar before he could reach her and jumped in. In her rearview mirror, she saw him coming toward her, so she threw the car in reverse and sped off, kicking up enough gravel to stop him in his tracks.

All the way home, she replayed her answers to the questions she chose to answer. There were plenty she'd sidestepped with a changed subject or distraction. Could she keep this up for eight weeks? The other guys in training seemed like a good bunch. *They* weren't giving her a hard time about being an Irish woman. Why should Ryan care?

"Yeah. Why does he give a feck who I am?" she muttered out loud. "As long as I can pull his arse out of a fire, he should be grateful."

And she'd proven she could—repeatedly. Although the fire was imaginary that day, their carries were not. They had deadweight dummies of various sizes from newborn infants to obese adults. She'd learned how *not* to carry a person too. The training film demonstrated the wrong ways, so no one would tweak their backs or pull out a shoulder. But even if she got hurt, she'd heal quickly.

"Morgaine," she muttered out loud. Morgaine could tell her what he was up to. She was a psychic.

The female half of her apartment building's management team read tea leaves at the Boston Uncommon Tearoom a few blocks away. Perhaps she could make a private appointment so she wouldn't have to talk with customers around.

Morgaine knew what Chloe was. All the residents did. Not that anyone knew much about dragons. The species had almost died out. But fortunately, there was one other dragon in Boston who'd proven he could be trusted, so her family had found a safe haven with people who accepted them.

The whole building was made up of several one-bedroom apartments and an exclusive paranormal club. She had never seen the penthouse, but she'd met the building's owners who lived there—a professional baseball player and his young family. They seemed kind but very protective of their privacy.

If only she could find a way to protect her privacy as well.

She glanced in the rearview mirror. "Is that him?" Ryan's Jeep kept pace behind her in the evening traffic. "Ah, feckers! He's following me."

Relax, Chloe. Maybe he's just taking the same route home. Now she was becoming paranoid. She had to figure out what his deal was and do it quickly.

She fumbled in her backpack for her cell phone.

Stretch. One. More. Half inch…

Her car must have swerved into traffic, because the vehicle behind her blared its horn. She popped up straight and grabbed the wheel with both hands. The drivers beside her weren't even glancing her way.

"What the feck?" Did Ryan just beep at her because she wasn't sitting up straight with her hands on the wheel in the ten-and-two position?

She glared in her rearview mirror and caught his darkened expression.

"Oh, this is going too damn far," she muttered. She saw an opening where she could cut over and take the next exit off the Southeast Expressway. They were near South Station, so if she wanted to, she could leave the car there and take the subway home.

She cut the wheel hard, but unfortunately Ryan followed right behind her.

"What is your problem?" she yelled, as if he could hear her.

At last she pulled into the parking lot and found the spots allocated for Zipcars. If Ryan wanted to park, he'd have to do it somewhere else. That should give her enough time to…

"Hey!" he yelled out the window as he stopped right behind her, blocking her in.

She was so tempted to hit reverse, but this wasn't her car to crumple. She'd just have to deal with the beast—for that's what he looked like at the moment. His intense eyes flashed and his dark hair shot out in wild directions, as if he'd just raked his fingers through it. He probably had.

She grabbed her backpack, slammed her door, and

marched up to his window. "What the feck is your problem, Fierro?"

"*My* problem? Where did you get your driver's license? Correspondence school? Did you know you almost caused an accident back there?"

"I did not."

"You did. If the car on your right hadn't swerved, you'd have hit him. What were you trying to do all bent over like that anyway?"

"Not that it's any of your business, but I was going to grab my cell phone, call you, and ask if you were stalking me." She slung her backpack over her shoulder. "Looks like you just answered my question."

"I wasn't following you," he said. At last his expression and his voice softened. "At least not like that. I don't know why it matters, but I just wanted to see that you got where you were going safely. Driving around here can be a bitch."

"Tell me about it."

They stared at each other for a long moment. At last Chloe said, "I wasn't actually planning to come here. I was going to leave the car closer to home and walk. From here I'll have to take the T. Now, if you'll just make like a tree and get the hell out of here…"

"Huh?" The light of understanding dawned in his eyes and he started laughing. When he settled down he said, "I'm not ready to leave. You can take any car tomorrow, right? It doesn't have to be this one."

"Yeah. So?"

"So, let me take you home the rest of the way. The car is already dropped off in a proper place." When she hesitated, he added, "I promise I'll behave."

She rolled her eyes. "You'll probably behave better if you're not criticizin' me drivin.'"

He grinned. "Get in."

She didn't want him to know where she lived, but she could always ask him to drop her off on the corner. In fact, she could choose a corner where taking her directly home would be impossible. Thank goodness for all the one-way streets in Back Bay. She heaved a sigh, then trotted around to the opposite side of the car and jumped in.

"Okay," he said as if he'd won a key battle. "Where to?"

"Marlborough Street," she said, feeling cagey.

"Ah, that's probably the prettiest street in Back Bay. Very little traffic, because it doesn't lead to anything but homes."

"Yeah," she said. "Only the residents have any business being there. You can leave me at the corner of Berkley and Marlborough and just keep going onto Storrow Drive."

He frowned at her.

Oh good. He realized he'd be going the wrong way to turn left onto Marlborough where most of the homes were.

"I don't take Storrow Drive to get to the South End. I can just shoot down Commonwealth Avenue to Kenmore Square after dropping you at your door. So, what block do you live on? I can always take Dartmouth and come back around."

Feck. Since her door was on Beacon Street, and he seemed like the type to wait for her to have her key in the lock, she might have to 'fess up to the "mistake."

She leaned back and let out a deep sigh.

"What?" he asked.

After a brief hesitation she said, "I don't live on Marlborough Street."

"Why would you tell me… Oh. I get it. You don't trust me." He scowled at the road.

"It's not that…"

It was exactly that. She didn't trust anyone who might want to come over. She lived with shapeshifters, vampires, witches, and a ghost. Not to mention the fact that her building housed a club for paranormals, and in the building next door lived another dragon and a minor goddess. It was all they could do to keep random passersby from witnessing any accidental, supernatural funny business.

She had just been planning to ask Morgaine to read her tea leaves.

It didn't really matter what the witch had to say, however. She knew her own fate. She was to remain alone for the rest of her long life.

Her grandmother had gifted each of her grandchildren with a precious or semiprecious stone upon their births. The stones were said to match their true loves' eyes. Shannon's husband Finn had eyes as blue as her sapphire. Rory's girlfriend was not only someone with amber eyes of the green variety and amber hair of the gold variety. Her name was even feckin' Amber! Of course, her stubborn brother needed to be hit with a sledgehammer of a hint.

But for Chloe's diamond, there was no match. No man's eyes were clear. She'd even tried to decide if her stone could be called a rare blue or brown diamond, but no. Any nuances were pure white. Ryan's eyes were dark brown, occasionally appearing jet black when he was angry. Like now.

"Look. It's not that I don't trust you. *You* have nothing to do with it. I just value my privacy beyond all else when I'm on my own time. I have the right to privacy, don't I?"

He didn't answer. He just kept driving toward the Back Bay. When he finally arrived at the intersection of the alphabetical streets at Arlington and Beacon, he said, "Where to? Or would you like me to close my eyes the rest of the way?"

"Oh, for feck's sake… Just leave me here." She needed to walk off some frustration.

―⁓―

Ryan had to blow off some steam too.

He knew where his brothers went to have a drink and shoot the breeze with their firefighter buddies. With any luck, one of them might be at the bar. It wasn't in the same part of town, but if anyone wanted to know what he was doing in the area he could always say he was visiting the local college in Charlestown to see if they had a major in fire sciences.

With the Internet and a thousand ways to access the information, it was a weak excuse at best. Hopefully no one would question his being there.

Upon walking in, he scanned the bar. Cool. One of his brothers was having a beer with the guys from his station. When he sensed Ryan, he looked up and waved.

Jayce slipped off his stool and strolled over to him. "Hey, bro. What are you doing here?"

"Can't a guy stop in for a beer? Or does this place only serve sissies?"

His brother laughed and punched him in the arm *hard*. "Is that sissy enough for ya?"

He grinned and didn't rub his arm until Jayce turned around and led the way back to his spot at the bar.

"I heard you started your training. Can I buy you a beer—or are you trying to be *healthy?*"

The way he said the word "healthy" made Ryan wonder if he'd been spotted at the health food restaurant the other night.

"Nah. I'll let you buy me a beer anytime."

Jayce ordered his family's favorite and introduced him to the other guys. Most of them he'd seen before, although he didn't remember their names, so reintroductions were helpful. One of them had a yellow streak in his hair. He'd have remembered that guy.

"So, you're training on Moon Island?" the guy named Drake asked. "I have a friend who's there now too."

"Oh? What's his name?" Ryan asked.

"Not a him. It's a her. Chloe Arish."

Ryan groaned before he could catch himself.

"What?" Drake asked. "Isn't she doing well?"

"It's not that. She's doing great. Showing up some of the guys, in fact. Not me, of course."

"Yeah, I can't imagine any chick topping a Fierro," one of the other guys said.

Ryan pictured Chloe in the girl-on-top position and his cock twitched. *Get a grip, Ryan. She's not even here.*

Drake was talking to someone else, so he leaned in and whispered to his brother.

"There's something up with that chick."

"Like what?" Jayce asked.

"She's scary strong, and she's from another country. Sometimes when she gets flustered, she sounds like she's fresh off the boat."

"Flustered? Oh, that's not good."

Drake turned around and said, "Who's flustered?"

"Oh, nobody," Ryan said. He didn't want what he said to get back to her.

"Chloe?" Drake persisted.

"Well, yeah. I was just talking about her accent. I guess she slips into it when she's nervous. Do you know anything about her background?"

"Yeah. She came here from Ireland a little over a year ago. My wife was one of the first people she met in town."

Oh, so she's friends with the firefighters' wives. That was an angle he hadn't considered. Women stuck up for each other. Ryan suddenly wondered how many firefighters' wives she may have met in the past year.

Drake went on to say that she had talked to him at length about joining the fire service. He sounded as if he'd supported her choice from the beginning.

"How well do you know her? I mean, why did you think she'd make a good firefighter?" Ryan took a long swig of his beer.

The other guys were paying attention now.

"Why wouldn't she?" Drake asked.

"Well, she's a tiny little thing…"

Drake leaned back and laughed. "Don't let that fool you. She's as strong, or stronger, than most guys I know."

"I can't wait to meet this chick," one of the single guys said. Haggarty, Ryan thought his name was. The look in his eyes made the hair on Ryan's neck prickle. Most guys would drool over her. But most guys didn't stand a chance with Chloe Arish. That weird protective part of him felt almost proud of her.

Ryan held his tongue and refocused his conversation

back to her country of origin. "Do you know what part of Ireland she's from?"

"Yeah. I think she called the town Ballyhoo. Her brother and sister came here with her, but her sister moved back."

"Why? She didn't like the United States?" Jayce asked.

"No. It wasn't that. She had a boyfriend back in Ireland. I guess he followed her here and convinced her to go back with him."

"Ah. So she still has family there," Ryan said. "Where is Ballyhoo, exactly?"

Drake shrugged. "Somewhere on the coast, I guess. They said something about taking a fishing boat to Iceland. I guess they spent a few weeks there."

"Iceland?" He sounded a little too shocked. He needed to keep it casual. "I thought Iceland was supposed to be beautiful. So how did they end up here?"

Drake laughed. "The language really tripped them up. Her brother said something about the eleven-letter words and odd consonants right next to each other. That would intimidate any English speaker."

"Ah. So why didn't they just go back to Ireland?"

Drake shrugged. "There was probably a reason they left in the first place, but I don't know what it was. Anyway, in Iceland they upgraded to a bigger, better boat. They arrived by yacht."

I'll be damned. She is *fresh off the boat!*

Suddenly Drake looked nervous, as if he'd said something he shouldn't have. "Don't say anything to her about it though. As an immigrant myself, I know it can be a touchy subject for some of us."

"Immigrant? I never knew that. Where are you from?" Jayce asked.

"Maritime Canada."

The guys around him laughed. "Yeah. You're real foreign," Jayce said. "If not for the state of Maine, we'd be neighbors."

Drake toasted to that and finished his beer. He had a wife and new baby to get home to, so he said his good-byes and left.

Ryan let this new knowledge roll around in his brain. *A fishing boat?* If Chloe liked to fish, they had something in common. The summer would be drawing to a close soon, so perhaps he'd suggest a fishing trip before the weather turned cold.

She can't storm off into the ocean if I come a little too close to the truth—or to her.

It was a good thing he'd run into Jayce. He shared ownership of their boat. Maybe they could make it a group thing and it would be less weird if more guys were invited. It wouldn't look like a date, which she'd refuse. But meeting some fellow firefighters might be a temptation she couldn't pass up.

"Hey, Jayce. What do you say? Want to go fishing this weekend?" he said loud enough for several of his brother's buddies to hear.

"Yeah, Jayce," one named Mike said. "We're off this weekend. Why don't you go and invite me too?"

Perfect. Meeting guys from the other houses wouldn't hurt him either. They never knew when a multiple-alarm fire might have them working together.

—∾—

Chloe sensed a change in Ryan. He seemed confident—
not that arrogant and conceited were different for him,
but it was the *type* of confidence that seemed new. He
was more self-assured. Less self-righteous. She found it
a lot sexier than his bravado, unfortunately. If the man
were any sexier, she might implode.

After that day's training, he didn't follow her to the
parking lot. Instead he said good-bye to the other guys
and then went straight to his Jeep. When he drove off
without giving her a backward glance, she wondered
why. And why did it matter to her?

Had she finally discouraged him? She should be
glad—she hated worrying about letting a guy down
easy. Her style was just to say, "See ya," and go on
her way.

Maybe she was getting a taste of her own medicine.

And she didn't like it.

As she drove home, she reminded herself why it was
important not to get involved with him. They'd be working together. She knew any relationship was doomed
anyway. Why start something she couldn't finish?

For the first time in hundreds of years, she cursed her
grandmother. "Why the feck did you have to give me
a diamond? Yeah, it's valuable, and maybe you were
trying to tell me I'm too valuable to be held down by a
bad marriage. But why isn't there a good one for me?
Am I that impossible to live with?"

She ended her rant by realizing she probably was. Her
siblings could put up with her because they'd learned
how…and they'd had to. Family was an odd thing in
Ireland. Brothers thought nothing of beating the tar out
of each other, but add anyone with outside blood to the

mix and watch how fast the brothers bonded and turned on the interloper—together.

Even marriage didn't change that. She loved her brother-in-law, Finn, but if he ever raised his voice, never mind his hand, to Shannon, he'd find both Rory and Chloe on him in a pile of fast-flying fists.

Irishmen and Irishwomen understood this on a subconscious level, even if they denied it. Blood—especially Irish blood—was much thicker than water.

Apparently Ryan had a lot of brothers. She wondered if the same held true for him and his siblings. Probably not. From what she'd seen, Americans seemed to weigh the pros and cons of an argument—then express themselves verbally. They rarely started fistfights in the streets. The laws were pretty strict against that here.

She chuckled as she remembered an argument between her apartment managers. She'd never witnessed anything so strange in her life.

They'd seemed to be having a staring contest. The wife had folded her arms and tapped her foot. The husband, with his hands on his hips, had just glared back. It wasn't until much later that Chloe had learned the two could communicate telepathically and were arguing their points in full view of everyone, with no one hearing a word.

Maybe she'd ask for that tea leaf reading from the wife/witch after all. Something about Ryan just didn't sit right with her. He wasn't acting as if he'd given up. He was acting as if he'd won!

Chapter 4

CHLOE PARKED THE ZIPCAR IN THE PRUDENTIAL Center's garage and strode home to her Beacon Street brownstone. She had planned to have dinner with Rory and Amber next door, but she was going to make a quick stop at home to change. If Morgaine had time for a reading, she'd call Amber and ask if dinner could wait a few.

When Chloe unlocked the front door, she was surprised to see Morgaine standing in front of her apartment.

"Is everything all right?"

Morgaine tipped her head. "I don't know. You tell me."

Chloe's brows knit. "Excuse me?"

"My psychic senses were telling me you needed to talk to me. In fact, your unspoken request was so loud it was almost shouting."

"Oh! I'm sorry. I was indeed thinking I'd like to talk to you. I guess I should think more…quietly?"

Morgaine chuckled. "Not at all. My senses pick up feelings, not volume. I sensed your need for my help might be urgent."

"Again. I apologize if I accidentally… Feck. You know what? It's not an emergency, but whenever you're available…"

Morgaine smiled and held up a small fabric bag printed with stars and moons on a midnight-blue background. "I'm available now."

Chloe felt a sense of relief wash over her as she unlocked apartment 2B and welcomed Morgaine inside.

Morgaine glanced around. "It looks nice. I haven't seen the place since your sister was here with you."

"I think it doubled in size after she left." Chloe chuckled. "It's a bit cramped for two, even two who are as close as sisters."

Morgaine laughed. "Believe me, I know. I shared the apartment upstairs with my cousin before she moved across the hall."

Chloe grinned. "And let's not forget Amber and Rory's mishap. Two total strangers claiming the same apartment and each refusing to leave."

When they stopped laughing, Chloe put on the kettle and took out a box of her favorite tea. "I'm afraid I only have one kind of tea to offer you. I'm not used to having company."

"Whatever you have will be perfect." Morgaine hummed and shuffled her tarot cards. "Do you want to do this at the dinette?"

Chloe hadn't seen her take the cards out of the bag, but the empty velvet pouch hung from her wrist. She shuffled as if they were attached to each other, like a sleight-of-hand magician.

"Sure. Sit anywhere."

Morgaine gracefully seated herself at one of four chairs around a glass-top table.

Chloe's stomach fluttered. *Do I really want to do this?*

Morgaine set the cards in a pile and said, "Cut the deck."

If Chloe wasn't intimidated by fire, she wouldn't let a little fortune-telling get the better of her. She reached over and picked up half the pile, and when Morgaine pointed to a spot on the table, she set them down beside the remaining cards.

"Did you want to ask a question or make a wish?" Morgaine put the small decks together and shuffled them again.

Chloe couldn't think of anything specific to ask... or even what she'd wish for. She shrugged. "I guess I'll just let you tell me whatever you see. How's that?"

"That's fine."

Chloe would guess Morgaine was in her early thirties, but she seemed a lot older and wiser. Which was odd, simply because Chloe was *so* much older than everyone she knew except her brother, Rory—and her cousin Conlan.

Each branch of the Arish family tree had three dragons on it. The Ulster branch was made up of three males, the Erin branch had two females and one male. And going back a generation, their mutual grandparents had another male child, whom everyone had lost track of.

But the banner with three dragons upon it remained in their castle built into the cliffs of Ballyhoo.

Morgaine spread the cards across the table and said, "Turn over three. We'll just do a quick reading to see if you need more information. I know you have somewhere to be."

"How did you..." She rolled her eyes. "Never mind. Psychic. I get it."

Morgaine smiled and sat quietly while Chloe performed the task.

As soon as she'd flipped over her three cards, the teakettle began to whistle. "Excuse me."

Morgaine gathered the cards and Chloe added tea to the pot, letting it steep. She gathered cups, saucers, biscuits, and napkins and set everything on a tray. She was glad there was a pass-through from the kitchen to the dining area, so she could set everything down within reach.

"Now what?" Chloe asked. "Drink tea or tell fortunes?"

"I'm good enough to do both at the same time." Morgaine winked.

Chloe took the seat nearest the pass-through. "Great! So, what have you found out?"

Morgaine leaned back and folded her arms. "Have you heard the saying, 'Just because you're paranoid doesn't mean they're not following you'?"

"Someone's following me?" Chloe jumped up and rushed to the bay windows.

Morgaine reached out. "No. Oh no. I'm sorry. I didn't mean anyone was literally following you. But someone is poking around your business, behind your back."

Chloe growled. "Nobody pokes me backside without permission."

Morgaine covered her mouth, but she was obviously trying to hide a smile. "Sorry. I just meant... Someone is interested in discrediting you. They may be digging into your background and trying to find some dirt."

"Why? I'm not runnin' for office. Wait." She slapped her forehead and returned to her chair. "It's probably the background check the fire department does on every employee."

Morgaine frowned. "I thought you already started the job. Wouldn't they get that done before you were officially hired?"

"Yes. Of course. Everything checked out. No felonies...yet," she added under her breath.

Morgaine snickered, then schooled her features. "I'm

not making myself clear. This is happening now. There's deception involved." She pointed to a card. "This card, plus my psychic warning bells going off, are sure this is not sanctioned activity."

"In other words, I *should* be paranoid."

Morgaine reached across the table and covered her hand. "Not at all. Just be aware. That's why people go to psychics in the first place. Everyone wants to know their future—and that's why I do what I do. It's important. Forewarned is forearmed."

"Another American saying?"

"Yes. Although it translates to any country."

Chloe nodded and mulled that over. Who could be delving into her background? Her immediate thought was Ryan…her rival. But what was the point, now that they'd both been hired?

Perhaps he was trying to discredit her before and forgot to call off the private detective or whatever… "I don't know. There was this bloke I was competing with for the job. They couldn't decide between us, so they got more funding and we were both hired."

Morgaine straightened and tapped a card. "Yes. It has to do with your job. See this card? Swords indicate a war of some kind and the staff indicates work. The very next card is coins. Money is closely involved."

Chloe took a good look at the cards. The swords were stabbing some poor schmuck in the back. *Shite. That poor schmuck is me!*

—∿∿—

Ryan had a small lounge in his parents' basement. Back when there were seven boys to house it was like a dormitory. Now it was a quiet place to study. But he couldn't keep his mind on the books.

He unfolded the picture he'd kept in his wallet for the past few years. It was from a Boston real estate magazine and included the view from floor-to-ceiling windows in a high-rise condo overlooking Boston Harbor. The picture had even gone to Afghanistan with him. His reduced rent at his parents' house was helping him save for that condo.

The following day the trainees would be sent into their first real fire. Granted, it was in a controlled setting, but they'd have the experience of using their equipment. But all he could think about was a slender blonde battling a blaze that could take her life.

Damn it. He *cared!* He didn't want to, but he had to admit it—at least to himself. Admitting it to anyone else would be probie suicide. He'd be transferred to another house before he started.

Yeah, they could run into each other again no matter where he was stationed in the city, especially if they picked up some overtime shifts. And he had to. The sooner he got out of his parents' basement, the better. If his fellow firefighters learned he was still living at home with mommy and daddy, he'd be teased mercilessly.

There were so many Fierros in the Boston Fire Department, they'd each been given a nickname. He'd be "Momma's Boy" for sure. He shuddered.

He wrenched his mind back to the book he was reading. He'd read it before. Hell, he'd practically cut his teeth on the binding.

It was no good. He tossed down the book and paced across the floor, raking his fingers through his hair.

What was it about her? He wanted to kiss her one minute and spank her the next.

He stopped in his tracks. *Oh…* A visual of her soft, round bum across his lap had him instantly hard. *Yeah, like that would* ever *happen.*

"Christ!" he sputtered out loud. "Damn, infuriating, liberated woman…"

He heard his father's footfalls on the stairs. Quickly retaking his seat on the couch, he laid the open book over the telltale tent in his pants.

"Is everything all right?"

"Yeah. Everything's fine."

"What were you shouting about?"

"Nothing."

His father stood with his hands on his hips, just below the spare tire he'd been sporting since he'd retired.

"You didn't run into Melanie, did you?"

"Huh? No. I haven't seen her since we broke up."

"Then there must be another infuriating woman you're upset with."

Ryan rolled his eyes. "Why did you ask me what I said if you heard me loud and clear?"

His father shrugged. "Just thought you might elaborate. That's all."

"Well, don't hold your breath. I'd rather not talk about this particular situation. At least not until I can take care of it."

The elder Fierro raised an eyebrow. "It sounds like you might need some advice."

"Not at all. What makes you say that?"

"I know you and I know women. You don't always think clearly when your heart is involved."

Ryan reared back and laughed. "Not to make you feel foolish, but the only thing attracted to this chick sits way below my heart."

"Interesting…"

He set the book on the coffee table. Clearly he wasn't going to get any studying done until he could convince his father he wasn't pining after some girl. "What do you mean by 'interesting'?"

"Nothing."

Shit. Now the old man was giving him back his own words.

"Look, I'll figure it out. Sometimes answers present themselves, if given time."

His father smirked. "Don't take too much time. If you're panting after this one, chances are other guys are too."

Fuck. Thanks, Dad.

―――∕∿∖―――

The training went on for several weeks, and Chloe sat in the back row—as far from Ryan as she could get. One day, he turned and frowned at her.

Waving her fingers at him, she hoped to keep him off balance. She was on to him, and with Morgaine's warning in her mind, she wanted to keep her distance.

The instructor sketched out the fine points of the fires they were to face that day. He stressed that the second job that afternoon would be kept purposely short and vague. Dispatchers would give out all the information they had, but with only a passerby reporting, the first crew on the scene would be going in with precious few details.

Their first fire was to mimic an apartment building with an explosion reported on the third floor.

As soon as they'd suited up, Chloe bumped Ryan with her elbow and said, "First one to the elevator is a boiled egg."

He laughed. "I think you mean 'rotten egg.'"

She shrugged. "Rotten or not, if an egg survives the fire, it's gonna boil."

The captain gave the order to enter the structure, and Ryan grabbed an ax and took off. His long legs carried him through the door first, but she was right on his heels. He was first on the stairs too.

Dammit. She had hoped by planting the word "elevator" in his mind he'd try to use it. That was stupid. *Yeah, he might make a rookie mistake, but not that one.* She'd have to figure out something else later. Right now she had a fire to fight.

They encountered a number of locked doors. Chloe pounded on them and yelled, "Fire department. Everybody out!" A few opened and fellow firefighters representing civilians rushed out. She pointed out the safest exit, and the captain nodded his approval.

Some doors, however, remained shut and Ryan pounded harder and yelled louder. Their protective equipment worked well, but tended to muffle their speech. He lifted his airpack just enough to shout and then clamped it over his mouth again.

Damn him. He was trying to show her up already. Well, she wouldn't let him. She grabbed the ax out of his hand and wielded it with near supernatural force, reducing the wooden door to splinters.

Ryan leaped through the hole and Chloe followed right behind him. They encountered a "body" on the floor. It was one of those deadweight dummies.

Ryan lifted the full-grown "man" properly and carried him over his shoulder while Chloe unlocked and opened the door wide. As he removed the body, a third firefighter joined her and she continued to the next closed door.

Her protective gear was working perfectly. She realized that Ryan may have fucked up already by trying to remove his, even for a second. In which case, she hadn't had to do a thing to trip him up.

She wielded the ax to obliterate another door and her fellow firefighter Ed used his foot to smash a larger hole. This time Chloe jumped through first. The smoke was much thicker here, but there was nothing apparent that would lead to an explosion. *Ah, the kitchen…*

Chloe had seen a gas range explode before. Shannon hadn't realized the pilot light was out until the oven she was preheating remained cold. When she tried to relight it… *Boom!*

Thank goodness dragons healed quickly. It took Shannon's eyebrows a couple of days to grow back, and Chloe couldn't help laughing at her sister's bald, red face as soon as she knew she was going to be all right.

Yup. A blackened dummy lay on the floor of the kitchen and the charred oven door was blown off its hinges.

She handed the ax to Ed and scooped up the badly burned "body" carefully. Carrying the heavy "woman" as if she were a baby, Chloe charged through the door Ed had opened wide and rushed down the stairs.

Ryan was headed back up. As she passed him their eyes met, and then the only thing that met her foot was air. Talk about being tripped up! She sailed over the last few steps and crashed onto the floor below. Dragons could defy gravity and fly, but not in human form.

Ryan whipped around and charged back down the steps where she was struggling to get up while still holding the body. He lifted both of them and charged out of the building.

Shite! She looked like a total incompetent, having to be carried out by a fellow firefighter. And he looked like a huge hero, carrying not one, but two bodies to safety simultaneously!

He laid them on the gravel, and she struggled to get out from under the body. Of course, he wanted to help her up, but she popped up onto her own two sore feet of her own volition.

"Feck! What the hell did you do? Trip me?"

"What?" he yelled. "You're accusing me of putting you and an innocent victim in danger?"

The captain jogged over to them. "Do you think you could put your argument on hold until the victim receives emergency medical attention?"

"Shite," Chloe muttered. She dropped to her knees and felt for a pulse while watching to see if the chest was rising and falling. Naturally it wasn't, so Chloe initiated CPR.

Meanwhile, Ryan located the firefighter paramedics and called them over.

Chloe reported what she'd seen in the last apartment and the captain seemed satisfied. He announced that the "gas" to the building had been shut off and returned to the scene to send in the men with a hose and observe how Ed was doing.

Chloe felt like a fool, but she should never have let her anger at Ryan interfere with the performance of her duties. She vowed it would never happen again. Then she cringed when she remembered there was another drill that afternoon.

———

The new recruits waited in a line after stripping off most of their turnout gear. Ryan wondered what had really happened. Was he somehow responsible for Chloe taking a header down the stairs? He certainly didn't do anything on purpose. He hadn't felt their bodies touch, but with all the adrenaline pumping, who knows…

The captain paced in front of the group, asking questions and sometimes adding information to their answers. When he stopped in front of Ryan and glared at him, he knew he was in trouble.

"Fierro, want to tell me what happened that caused you to carry two bodies out of the building simultaneously?"

Shit. What could he say? He didn't know?

"Is there some reason you're not answering my question?"

"No, sir. I—I assisted Firefighter Arish when she fell on the stairs."

"Was Firefighter Arish unable to walk after you helped her up?"

"No."

"Did she ask you to carry both her and the victim to safety?"

"No, but…"

"Stop." The captain sighed. "I'm aware of the reputation your family has. Some call it the Boston Fierro Department…"

That was true. Ryan had heard it when three or four of his brothers were together at cookouts or on fishing trips with their buddies.

"But if you feel like trying to be a hero because you're holding yourself to some kind of higher standard to gain their approval, well, just forget it. I've had this conversation before and frankly, I'm getting a little tired of it."

What the… Was that what he was doing? Or was he trying to show up Chloe? Suddenly a new realization crossed his mind. Perhaps he was *showing off* for Chloe?

"Shit," he muttered under his breath.

"What's that, Fierro?"

"Nothing, sir. I just hadn't thought of it that way."

"Then how *did* you think of it? Tell me. I'm curious."

He took a deep breath and tried to process possible answers and their consequences in those two seconds. Finally he bit his lower lip and shook his head.

"You have no answer, do you?"

Chloe straightened her back. "Sir, may I speak?"

What the hell is she going to say? Ryan eyed her curiously.

"Sure," the captain said. "Why not? Maybe you can explain what your fellow firefighter was thinking."

Was that sarcasm or not? Ryan wasn't sure, but he had a sinking feeling it was and would come with some kind of rude lesson.

"There's been some, uh…friendly competition between Firefighter Fierro and me, sir. I think it was his way of one-upping me."

To Ryan's surprise, she added, "It's as much my fault as his."

The captain stopped pacing in front of her and faced her squarely. "I was getting to you next, but let's talk about that now. I'm aware of the competition. I'm fairly sure I know the reason for it too, but we won't discuss that now. What I want to know from you is, how did you fall?"

She chewed her lower lip before she answered. "I don't know, sir. I guess my foot just missed the step."

"So, you don't think you were tripped?"

"No. Not really."

The trainer crossed his arms. "Not really? What does that mean?"

"It means I've had a chance to reflect on it, and I don't think I was tripped by Firefighter Fierro. I may have tripped over meself. I mean…*my*self."

The captain just stood there, staring her down. To her credit, her posture and gaze didn't waver.

At last, the captain let out a snort and resumed pacing. "It happens. Although if it happens too much, you risk becoming a liability. Be aware that you could be sent for neurological testing to be sure there's no physical reason for being a klutz."

Klutz. Oh crap. If that story got back to the firehouse, she'd have a horrible nickname waiting for her. Even Ryan couldn't hate her enough to let that happen.

"Sir, if I may…"

"At last he has an explanation…"

Ryan launched into the least problematic truth he could think of. "As I passed her on the stairs, I may have coughed. She turned, possibly thinking I was going to say something to her. That's when she missed her step. I don't think she's a klutz."

Instead of looking mollified, the captain appeared even angrier. "That brings me to another important point. Why did you remove your mask in the building?"

"To make sure the occupants heard us." As an afterthought, he added, "sir."

"Yeah, that wasn't smart. If you coughed after that, it may have been because you inhaled smoke or toxic gases. You won't last long if you keep breathing that crap."

He nodded. "Understood."

The rest of the trainees seemed to have done their jobs adequately and without incident. So much for having special powers.

The captain glanced between Ryan and Chloe and finally said, "For Christ's sake, don't fuck up this afternoon."

———

During lunch in the classroom, Chloe spotted Ryan striding toward her. She thought everything had been hashed out. It was humiliating to be called a klutz in front of her fellow trainees, but she imagined this was the time to make mistakes—not as a probie in her own firehouse. What could he have to say to her now?

"Uh, Chloe… May I sit down?"

She hesitated, but didn't want to look like she was harboring a grudge. "Suit yerself."

"I'm sorry about this morning."

Her eyes grew wide and she whispered loudly, "So, you're admittin' you tripped me?"

"No!" He lowered his voice. "Not at all. I'm just sorry the whole situation took place. I still don't know how it happened. I hope we can strike a truce."

She leaned away from him and said quietly, "I didn't know we were at war."

"We're not. Whatever competition existed before, I think we'd both be better off to let it go. I want to extend an invitation. Some of us are going fishing on Sunday. Would you like to join us?"

She groaned. "I hate fishin' boats. There's probably no privacy for ladies, is there?"

"Oh. We can stay out of the way if you need to use the head."

She laughed. "Sure you will." She hoped her sarcasm came through loud and clear.

"Look. I may not have acted like it at times, but I really am mature enough to treat you properly."

"What does that entail?"

"As an equal, but with dignity."

She had to admit he was saying all the right things, but she still hated fishing boats. Being cast adrift on one with her brother and sister, then told by leprechauns they could never return to their native land, had left a bitter taste in her mouth.

"I'm sorry, but no. And it's not because I wouldn't be open to socializing with you and your mates. I just really do hate fishing."

He nodded. "Okay. Well, if we do something else sometime, I'll be sure you're invited."

"Thank you kindly." She smiled to let him know she appreciated his effort to make peace.

Maybe Ryan wasn't the backstabber she should be wary of. She glanced around the room but didn't notice anyone else paying special attention to her.

Maybe Morgaine had been wrong. After all, psychic

predictions weren't an exact science. Hell, psy ability was called a pseudoscience. She didn't think she could relax yet, though.

The afternoon went a lot better. Chloe was glad she and Ryan seemed able to work together without any more mishaps. The trainer seemed relieved too.

Chapter 5

AT THE END OF THEIR LAST DAY, THE CAPTAIN SHOOK everyone's hand and wished them luck in their new assignments or EMT training if they were continuing on. As they were about to walk out to the parking lot, the trainer called, "Fierro. Arish. Wait a minute."

Ryan glanced at Chloe and she looked as perplexed as he was. Were they going to get another talking-to? Hadn't they been thoroughly chastised?

They waited until the last guy was gone and the door had slammed after him. Then the captain stood in front of them with his arms folded.

When no one said a word for several seconds, Ryan cleared his throat. "Is everything all right, captain?"

"Yes and no," he said. "You two are going to be working together in the same house."

"Yeah... Not for a while though. We still have EMT training to finish."

Chloe interjected, "We were told we'd probably be on different shifts either way though."

The captain's mouth formed a straight line. It may have been a smile, but it was hard to tell. "That's what I thought too. But I just got the word that a couple of guys used this opportunity to change their shifts and now you'll be on the same one."

Chloe's jaw dropped, and she stared at him with what could be interpreted as fear or surprise. Ryan tried to school his features, but it may have been too late. The captain was snickering.

"What's so funny?" Chloe asked.

The captain scratched his thinning scalp and hesitated. Finally he said, "I don't usually get involved in these things, but I can tell you two are like oil and water. You admitted there was competition between you, and I'm aware that at one time you were competing for the same job. That's not the case anymore. You both have jobs, and if you want to keep them, you're going to have to find a way to work together as a team. On the *same* team."

Ryan nodded. "Got it, Cap'n."

The older gentleman chuckled. "I don't think you've got a clue, Fierro."

That stung. He straightened and waited for the guy to explain himself. All he did was stand there, glancing from one probie to the other.

Chloe narrowed her eyes. "I feel like there's somethin' you're not sayin'. If you want us to hear it, perhaps you should speak plain."

Uh-oh. Her Irish accent's coming out.

The guy started to pace and shake his head. Finally he stopped and tossed his hands in the air. "I give up. If you two are so thick you can't see it, I'll just have to make it simple. You're attracted to each other. And you're about as subtle as seagulls following fishing boats."

Chloe gasped, then burst out laughing.

Ryan's first reaction was to protest, vehemently, but would that help? It might just prove the old man's point.

By the time Chloe was able to calm herself to the point of mere giggling, her eyes were leaking tears. "Sir.

I mean no disrespect, but maybe you should have your eyes checked."

"There's nothing wrong with my eyes. I have five teenagers. I know what I'm looking at."

She slapped a hand over her mouth and tried to hide the smile that remained.

Ryan felt like a complete idiot. Should he argue with the guy and back up Chloe? He had a feeling no matter what he said it wouldn't make any difference. The captain thought he knew what he knew and saw what he saw. But standing there with his thumb up his ass wasn't helping either.

"Sir. I'm not one hundred percent in agreement with you, but I'm sure that Arish and I will keep our working together on a professional level."

He nodded slowly and seemed satisfied. "Okay. I just wanted to get that out in the open. Things come up in a house that change the balance sometimes. I'm not maligning your gender, Arish, but a woman on the crew is one of those factors."

"I was told I'm going to a house that has had a woman in it before."

"Yes, and I'm glad. That should help. But if any of the guys want to test you, try not to take it personally." Then he whirled on Ryan and jabbed a finger into his chest. "And you let her fight her own battles."

He backed up a step. "Of course. Why wouldn't I?"

"I don't know. Why wouldn't you let her complete a botched carry on her own two feet?"

He dropped his gaze to the floor and shuffled his boots. The captain was much too shrewd. The protective side of Ryan's personality came out, yet he thought he was hiding it in competition.

"I thought he was tryin' to make me look bad, sir," Chloe said.

The captain smirked. "Not at all. He was trying to *take care of* you."

Chloe gazed at him with rounded eyes. Now she knew the truth too. *Damn it*.

She turned on her heel and marched toward the door. "I can take care o' meself." Before either of them could comment, she strutted through it and let it slam behind her.

"Should I go after her, sir?"

"Nah. Let her go. That fighting spirit may help her deal with a lot of shit. You're going to have to figure out another way to handle it though."

"Handle what? The probie teasing?"

"Yeah. That and…if you get involved with her, teasing will be the least of your worries."

Chloe immediately spotted Ryan on their first day of EMT training. It was as if her radar was automatically attuned to the man. Or maybe it was just because he was the tallest of the few trainees who were earning their EMT certificate. His luscious backside was right in her line of sight as he faced the ambulance in the hospital parking lot.

When he turned around, she wondered if he could sense her too.

The guy with the clipboard glanced up. "As soon as the last trainee arrives, we're going into the classroom. Meanwhile, feel free to take turns climbing into the back of the ambulance. As first responders you'll be responsible for knowing what and where everything is on your particular vehicles, but you can get an idea of how most ambulances are set up."

As soon as the first two trainees exited, Chloe approached the open doors. Ryan extended his hand.

"Can I offer you some assistance, m'lady?"

She rolled her eyes and hopped into the ambulance, ignoring his "kind" gesture. She still wasn't quite sure where he was coming from when he called her princess or some version of that, but it wasn't the worst nickname in the world—especially since it was true.

The last trainee arrived and the group moved to a meeting room inside the hospital. Ryan plunked his awesome butt in the chair right next to her. When she glanced over at him, he winked. She really didn't know how to react to him anymore, but her body was reacting to him whether she liked it or not.

She forced herself to ignore him and concentrate on their instructor, who was handing out pamphlets on CPR and first aid.

"You'll be expected to know everything in these booklets for the certification. Oh, and by the way, your first test is tomorrow."

Some of the trainees groaned. Chloe imagined that many had prior obligations or busy lives and might have difficulty finding the time to read all that information overnight. However, she had no life, so she welcomed the challenge.

"Before you stress about it," the instructor added, "this test is just a baseline to see what you already know. You don't have to choke down all this information at once. I have a video to show you. Give me a minute to get it going."

Chloe glanced over at Ryan. He was already reading the booklet—like he didn't have enough of an advantage coming from a large firefighting family. Some of them must be EMTs.

"Well, I know what you'll be doing tonight," he said without looking over at her.

"Do you now?"

"I'm pretty sure you'll be cramming for this test. Your competitive nature practically demands it."

Feck. When did he become such an expert on me?

Before she had a chance to come up with a verbal response, he smiled at her. "Maybe we could study together."

Well, that's a surprise. "I, uh…I'm afraid I have something I can't get out of." *Like this crazy attraction to you.* If she were a normal young woman, Ryan's attention would be flattering and probably welcome. But she wasn't normal. She was a dragon—more used to setting fires than extinguishing them. Imagine his surprise if he came down one morning to find her reheating his coffee with her breath.

The video was ready and the instructor shut off the lights.

Ryan leaned close. He smelled like the great outdoors. Trees, grass, rain… He smelled good. Too good.

"Come on, Arish," he whispered. "We're going to have to find a way to work together eventually…"

"Shhh…" was all she had time to say before the video started.

This attraction was not only inconvenient, it was potentially tragic. Her grandmother's predictions were never wrong. She remembered her mother telling everyone about her father's aquamarine matching her eyes and her uncle's fluorite matching her aunt's eyes. If she had indeed received a diamond at birth, it couldn't be any clearer—no man had eyes for her.

Maybe I should have become a nurse or a teacher… That annoying thought was quickly squashed when she pictured working with a bunch of bitchy females. She hadn't been raised like most kids, that was true, but whenever the opportunity to interact with girls presented itself, the results were puzzling. Instead of making friends, she was treated as a threat. Her brother thought it was because she was too brash, so she tried adjusting her behavior to fit in, but it never worked.

Finally, a young woman who was just passing through the village noticed the way she had been ignored after one of their musical sessions at the pub. Her brother and sister were being treated to pats on the back and free pints. Chloe was by herself, breaking down her flute and packing up the other instruments.

The stranger invited her for a walk and they got to talking. Apparently it took an outsider to spot something she and her siblings might never have noticed: Chloe was beautiful. "Drop-dead gorgeous" were the words the stranger used. A pretty blonde with a willowy figure, she was indeed a threat to insecure women.

All Chloe saw were her faults. She thought her limbs were too thin, her hair was too straight, and her freckles marred her ivory complexion. She envied her sister's curly red hair and barely-there freckles that added a touch of warmth to her peach skin.

The woman laughed. She was older than the girls Chloe tried to befriend, so maybe she was more mature too. She offered Chloe sympathy. Sympathy! For her beauty! It was a crazy idea to her at the time, but she understood better as she thought about it. Boys wanted to "date" her—code for get into her pants—until she showed her assertive side. Girls just wanted to drown her. She wrestled her mind back to the moment.

After the video they had a short break. In the EMT class there was only one other woman, and she was wearing a wedding ring. Chloe might be able to find a friend and put some distance between herself and Ryan. She'd try anything at this point.

She strode over to the woman and introduced herself. "Hi. I'm Chloe Arish." She stuck out her hand.

The woman glanced at it and said, "Hi. I'm Beverly. Excuse me. I have to find the ladies room."

The woman took off and left Chloe feeling rejected. Ryan strolled over to her. As much as she hated to admit it, male friends were better than no friends. She offered him a smile.

"Pretty inspiring video, wasn't it?"

"Huh? Oh, yeah."

"I guess they figured they'd appeal to our hero complexes first, and then get into the nitty-gritty of how it's done later."

Chloe had barely watched the video. It consisted of a succession of clips showing ambulances responding to desperate people, and the quick, efficient workers doing their jobs. EMTs were never thanked for their efforts, but the broad grins on their faces afterward said it all.

If there had been pertinent information given, she could have concentrated on that. She didn't need her "hero complex," as Ryan called it, stroked or inspired.

But it was nice to know that someday she might be greeted like a savior instead of a pariah.

"Was there something you wanted?" she asked him.

He laughed.

What the feck was so funny?

"Sorry…" He shook his head, but the smile remained.

"Is there some kind of private joke being had between you and yourself?"

"No." He blew out a frustrated breath and the smile disappeared. "Look. I'm trying. We can be friends or not. I'd like it if we could work together as friends, but it's your call." He turned and strode away. Oh God. She knew that feeling. She knew that stride of shame.

She followed. "I'm sorry," she said when she caught up to him.

"What are you sorry for?"

She threw her hands in the air. "I don't know. Bein' a bitch. Treatin' you crappy. I don't know what to call it, but I know what it feels like…and I'm sorry."

He stood still and the smile returned.

Oh, please don't tell me I just made a big mistake.

He strolled over to her. "Thank you. You haven't been a bitch though. You've been…private. Soon, you'll discover how little privacy firefighters have. I think I'll give you your space for a while and let you get used to the idea of living and working with a bunch of guys, day in and day out. It's what we'll do—until you quit, get promoted, or retire."

Shite.

————

Chloe had dinner plans with Rory and Amber. They

wanted to take her out to celebrate the end of her training, but she didn't feel like going anywhere.

She had changed into her little black dress and waited on their stoop before ringing the doorbell. When she looked down the street, it appeared as if nothing had changed since the nineteenth century. Well, electric streetlamps and cars instead of horses and buggies, naturally, but other than that, this place seemed like stepping back in time. It could be a residential street in long-ago Dublin.

Yet, so much had changed for her in a year. Just the fact that this building she was about to enter had gone from a seventies disco palace to an elegant bed-and-breakfast was amazing.

Now her brother was welcoming the city's paranormal visitors to his B and B, and she was Firefighter Arish. How different their lives were from living in a caretaker's cottage in sleepy little Ballyhoo, Ireland.

They still played sessions at the Boston Uncommon Tea Room, and the public flocked to the place on their Irish folk songs night. Life was good.

She could have relaxed and done nothing but play her flute, tin whistles, and violin once a week, but that person would not be Chloe Arish. She had needed more, and the fire service certainly fit the bill.

The door flew open and Rory grinned. "Well, are you goin' to stand out here all night?"

She chuckled and said, "What if I am?"

He snorted. "Then I suppose I'll have to push you to the restaurant."

She became somber. "I was just feelin' nostalgic. Would you be opposed to eatin' here instead of at some fancy restaurant? I'll help Amber cook."

He cocked his head and stared at her curiously. "You don't have to help a minor goddess do anythin', Chloe, but if you'd rather stay in, we can certainly accommodate you. It's your night."

She smiled gratefully. "Thanks."

She followed her brother inside, and he took her coat and hung it in the closet next to the front door. The long winding staircase led to the second floor where the kitchen and office were located. The main floor housed the large parlor and dining room. A dumbwaiter brought food downstairs when Amber didn't just "poof" it down there directly.

Four guest rooms were located on the third floor, and Rory and Amber occupied the top floor. There had been maids' quarters above that in what was now considered the attic. It was mostly for storage. Amber insisted maids weren't necessary as long as she could make the beds with a snap of her fingers.

Rory looked up and raised his voice, "Amber?"

She appeared beside him. "No need to shout, hon." Then she hugged Chloe. "You look gorgeous. I don't think I've seen you in a dress since Shannon's wedding in Ballyhoo."

Chloe chuckled. "I don't wear a lot of fussy dresses. I prefer to be comfortable."

"Dresses can be very comfortable. We should go shopping sometime."

"Why? Is this dress not fittin' the tab?"

"Um. I think you were going for 'fitting the bill,' but that's not what I was saying. It's perfect. I just thought you might like to have a couple of dresses in pretty colors, just in case. You'd look fabulous in hot pink or electric blue."

"Just in case of what?" Rory asked, looking genuinely perplexed.

Amber bumped his elbow. "In case she has a hot date."

Rory made the mistake of leaning back and letting out a deep belly laugh.

Chloe crossed her arms. "I think I'm insulted."

"You think?" Amber stomped on her boyfriend's toe until he picked up his foot and hopped around. He didn't stop laughing though.

"Do you think no one will ever ask me for a date, Brother? Am I hideous?"

"You're not hideous, Chloe. But history has shown that any poor bloke who asks you for a date gets told to go on his way and never bother you again. If they don't listen the first time, I usually see 'em runnin' for their lives the second."

Chloe snickered. Her brother was right, but that was back in Ballyhoo where sons of sheepherders and fishermen held no appeal. Now things were different. *She* was different. And one Ryan Fierro was responsible for some of the uncomfortable changes.

"I could date," she said. "I was asked out recently."

Rory's eyebrows shot up. "Is that a fact?"

"'Tis indeed."

Amber clapped her hands. "Awesome! Let's go shopping on your next day off. When will that be?"

Chloe let out a sigh. "I'm not feelin' much like shoppin'. It's not like I was asked to go to the ballet or symphony. I was asked to go on a fishin' trip."

"Fishin'?" Rory said. "After all the fish we had to catch and eat on our way to Iceland? I thought you said you'd never eat fish again."

"I did. Which is why I turned down the invitation."

"Oh…" Amber said, sounding disappointed. "Well, maybe someday…"

Her brother and his girlfriend were really irritating. They seemed to think that her being asked for a date was a fluke that would never happen again. Well, she'd just turn the tables on them.

"So, when are you two gettin' married?"

Rory barked a laugh. Amber didn't seem quite as amused.

"It's not that we won't, someday…" Rory said.

"Well, I can't imagine what you're waitin' for. Hell, you've been inseparable since the day you met."

She couldn't hide the smirk creeping into her smile. The two of them had begun their relationship fighting over the same apartment, each of them refusing to leave.

Suddenly Chloe realized she and Ryan had been thrown right into a similar situation. They had been competing for a single job.

A year and a half ago, it had been clear to everyone *except* Rory and Amber that their struggle involved more than an apartment. The way they'd looked at each other, even when angry, couldn't hide a smoldering sensuality.

Is *that* what the captain saw when she and Ryan were glaring at each other?

"Holy shite," she muttered under her breath.

Amber put her arm around Chloe's shoulder. "There's no need to stand here in the foyer. Let's go sit in the living room."

A split second later she wobbled, light-headed, when she and Amber appeared in the fourth floor apartment in front of the sofa. "I may never get used to teleportation."

Amber smiled. "Have a seat. I'll be right back."

She disappeared into thin air and a moment later returned holding Rory's hand.

"You didn't have to do that. We can take the elevator like normal people," Chloe said. "In fact, you-know-who would be very upset if she saw you usin' your power where anyone walkin' by could see."

"It's still light out. People can't see in, and we don't have guests at the moment." Amber set a tray of hot appetizers on the coffee table. Appetizers that hadn't been in her hands a moment ago.

"Now, tell us what's bothering you."

"Who said anythin's botherin' me?"

"You did. You want to stay in and your accent is back."

"That's just because I'm with me brother. It comes floodin' back in the presence of a fellow Irishman."

Amber folded her arms. "Do I need to loosen your tongue with some Irish whiskey?"

Chloe grinned. "I'll certainly let you try."

Rory laughed and took that as his cue to fetch the Bushmills. He poured two fingers for each of them and set one in front of his sister.

She downed it in one gulp.

"Jaysus, Chloe. Amber's right. You must be upset. Since you've never done that unless dared, I assume it's somethin' terrible."

"It's no biggo."

Rory's glass paused on the way to his mouth. "Biggo?"

Amber pushed away her drink and said, "I think she meant to say *biggie*. 'It's no biggie.'"

Chloe's face heated. Just when she thought she had

all the American expressions down, she screwed up another one.

Rory laughed. He stopped quickly though. "So, little sister. It doesn't matter if the problem is little or biggo. If it's a problem of yours, 'tis a problem of mine."

She stiffened. "Says who?"

"Says someone who loves you."

As if the air went out of her, she sagged against the couch. "I'm sorry." After a long pause, she blurted out, "There's this man…"

<center>~~~</center>

At Sunday dinner, Jayce announced to the entire Fierro clan, "So, I hear Ryan has a new girlfriend."

Ryan sputtered, almost choking on his mother's excellent manicotti. After the catcalls, congratulations, and lewd comments had died down, he said, "You heard wrong."

"Really? Because a couple of the guys have met her and whooeeee…" He waved his fingers as if they were on fire. "They said if they had seen her first…"

Ryan narrowed his eyes at Jayce. "If they'd seen her first, they'd what? Ask her out? Tell those fools she'd eat 'em alive."

Mr. Fierro laughed. "It sounds as if my middle son might eat 'em alive."

Ryan shook his head. "Not at all. I'm just trying to save your buddies an unnecessary rejection…but if they like being shot down, tell 'em to go for it."

"So, she's not looking for a hot date?" his youngest brother Luca asked. "Why not? Is she already seeing someone?"

Ryan was silent. He could pretend he didn't know, but Chloe had told him she didn't have a husband or boyfriend.

"I don't know," Ryan started. "But she has kind of a prickly vibe. Nice enough to the married guys, but she definitely gives out the 'back off' message if anyone tries to get too friendly. And her favorite phrase seems to be, 'I can take care of meself.'"

As the majority of the men guessed that meant Chloe was gay, his mother raised her hands. "Now, now, Jayce, Miguel, Gabe, Ryan, Dante, Noah, and Luca… don't forget…it's not about a person's sex or sexual orientation. If they can do the job, that's all that matters."

The Fierro patriarch shook his head. "How do you remember all their names? And in order, no less."

The sons chuckled. Good ol' Dad could be counted on to bring the comic relief to any situation—whether he meant to or not.

Dante folded his arms and focused on Ryan. "Maybe she's just independent. So, you're saying you wouldn't go out with her if she asked you?"

Ryan tried to keep a straight face. "Yeah, that'll happen when hell freezes over."

Gabe, his next older brother, the one who probably knew him best, asked, "So if we set you up on a blind date, you'd go?"

"Hell no. I don't go on blind dates. You know that."

He shrugged. "I just thought I'd ask. It's been a long time since Melanie. Now that you're in a pretty much all-male job, you might need help meeting eligible females."

Ryan snorted. "I don't need any help in that department."

Miguel, the second son, who was happily married,

said, "There's always the girls who hang around the station hoping to snag a date with a firefighter."

Ryan's brows shot up. "The *Fire Hoes*? No way."

His dad laughed. "In my day we called them Jake groupies, but I like your term better."

"Leave him alone, boys," his mother said. "Ryan may not be ready for love, despite what you all think."

"Thanks, Mom."

"Who said anything about love?" Noah, the next to the youngest, asked. "It's just weird he's been celibate for a year." He leaned out enough to see Ryan. "You must be ready for a little fun."

"Again, I can find my own fun." Ryan drained his wineglass. "May I be excused?"

"You may not," his father said. "Your mother works hard to put together Sunday dinner each week. The least you can do is sit and suffer through it."

His mother glared at her husband. "Suffer through it?"

"Sorry, hon. I didn't mean that the way it sounded."

She rose. "I'd like Ryan's help in the kitchen, if you don't mind. There's still dessert to 'suffer though.'"

Her sons protested that her tiramisu was nothing they had to suffer through, and they all offered to help.

"The only one I want in there right now is Ryan. Thank you for the offers, though." She smiled at her sons and shot her husband a parting hairy eyeball.

"Oh boy, Dad. You really stepped in it," Gabe said.

"Yeah." Mr. Fierro placed his elbow on the table and cradled his chin. "I'll probably get the smallest piece and a lecture about my waistline."

Chapter 6

"CHIEF, MAY I TALK WITH YOU PRIVATELY?" Haggarty asked. "It's about Firefighter Arish."

"Already?"

John Haggarty hadn't expected the district chief to drop in and welcome Chloe and Ryan to the firehouse personally, but now that he was here, seizing the opportunity seemed like the right thing to do.

"Uh. If you have time... It'll only take a couple of minutes."

"Sure. I like to say my door is always open, except when it's closed. Looks like it's open at the moment." He ushered Haggarty into the office he used when he was at this particular firehouse. His position covered more than one.

As they sat, John said, "First off, I want to thank you for hiring two firefighters. I know it couldn't have been easy to get the extra funding."

The chief chuckled. "Don't worry. We'll have a bake sale or something."

The guy seemed to be in a good mood, so Haggarty relaxed. "This is kind of related to that, actually. I was just wondering if Firefighter Arish's background check was...well..."

"Spit it out, Haggarty."

"Thorough," he said. There. He might not have to worry about his position in the department, but he still wanted to be sure he stayed alive. A petite female firefighter could never rescue his six-foot-two, slightly pudgy frame.

The chief leaned back in his chair and clasped his hands. "What makes you think it wasn't?"

"I don't know anything for sure, but one night me and the guys were out for a drink and Fierro came in. He was talking about the blonde being fresh off the boat. And just a little while ago, I asked her if she'd ever been to Trinity College in Dublin. She acted as if she didn't know the school. I thought it was world-famous."

"Hmmm... It could be that she didn't travel much in Ireland. She's from Northern Ireland, you know. Have you noticed anything that can't be explained by individual preferences?"

"Well, maybe. When I was talking to a firefighter from District 3, he said his wife met her on the day she arrived—by boat."

The chief shrugged. "And?"

"Well, I thought that was kind of suspicious. She hates boats. She turned down a fishing trip because of it."

The captain laughed. "Ever heard of a white lie, John? She was probably just letting you down easy."

"I don't think so, sir. Besides, I'm not the one who asked her. She said she'd be willing to do something else with the guys, but no boats."

The chief frowned. "I really don't see what this has to do with her background check."

He hated to spell it out, but the chief wasn't getting it. "Are you sure she came into the country legally? If someone hates boats and has to cross an ocean, they'd probably fly. Wouldn't they? Unless they didn't have a passport or were on a no-fly list."

Chief O'Brien raised his eyebrows. "Are you saying you think she's an undocumented immigrant—or a terrorist?"

"I don't know, sir. I just wondered."

The chief rose and strolled to the door. "Well, don't worry about it. All naturalized citizens are investigated thoroughly. Her documents were checked and nothing out of the ordinary was found."

Haggarty realized the conversation was over when the chief opened the door. "Yes, sir." He crossed in front of him and left, but the officer didn't follow. Instead he returned to his desk, and Haggarty was somewhat gratified when he saw him reaching for the phone. Perhaps he'd planted a tiny seed of doubt.

Hopefully he hadn't made it look like he simply disliked her and wanted her gone for that reason. He knew full well that working closely with other people was a crapshoot. Sometimes you liked each other and sometimes you didn't. As long as it didn't affect the work, the top brass didn't give a shit.

Maybe his next move should be to invite her to do something else with them. If he didn't like her, he'd avoid her company, especially on their days off, right?

When he reentered the kitchen, the guys seemed a little more interested in their new female probie than he'd expected them to be. Not just interested, but downright charmed. Chloe was smiling and seemed more relaxed than when he'd left.

So why did that bother him?

"Hey, Arish," he said. "We hang out sometimes. Is

there anything you like to do besides sewing circles and shopping?"

One side of her lip turned up slowly. "I'm not much for either sewing or shopping. Can't you see a woman doing anything else?"

"Don't worry. I won't ask you to go fishing." He winked.

Ryan Fierro rose and approached him slowly. "She knows how to 'hang out,' Haggarty." He used air quotes and his tone sounded downright offended.

"Are you saying you and Arish are hanging out, Fierro? As in dating?"

Chloe snorted. "I won't be datin' any of me coworkers, boys. That's a recipe for disappointment."

"I think you mean 'a recipe for disaster,'" Ryan corrected her.

She looked at him wide-eyed. "I'd hardly call a bad date a disaster. No one should matter *that* much."

The guys laughed.

Lieutenant Streeter spoke up. "I won't be asking. I'm married, and my wife is disappointed enough."

More laughter filled the kitchen.

"So it sounds like you're expecting a date with a firefighter would be a disappointment," Haggarty said.

Ryan whispered something to the guy next to him. It sounded like, "If he's genuinely thinking of asking her out, I can't wait to see her shut him down."

"Not a'tall," Chloe answered. "I simply wouldn't want it to be awkward, workin' alongside any of you fine fellows *if* things went pear-shaped. I imagine it might affect the workplace."

"Pear-shaped?" Haggarty mumbled.

"You're probably right," Ryan said. "But if things got that bad, one of you would be transferred to another house."

"And I don't want it to be me," she asserted. "I live within walkin' distance, and I like it that way. Drivin' around Boston *is* a 'recipe for *disaster*.'"

They all laughed.

"You got that right," Streeter said.

She looked up at John innocently. "So, what were you thinkin' when you mentioned hanging out?"

He shrugged. "I don't know. I heard you didn't like fishing when you were invited. So what *do* you like to do?"

She hesitated. "Up until now I enjoyed helpin' me brother remodel his B and B. But it's finished. I miss the physical activity."

"We could go to a gym," Ryan suggested. "Spot each other, lift weights. Maybe try out some equipment we don't have here at the station."

Haggarty snorted. "That wouldn't interest me much. I like to box, but I won't be hitting a woman."

Chloe seemed to perk up. "I'd like to see a first-class gym. The few donated things they have here wouldn't keep me occupied for long."

"Great," Ryan said. "I used to go to a place in the financial district. They had ProForm equipment, treadmills, hybrid trainers, Tour de France exercise bikes, ellipticals, and all kinds of weights. Anyone else know of something like that nearby?"

The quiet ones shook their heads, but Streeter suggested a place in Kenmore Square. "They have some good weight training equipment," he said, looking directly at Chloe.

At that moment, the tones rang out. A dispatcher announced over a loudspeaker where they'd be going.

"Shit," the lieutenant muttered as he jogged around the corner to where the pole was. "Probies, follow me."

Chloe and Ryan grabbed for the pole at the same time. He stepped back and gestured toward it. "After you."

"Ah, no. You go first," Chloe said. "I insist."

The lieutenant's voice boomed up toward them, "Is there a problem, Fierro?"

"No, sir," he called down. He nodded to Chloe and she rolled her eyes, then grasped the pole and disappeared down below.

There was something going on between Fierro and Arish. John was sure of it. Some kind of not-so-friendly competition, and yet he seemed ready to jump in and defend her.

Haggarty hadn't been at this station very long and hadn't worked with the other female—or any female for that matter. He had transferred in when the woman was promoted.

And having women out of the way was the way he liked it.

———

The call turned out to be a false alarm. One of the area hotels had a smoke detector malfunction. Still, the fire department had to be sure, so they did a thorough check of the place. A lot of area businesses required regular inspections anyway, so it was good for Chloe to see what that entailed.

When they pulled back into the fire station, the lieutenant asked to see them both in the captain's office.

"Are we in trouble, sir?" Chloe asked.

"Not at all. I just want to address something before it becomes an issue. The other guys have already heard it, so you two are the only ones I need to talk to."

She relaxed and followed him into an office strewn with paperwork and fluttering bulletin boards.

The lieutenant took a seat by one of the desks facing the window. Then he pointed out a couple of chairs they could drag over.

"Get comfortable. This is about having a female firefighter on the crew," the lieutenant said.

"Oh." Chloe was surprised. She thought…well, she didn't really know what to think. She'd hoped to be treated like any other firefighter.

"Relax, Arish. There's nothing especially wrong with having a woman around."

Nothing especially *wrong?*

"But there are factors that need to be acknowledged," he continued. He nodded to Ryan. "In your father's day, a female firefighter was rare. The few we have now still face some prejudice at times, and it's best to just get it out there."

The lieutenant stretched out with his hands clasped behind his head, as if settling in for a long discussion. "As far as we know, the first woman to be paid for fighting fires was Sandra Forcier, who was hired as a public safety officer—a combination police officer and firefighter—by the City of Winston-Salem, North Carolina, in 1973."

"'73, sir?" Ryan exclaimed. "Not until 1973?"

"That's right. Forcier moved into a fire-only position four years later. Battalion Chief Forcier, now Waldron, retired from Winston-Salem in 2004."

He paused and looked directly at Chloe. "A lot of women have bravely faced situations that people have previously considered a man's responsibility. And that's what I'm addressing now. It's not your fellow firefighters, but the public at large who may view you with anything from awe to distrust."

She nodded slowly. "I never gave much thought to the public not trustin' me, sir."

"I know. The first time it happens, don't be shocked. Sometimes people in danger blurt out all kinds of stupid things. I don't think you have to worry about the guys here. They know you can do the job. You wouldn't be here if you couldn't."

Ryan's eyes narrowed. "I don't know about that, sir. I've learned she can do the job, but the other guys haven't had a chance to see her in action yet."

"Throughout training each of you were watched and tested carefully. The guys all know this, because they've been through it. And if women wash out, quite often it's because of their own fears and doubts."

"I have no doubts, sir."

"And from what I've seen," Ryan interjected, "very little fear."

She turned and smiled at him. It was the first time he'd ever acknowledged her bravery. He didn't know about her natural advantage—namely being a fireproof dragon—but it was still good to hear.

"So, you trust me now?" she asked.

"With my life."

The lieutenant smiled, apparently satisfied that any rivalry he'd been warned about between these two wouldn't cause a problem.

"And I trust you, with mine," Chloe said. *But not with my heart.*

"Are you sure you're up for this?" Ryan asked.

Chloe had her gym bag over her shoulder and laughed. "Why? Did that little hotel fire yesterday tucker you out?"

He grinned. "What fire?"

"Exactly. I thought a big city like this would be a lot busier."

"I know from listening to family members that it can be crazy busy. Sitting around and waiting for something to happen was the hardest thing about yesterday."

"I'm looking forward to the physical exercise," Chloe said.

"Me too." He held open the door for her.

She had almost given up on trying to change his "ladies first" mentality. It seemed as if that was ingrained in his makeup. Obviously he'd had no sisters who were willing to run up and over his back to be first.

"So, what do you think of this twenty-four hours on and four days off schedule?" he asked as they waited for the elevator.

She laughed. "Yeah, the schedule is feckin' crazy. But I guess we hit it right. It could just as easily have been three or four days round the clock, and then a day off."

"That would have been fine by me. I get bored easily."

The elevator arrived and they stepped inside. Chloe didn't address his comment. It was hard to tell if it was his competitive nature again, or if he just meant it as an innocent comment.

She would see if his competitive streak showed itself again soon enough. They changed in their respective locker rooms and met at the weightlifting equipment.

As she spotted him, he lifted more weight than she thought the average man could manage. But Ryan was proving he was anything but average.

The weight he kept adding to the barbells was bordering on ridiculous. His skin glistened with a fine sheen of sweat, and she couldn't help noticing his muscles. Damn it all, her mouth watered. *Don't drool, Chloe. He has enough of an ego without you feeding it.*

At last it was her turn. He started removing the weights, and she said, "Leave 'em."

He cocked a brow. "Seriously? You think you can lift this?"

"I can."

He smirked. "All right, princess. I'll let you try…but just so you know, I'm going to hover. You don't need an injury before your next shift."

She rolled her eyes. "Fine. Hover all you want. I'm tellin' you, I can do this."

As he stood behind her and she lay on the bench below the barbell, he chewed his lower lip. *Ah, a tell.* Now she knew when he was nervous.

Her toned arms looked even leaner as she reached for the barbell.

"Don't," he said and clamped his hand over the middle of the bar.

"Excuse me? It's my turn."

"I know, but I can't let you do this. Even if you did manage to lift it, the strain isn't worth it. You need your arm strength for the job."

At that moment a woman appeared, dressed as if she were auditioning for a remake of the '80s movie *Flashdance*—complete with leg warmers and a poofy perm.

"I need to speak with you, miss," she said.

"I'm in the middle of—"

"Now!" The woman grabbed her hand and all but yanked her off the bench, then marched her to the ladies' locker room. When they saw a couple of women chatting, the staff member barked, "Leave!" They immediately scurried out.

"Jaysus, there's no need to be—"

Suddenly the woman transformed into none other than Mother Nature herself. Her hair turned white, long, and loose, and she wore her signature ivory robe, belted with a vine.

Chloe gasped. She had only met the deity once, but it was a meeting she'd never forget. One isn't often lectured by the Goddess of all. And here she was, almost breaking the rule she'd been lectured about.

"What do you think you're doing?"

When she recovered her decorum, Chloe answered, "Defending the right of women to be as strong as a man."

Mother Nature paced, staring at her with narrowed eyes. "Are you an 'idjit,' as your people would say?"

Chloe folded her arms. "Not a'tall."

"I beg to differ. What if I had been a real staff member? Without the muscle to back up your ability, you'd reveal that you're supernatural. You *know* that's not allowed."

"I—I…"

"Yeah. I-yi-I! Not. Good. Downright stupid."

"I get it! You don't have to insult me intelligence."

"Oh, I think I do. If I were sweet about it, would you listen?" She mockingly said in a meek voice, "If it's not too much trouble...that is, if you wouldn't mind...would you kindly refrain from trying to show your strength?"

Chloe had to agree. She'd steamroll a request like that and do whatever she wanted. And she wanted to show Ryan she was his equal.

"I understand your competitive nature. Hell, I gave it to you! I thought women might need it, being the smaller, gentler sex."

"So you knew we'd have to prove we're equal?"

Mother Nature rolled her eyes. "Again. Just who do you think you're talking to?"

"Oh."

"Now, go out there and take at least half the weight off that barbell. If you can't do that, make up an excuse to leave."

Chloe sighed. "Yes, ma'am. I'll make up an excuse and go home."

Mother Nature's eyes widened and she rose about a foot off the floor. "I *hate* being called ma'am! It's Goddess, or Gaia, or Mother Nature. Understand?"

"I do. My apologies, Goddess."

She nodded and floated to the floor again. "That's better." She patted Chloe on the head. "Now be a good little dragon and pretend to be *normal*."

Oh, that rankled. But when dealing with the Goddess of All, the least of her problems was a little patronizing behavior—or would it be matronizing? Whatever. The woman could reduce her to ash if she wanted to. Her fireproof gift could be removed in the blink of an eye, and then where would she be? Reduced to competing with the others on a *human* basis. Ugh.

Chloe changed into her street clothes and found Ryan. She waved her cell phone. "Sorry. I got a call from my brother. Apparently he needs me right away."

"Oh. Sure," Ryan said as he put the free weights back in the rack. "Just give me a minute to change and I'll drive you home."

"Not necessary. I can find my way."

"Are you sure? I don't mind leaving early. Maybe I can help."

"Ah, no. It's a family matter. I'll see you at work in a few days."

When she saw the disappointed look on his face, she impulsively invited him to their session at the Boston Uncommon Tea Room the following night. During training she had told him that her family formed a small Irish folk band and he'd said he liked that kind of music.

Now she had to think up a plausible family emergency and ask Rory and Shannon to play along.

—⁓—

Ryan walked up to Chloe at the tearoom before finding a seat—if he could. The place was packed. "You know, I was surprised you invited me here. I thought you were hiding your family. Maybe you have a crazy uncle in the attic or something…"

She laughed. "No. The crazy one is me." She gestured to her brother and sister. "Rory, Shannon, this is one of my fellow firefighters, Ryan Fierro."

"Ah, Ryan," Rory said as he shook his hand. "A good Irish name."

Ryan chuckled. "I don't think I have a drop of Irish blood running through my veins. I was named for a firefighter who saved my father's life when he was on the job."

Shannon shook his hand. "Sounds like an interesting story. We Irish love stories. You'll have to tell us all about it sometime."

He smiled. "I'd be glad to. I just have to get Chloe to invite me to your home sometime."

"Oh, well that may be—"

To his surprise, Chloe clapped a hand over her sister's mouth. "Impossible. Me sister lives out of state. And she doesn't have a big enough place to host everyone."

Shannon peeled Chloe's hand off. "I can speak for meself, if you don't mind."

Chloe raised an eyebrow at her sister. "Maybe I do mind."

Rory sighed. "Jaysus, girls. Leave it." He turned to Ryan and said, "I have a place that's plenty large enough to host a family dinner. We'll have Chloe tell you when. I assume she knows your schedule."

Under her breath Chloe muttered, "Now you've gone an' done it."

Ryan raised his brows. "I'm being invited to dinner?" He stared at Chloe. She nodded, albeit reluctantly. "Sure. I'd love to come. My schedule is the same as your sister's."

"Grand. I'll tell Amber when she gets here later. She's on a short errand."

Chloe pointed to an empty seat. "Ah. Someone just left. You'd better grab his chair before someone else comes in."

Ryan excused himself and took the chair across the room. He noticed Chloe whispering furiously to her brother, but with the background noise competing, he couldn't hear what was being said. At last, Rory held up his hand and the place quieted.

"Good evenin' to you, one and all," he said. "Tonight we're goin' to play a selection of our favorite songs. Some you may know, so feel free to sing along. First up is 'My Wild Irish Rose.'"

Ryan thought Chloe certainly fit the song's title. He didn't know the words, but many in the room did. They sang along with Rory's melodious low voice.

It was a love song. He was sure of that much. Chloe peeked up from her flute once, then glanced off in another direction. When the lyrics spoke of the singer hoping someday to take her flower, Chloe's face reddened.

Could she be a virgin? That thought startled him. Yet the more he thought about it, the more sense it made. She was prickly around any man who hit on her. And even though she was beautiful, not many tried. She gave off a "leave me alone" vibe that was unmistakable.

Crap. Did he want to be the one to "take her flower"?

After an hour of watching her handle the flute, violin, and tin whistles with such reverence and love, he realized he did. As soon as she settled in at the job and relaxed, he was sure she'd lose that brittle edge.

After their set, Rory brought Amber over to him and introduced them. "Amber's me luv, and she decides how many she'll cook for."

Amber's hazel-green eyes twinkled. They weren't the same green as Chloe's light jade. "Chloe is coming over tomorrow night, anyway, and we'd love to have you."

"Well, thank you for the offer…but does Chloe want me to come?" *Yikes. I just heard myself.*

Amber smiled. "Chloe doesn't know what she wants when it comes to guys. I think you'd be good for her— even if you're just her friend."

He took a deep breath. "I can be that to her." *With benefits.*

"Good," Rory said. "We'll see you at seven. Do you know where we live?"

"Ah, no. I've offered to drive Chloe home, but she prefers to walk."

"That she does," Rory said. "I worry about her, even knowin' she can take care of herself."

"That seems to be a theme with her."

Rory laughed. "You've got the right of it."

Amber put her hand on Ryan's arm. "You may be just what she needs. Perhaps you can take her home tonight."

"I took the subway, but I can certainly walk her home and catch it at Copley."

"That would be grand," Rory said. "I'd feel better if she had an escort." He winked at Amber. "My lass will see me home as she usually does."

———

Chloe couldn't believe Rory and Amber were playing matchmaker. They knew full well there would be no long-term lover in her future. She avoided heartbreak by avoiding short-term relationships in the present.

But Ryan said he needed to know where she lived, so she'd take him to her brother's stoop and never mention she lived next door. At least he wouldn't show up at paranormal central. It was bad enough that her brother and his intended were supernatural beings, but at least they knew enough to keep that to themselves. Chloe had seen her neighbors assume everyone entering the paranormal club on the second floor had to be supernatural whether they knew it was true or not.

So far, they hadn't been wrong, but if they saw Ryan and assumed… Well, a mistake like that would be awkward to say the least.

When they arrived at Rory and Amber's Beacon Street brownstone she turned and said, "Well, here it is…"

He looked up and whistled. "What a beautiful building. I understand why you enjoyed your time renovating it."

"How do you know I enjoyed it?"

He smiled at her. "By the nostalgic look in your eyes when you talk about the work you did, and the sadness in your voice when you say it's finished."

She stared at the sidewalk and nodded. "To be sure."

He tipped her chin up. "Your brother and Amber must have been grateful for your help and proud of the work you did."

"They are, but heck, I'm proud of meself."

He was quiet. Too quiet. "Is something wrong?" she asked.

"No. I just…" He took a deep breath. "I know we don't know each other very well—yet." He smiled. "But I really, really want to kiss you right now."

"Oh." Chloe wanted to kiss him too. In fact, just how badly she wanted to kiss him surprised her.

He wrapped his strong arms around her and it felt safe—right. Instead of giving him verbal permission, she leaned in, closed her eyes, and tipped up her face.

In less than a second, their lips collided. He pulled her against his chest and she slipped her arms around his neck.

She had no idea how long they stood there on the sidewalk, kissing. His mouth moved over hers with purpose. Eventually, she parted her lips and allowed him to deepen the kiss. He pulled her closer and cupped the back of her head. When he slipped his tongue into her mouth, she swirled her tongue with his. He tasted like cinnamon.

"Hey, get a room," a passerby joked.

He didn't end the kiss and she was glad. Kissing him was different than she had thought it would be. It was then that she realized she had fantasized about kissing him—and that his real kisses could become addictive.

Chapter 7

RYAN FOUND HIMSELF WONDERING IF HE'D DONE the right thing by accepting the Arishes' dinner invitation. Sure, his dad had accepted many dinner invitations of friends in the department over the years, but never at the home of a female firefighter.

Especially not one he'd kissed.

Ryan had puzzled over what to bring as a hostess gift. A bottle of wine seemed like a safe bet, so he clutched that in his left hand. He had seen some poor sap selling flowers by the side of the road in the chilly evening air, but decided against buying a bunch. Even if he said they were for Amber, Chloe might be upset thinking they were for her…or disappointed when learning that they weren't.

Regardless, he was annoyed at himself for second-guessing everything. He finally asked himself how he'd behave if she were a guy, and made decisions accordingly.

That theory died the minute she came to the door in a little black dress. Her shiny blonde hair fell softly over her angled jaw, but it didn't hide the long earrings she wore. Sparkling gold triangles cascaded almost to her shoulders. His gaze began to wander farther down to her apple-sized breasts, but he quickly snapped his eyes up to her face.

As she opened the door, he told himself to focus on her earrings. It looked like some kind of Celtic design had been carved in them.

"Evening, Chloe. I didn't realize you were going to dress up." *Damn, Ryan. What a stupid thing to say. She probably primped all afternoon.*

"You don't look too shabby yerself, Mr. Fierro."

He glanced down at his black Dockers and black sweater. "Hey. We match."

She rolled her eyes, but at least she was smiling.

"My brother and his wife are upstairs doin' the cookin', but they charged me with gettin' you a beer or…" She pointed to the Chianti he had brought. "Is that wine?"

"Yes. In my family we usually drink wine with dinner. I wouldn't mind a beer though."

"Well, come in." She waved him toward the living room on the left. "I'll run this upstairs and be down with your beer in a minute. Do you like Guinness?"

He didn't. It was so dark and thick he was reminded of molasses. "Why don't you just open the wine? Then you don't have to run anywhere." He winked. *Christ, Ryan. Now you're winking at her. Just stop thinking of her as a woman.* He eyed her round bum as she sashayed over to a freestanding mahogany bar. *Yeah, right.*

Wandering around the room, he tried to focus on something else—anything else. The furniture was traditional and elegant. A tufted cream-colored sofa was flanked by a couple of armchairs that didn't exactly match, but went with it as if a designer had picked them out. Hell, the whole place looked like a designer had been there.

"Did you do all this?" he asked.

"What? The furnishings and such?"

"Yeah."

"I didn't. That was all Amber's department."

He picked up a gold vase from a plaster pedestal. It looked extremely old and also sported some Celtic designs. "She has good taste," he said.

"Ah, that she didn't furnish. Me brother brought that from home. We had some antiques passed down from older generations." She extracted the cork from the wine bottle and poured two glasses.

He replaced the vase gently, even though it looked sturdy enough. "Hey, do you like basketball?" *Changing the subject much, Ryan?*

"It's one of those American sports I haven't really followed yet," she said, handing him one of the glasses.

"Well, it was invented right here in Massachusetts. Our team is called the Boston Celtics. The designs on your jewelry and the vase just reminded me."

She cocked her head. "Are you thinkin' of askin' me to attend a game with you?"

He hadn't been, but why not? As long as the kiss cam didn't land on them, they'd be okay. And really…what were the chances of that happening?

"Ah, yeah. It might be fun sometime. The season is just starting."

"Are the Celtics a good team?"

He shrugged. "Depends. There were years when they were unbeatable. Lately, they've been, well…"

"Beatable?" she supplied.

He chuckled. "Yeah."

~∾~

Amber descended the staircase, carrying a tray. "I thought I heard Ryan's voice," she said. "I brought some cheese and crackers. Dinner won't be for another few minutes."

Rory jogged down the stairs a few seconds behind her. "Hey, where are you goin' with me cheeses, luv?"

She set them on the bar. "Oh, now they're yours?"

"I picked out the good ones, didn't I?"

"You picked the Irish cheddar. I got the French Brie."

"As I said…" He grinned at her.

Amber chuckled. "He's so easy. I could feed him cheddar cheese and Ritz crackers every night. As long as it came with a Guinness, he'd be in heaven."

Oh great. I had Ryan thinking we were elegant people, and now my brother goes and shatters that idea. Why did she care what he thought? This wasn't a date and there was no need to impress him.

"You'll have to pardon me brother," Chloe said. "We've been on our own since we were young. No one to teach us proper manners and such." *And we really did grow up in a cave.*

Ryan's face betrayed what she hated most — sympathy. Then he put on a quick smile. "I'm a man of simple tastes, myself."

At least Rory waited until their guest took some of the appetizers before he loaded up a cocktail napkin.

Amber excused herself and returned upstairs while the three others settled into the living room. Ryan took the end of the sofa closest to the armchair, which Rory plopped himself down on right away. That left Chloe to sit on the other end of the couch, or the opposite side of the room.

Might as well look *friendly, at least.* She sat on the sofa, leaving one cushion between herself and Ryan.

"Why so far away?" Rory asked.

She gave him the stink-eye.

At last he shrugged, asked Ryan how he liked the training, and then tucked into his cheese and crackers.

"It wasn't bad. Actually, I enjoyed it." He glanced at Chloe. "I think your sister did too."

"I did," she said.

"Have you experienced any hazing yet?" Rory asked with a sly smile.

Ryan laughed. "Yeah, but only one incident…so far."

Chloe's brows went up. "Really? I haven't. What did they do to you?"

Rory grinned. "I don't know if you should tell Chloe. They might do the same to her. T'would be a shame if she missed the surprise element."

"I doubt it, since it involved the men's bathroom."

Rory leaned forward. "Ah, this is gettin' interestin'. What did they do to you?"

"They have a very lifelike plastic baby alligator. It was in the toilet bowl, propped up like it was crawling out. I admit, I was pretty startled at first."

Rory leaned back and laughed, long and loud. When he settled down, he wiped a tear from the corner of his eye.

Chloe couldn't help chuckling too. "Thanks for the warnin'. I imagine they could put that thing in other places where I might come upon it."

Rory snapped his fingers. "Ah, feckers. Now she's ready for it. I bet they'll put it in your bed and be hopin' you'll scream like a little lassie."

Chloe folded her arms. "I wouldn't scream at a baby alligator, in me bed or anywhere." *Rory should know that.*

Dragons were fond of reptiles, being part of the same family themselves. Maybe he was just playing along.

Ryan smirked at her. "Don't feel bad if you do scream. I almost screamed like a little girl, myself."

She couldn't help liking the guy. He was no longer the pompous ass she'd met in the beginning. He wasn't afraid to show he had a sensitive side now and then… like during their EMT training. When they were told they might be called upon for a SIDS case, sudden infant death syndrome, he hung his head and said he couldn't imagine anything worse.

Suddenly, she thought, what if he wanted children? She couldn't provide him with any. Dragons could only reproduce with other dragons—and only once every five years. *Now why on earth did that thought pop into my head? We won't be getting married.*

Amber descended the stairs and announced that dinner was ready. Chloe almost let out a sigh of relief. She needed a change of subject—even though the subject of having a lover and children was only in her mind.

—∿∿—

The day they were to return to work for several consecutive twenty-four-hour shifts finally arrived. Ryan couldn't believe how ready he was to get back to the firehouse. Or was it back to Chloe?

That night he was pranked again. A big, hairy plastic spider waited for him in bed. He threw back the covers with the bedside lamp on, almost expecting something of the sort. When he saw that the tarantula wasn't moving, he chuckled.

"Nice try, guys," he called out.

A few male chuckles followed. Chloe appeared in his doorway, dressed in a long T-shirt and sweatpants. *How the hell does she make activewear sexy?*

"I take it you've been hazed again," she said.

"It was a valiant attempt." Some of his phoenix ancestors were from the deserts of the Southwest, so a big-ass tarantula was nothing short of nostalgic. "I haven't heard you scream like a 'little lassie' yet. Have they tried to do anything to you?"

"Not a thing." At first she shot him a smile, but her expression soon turned to sadness.

"Feeling left out?" he asked.

"A little. I had hoped they wouldn't treat me any differently just because I'm a woman, but clearly that's their intent."

He saw two of the guys sneaking up behind her with a bucket of water. Without letting on, he said, "Maybe you should be grateful."

She shrugged. "Mayhaps I should."

At that moment, the guys dumped the bucket over her head. It wasn't just water in that bucket. It was ice water! Her openmouthed, shocked expression was priceless.

Whoa! It wasn't just a prank. It was a wet T-shirt contest!

She whirled around, looking like she was ready to give the guys a piece of her mind. Suddenly he saw their eyes bug out of their heads as they stared right at her nipples. She glanced down and wrapped her arms over her breasts.

Ryan jumped in front of her. "Very funny, guys. I know Arish wanted to be treated as an *equal*," he said, hoping they'd get the implication that dumping ice water over a braless woman was anything but fair.

They grinned. "Welcome to the family, Arish," Haggarty said.

The lieutenant's warning popped into Ryan's head and gave the word "brotherhood" a whole new meaning. Haggarty seemed to be the only one noticing the difference, and he'd bet money the asswipe had come up with the *ice* water idea.

"That's a grand welcome, guys," she said with a chuckle.

Whew. She wasn't losing it. He was afraid she might go apeshit and really stand out—in a bad way.

"Now, if yeee'll excuuuse me." Her teeth chattered as she sprinted to her bedroom.

Once the door was closed, Ryan narrowed his eyes. "Not cool, guys."

"Or maybe it was a little too cool," the quieter of them said with a grin.

Ryan couldn't help the smile that spread across his face. He could never unsee her perky breasts stuck to the soaked white T-shirt. Unfortunately, the other guys wouldn't soon forget it either.

Chloe didn't know what to think about her "grand" welcome. Was she being treated as an equal, or were her male cohorts treating her to some good old-fashioned chauvinism? She almost had to admire them for thinking up a way to do both at the same time.

Oh well, at least I didn't scream like a ninny.

Haggarty, her partner, hadn't been very forthcoming

with information. Oh, he'd answered her questions, but didn't volunteer anything. She got the distinct feeling he didn't want her there.

She couldn't wait for a chance to prove herself. The sooner she carried one of the guys over her shoulder to safety, the better.

But she wasn't sure she'd ever get a chance to. They'd assigned her to the first ambulance. "Seniority" was supposedly the deciding factor. She and Ryan had been hired at the same time. So why was she one slot higher on the totem pole than he was?

She suspected it was her gender again, but when she asked the captain about it, he claimed they'd decided the tie alphabetically. Arish before Fierro.

That put Ryan in the front lines. And she wouldn't be there to protect him. *Feck*. At least he was an outstanding firefighter in his own right. Chances are she had nothing to worry about.

So why was she worried?

That night, she slept lightly…the way dragons used to when they were guarding their piles of treasure from greedy, thieving humans.

Dispatchers were at the ready all night, and she was told that most firefighters got used to tuning out background noise, while being hyperaware of the need to wake up and listen to any announcements over the loudspeakers.

Her first overnight had been quiet, but the others had warned her that tonight might be different. It was an American holiday they called Halloween.

Her ancient roots took her back to the pagan holiday Samhain—celebrated at this same time of year. For those people, it was a solemn occasion when they honored their ancestors. Her only experience with Halloween had been last year when she had seen a few college students dressed in costumes, walking to and from the local dorms. It seemed peaceful enough.

Famous. Last. Words.

—⁓—

The alarm blared and the dispatcher's voice announced a fire at a nightclub in the Kenmore Square area.

Chloe was dressed and had her boots on before footsteps were heard on other bedroom floors. She reached the pole first and sailed down it to the equipment below. Ryan and three others were right behind her. They all suited up in their turnout gear as the bays opened, allowing them to drive the engines and ambulances out onto Boylston Street.

The night sky flickered orange and black only a few blocks away. Those were Halloween colors, she'd been told, but tonight they were the colors of a fully engulfed building inferno.

The sirens screamed and her adrenaline kicked in. A couple of police cars raced to the scene at the same time. Good. They'd be needed for crowd control. The number of people standing on the sidewalk just outside the block of buildings would be a hazard by themselves.

Chloe didn't wait for the ambulance to make a full stop. She was on the ground, asking if anyone was hurt. Before she could learn much, she felt a large weight on her shoulder.

"Whoa there," Haggarty said. "I'll handle this."

He asked the exact same questions she just had. *Infuriating man.*

When someone indicated there were several people still inside, Chloe looked to Haggarty for instructions. He didn't say or do anything in response.

Really? I'm supposed to read the idjit's mind?

She observed the lieutenant as he was barking out orders for the firefighters. The cops had begun clearing people from the sidewalks so they could run hoses. Not one to just sit around, Chloe also began asking uninjured people to move out of the way.

"That's not your job, Arish," Haggarty said.

She stomped over to him and asked, "Then what *is* my job? What am I supposed to be doing while everyone else is running around like chickens?"

He snorted. "You're supposed to know your job by the time you come out of the academy."

She felt her face heat. She whirled away from him, realizing he could make her shoot smoke out of her nostrils if she got angry enough. *Damn.* This guy seemed determined to make her angry.

How had she managed to keep her fury under wraps with Ryan? Oh yeah. She ignored him. Chloe couldn't very well ignore her partner—although that seemed to be exactly what he was doing to her.

She moved closer to the lieutenant and the door the firefighters used to enter the building. Maybe one of them could use her help.

A moment later, Ryan appeared with a victim in his arms. She stepped toward him and he willingly handed over the adult male. She had him secured and was just turning toward the ambulance when Haggarty burst forward. "Are you crazy? She can't handle a heavy patient by herself."

He tried to grab for the man in her arms, but Chloe

swiveled her body away from him. "I've got him. Grab a stretcher."

The look Haggarty gave her could only be called "poisonous." Then he glanced over her shoulder and she heard the lieutenant say, "Is there a problem, Haggarty?"

"No, sir," he said sharply. Chloe carried the man to the ambulance and waited for her partner to produce a stretcher. As soon as she laid him down, she began assessing his vital signs and Haggarty disappeared.

A few moments later, she had an oxygen mask over the guy, who had apparently fallen inside. She applied a C-spine to stabilize him. Fortunately he hadn't lost consciousness and didn't seem to have any broken bones. Suddenly Haggarty appeared with a woman in his arms. "Do you think you could grab another stretcher—you know, when it's convenient?" he sneered.

Chloe did her best to ignore the sarcasm and made her duty to the injured her priority.

"So, do we take these two to the hospital?" she asked Haggarty.

He rolled his eyes but never answered her.

As soon as she was sure the second victim was secured, she rushed back to the lieutenant. "Should we take these patients right away or see if there are more serious injuries, sir?"

He glanced at Haggarty and frowned, then gave her a brief smile. "If the two patients you have are stable, hang back a bit to be sure there's nothing more serious. Ambulance 2 is on the way. When they get here, you can take off."

She nodded once. "Yes, sir."

"Keep up the good work, Arish," the lieutenant said.

She assessed and treated another four individuals, all of whom were walking and talking; meanwhile, her coworkers fought the flames with everything they had.

She knew she could do more. She wanted to be inside the structure with her superior senses and fireproof scales. This club encompassed the basement and ground floor only, and the fire was quickly contained.

Okay, Chloe. So you weren't needed inside this time. But there will come a day…

She glanced behind her to see if Haggarty needed anything. He stood by the ambulance with his arms crossed.

Scowling, he barked out, "Anytime you're ready, Arish…" As if she'd been waiting for her nails to dry.

"Feckin' arsehole," she muttered under her breath. As soon as they loaded the stretchers into the ambulance she said, "I assume you want to drive," and swung up into the open back.

"Ordinarily I would. But you should probably do it to get some *experience* finding the Brookline Avenue hospitals."

Who the hell couldn't find the Brookline Avenue hospitals? Might they be on, oh, say, Brookline Avenue? Chloe doubted he wanted her to get experience as much as he wanted to show her who was boss. He seemed to tell her to do the opposite of whatever she was planning to do at any juncture—probably for no other reason than to create doubt in her own assessments and decisions.

Well, she wouldn't give him the satisfaction. She was a good EMT and firefighter. If Haggarty wanted to, he could turn her into a great one. It seemed as if he wanted her to fail instead…but why?

At least Ryan had a reason for hating her back when they were locked in competition. One job. Two candidates.

His family pride had added pressure to his need to succeed. Even his fear of being "bested by a girl" was less of an issue once he understood that the welfare of the public took precedence over everything else. Eventually, whatever competition that remained had become friendly.

Was Haggarty coming from the same place? If so, would he eventually get over himself? They weren't in competition for the same job. He clearly had seniority, and if he wanted the second ambulance position, making her look bad wouldn't do a damn thing.

Clearly he had issues, and she might never learn what they were. Maybe even *he* didn't know.

———

Ryan had made a complete sweep of the station—twice. Where the hell was Chloe? The way she'd stormed off after they returned from the nightclub fire had him worried. He gave her a few minutes to calm down before going to her room, but the door was open and she wasn't there.

Where could she be hiding and why? He thought she lived for that sort of excitement. His own inner adrenaline junkie was still riding high. But that high was rapidly fading the more he became concerned over Chloe.

"Has anyone seen Arish?" he asked the others gathered in the kitchen.

He saw a few grins and heard a snicker or two.

"Oh no. What did you guys do?"

Haggarty sipped his coffee. "Nothing. Just sent her off to do the rest of her job."

By now some of the guys were laughing out loud.

"C'mon, guys. Where is she?"

One of the quiet ones, Henry was his name, finally answered him. "Check the basement. She's doing everyone's laundry."

"What?" Had Chloe lost a bet? Or had they duped her? *Oh shit. If they made her think she had to do the laundry because she's a woman, there'll be hell to pay.*

He jogged down the two flights of stairs to the basement laundry and found her angrily cramming clothes into one of the heavy-duty washing machines.

Ryan approached with caution. "What are you doing, princess?" he asked, trying to seem casual.

"What the feck do you think I'm doin'?" She slammed the door shut and added the soap to the washing machine.

"It looks like you're handling more than your share. We're all responsible for washing our own stuff, you know."

She swiveled her head toward him. "Each time?"

Uh oh. She *had* been duped.

"Yeah. Why? What did you think?"

"Me partner—I mean, *my* partner, that asshole Haggarty, said we took turns doin' everyone's laundry after a fire. Bein' I was a probie, he said it was *my* turn."

"God dammit," Ryan muttered under his breath.

Apparently Chloe had figured out she was being hazed again, but this time she wasn't laughing. Her eyes flashed with something that looked like fire.

She strode toward the stairs.

"No, Chloe. Don't give them the satisfaction..."

She ignored him and began stomping up the steps.

"Whoa." He raced up after her and before she reached

the door, he whisked her off her feet and into his arms. "I'll help you. Just don't go up there. Please."

"Why the feck not?"

"Because I'm afraid you're homicidal right now."

That got her to burst out laughing. "I just want to give them a piece of my mind. I wouldn't kill anyone."

He turned and carried her back down the stairs. "I don't know… They were laughing pretty hard when they told me where you were. Listen…let's just finish our own and leave theirs in a big wet pile on the floor."

She grinned. "I like that idea."

And he liked the idea of helping her. Maybe it was that protective streak coming out again, but it wasn't without a benefit to him too. He got to be alone with her for a while.

Ryan grabbed her hand and pulled her into the empty space under the stairs. Before she had a chance to ask what he was doing, he captured her mouth, fully intending to kiss her until her toes curled.

She returned the heat of his kiss with her own. *Jesus*.

He didn't know how long they made out under the stairs, but he felt they'd better cool it before she had to go upstairs with swollen lips and stubble burn. He reluctantly pulled away.

"Ah…that was an unexpected benefit of doing the laundry," she said.

Fortunately, the wash cycle finished and they yanked out their own clothes, putting them in the large capacity dryer. Then they piled the rest of it in a heap on the floor off to the side. Soon a lake surrounded the pile. To his surprise, she filled the washer with the next load.

Was she over it so quickly? He was glad to see she

had calmed down. Her accent was all but unnoticeable, but he was surprised by how much he missed it. The capacity for that kind of forgiveness was impressive. Ryan gazed at her and smiled.

She shrugged. "They said to do the washing. Not a word was said about the drying."

He laughed. "That's the Chloe I know and lo—"

Shock rippled through him. *Was I about to say I loved her? Crap.* She'd probably laugh in his face—or worse. Avoid him at every turn.

Fortunately, she acted as if she had no idea what he was about to say. She leaned against the dryer. "Why aren't you upstairs laughing with the rest of them?"

"It didn't seem right. I was afraid they'd said something about your having to do the laundry just because you're a woman, or something along those lines."

She laughed. "No. If those words had been spoken, you'd have seen a bunch of bloody noses. They said after a fire it got so crowded down here, and there was such a long wait for the washer or dryer by doing it individually, that they'd just changed the policy amongst themselves and now took turns doing the whole thing. It made enough sense for me to believe it."

"I should have known you wouldn't fall for it any other way."

She strolled across the room to get more soap out of the supply closet. "I could fall for you," she whispered to herself.

Holy shit. If he hadn't been paranormal with superior senses, he'd never have heard her…or believed she could ever utter those words.

Chapter 8

THE NEXT DAY, LIEUTENANT STREETER CALLED Chloe into one of the private offices.

This had better not be about leaving the laundry damp. She couldn't imagine the guys tattling on her, especially because it was the result of their hazing, but she wouldn't put it past Haggarty to find a way. She was rapidly tiring of her so-called partner.

"I'll get right to the point, Arish," he said as they sat opposite each other. "Two of our guys have been on light duty, healing from minor injuries. Nagle is ready to return to the field. His previous assignment was on Ambulance 1, and he'll be returning to that position. That will move you down a rung and place you in the front lines. Do you have any problem with that?"

Front lines? And away from Haggarty? Hallelujah! "No, sir. No problem at all. In fact, I welcome the challenge."

"Good. That's what I like to hear. So…how's it been for you here?"

Ugh. "Well, there's not much I can tell you that you don't already know." *And not much I can divulge without getting the others in trouble and being labeled a tattletale.*

He rocked back on the chair legs and looked at her askance. "I'm here 24–7, just like you are, but I can't get inside your head. Do you like the job?"

"Oh! I love it. And as soon as I feel like I'm contributing fully, I'll probably love it even more."

His eyebrows raised. "That's good. I kind of thought the guys might take it easy on you, but I know they haven't."

Oh. Is that what Haggarty was doing? Not taking it easy on me? "No, sir. But I didn't want to be treated any differently from other new firefighters."

He smiled and rose. "Good attitude, Arish. I thought I noticed you scowling from time to time and wondered if you were okay."

"I'm A-one." She smiled back.

He scratched his head. "That's a steak sauce…"

She felt her face heat. She must have butchered another American expression. "A-OK?"

"That's the one." The lieutenant opened the door for her to leave and followed her to the kitchen, then asked Ryan to come to his office. Chloe wondered what he was being called in for. She wanted to wait for him, but Haggarty was camped out next to the stove, watching Nagle make stew.

"Hey, Arish. This should make you homesick. Nagle's making Mulligan stew."

"As long as that's the only kind of sick it makes me, I'll be fine," she quipped. The other guys around the table laughed.

"Good one, Arish," Nagle said. "But insulting my cooking isn't something I want to hear again…especially from a probie."

"Usually anyone who has a problem with Nagle's cooking gets to make the next meal," Haggarty said. Then a grin that could only be called evil crossed his face.

Feckers. What's he "cooking up" now?

She noticed the bowls stacked beside the stove. If there was spit in the top bowl and they insisted it was "ladies first," she'd have none of it. *I ought to check that top bowl.*

She wandered over, appearing to take a look at the stew, but glanced in the top bowl as she passed. It appeared clean. If there was something funky in the brew, they were all getting it.

"It smells delicious," she said.

Nagle smiled at her. "Thanks. I hope it's just as good as what your mother used to make."

Chloe laughed. "Mother never made…" She broke off quickly, remembering they couldn't and shouldn't know that her mother was an Irish dragon queen and had cooks for that. She returned to her seat at the long table.

Nagle cocked his head. "Your mother never made Mulligan stew?"

"I—uh. I don't remember. We lost our parents at an early age. Me brother raised us."

The kitchen fell silent. A couple of the guys shot disapproving looks at Haggarty.

Under his breath, Haggarty muttered to Nagle, "Oh, boo hoo. A lot of people were raised by *strangers*. At least she had some family."

She suddenly wondered what his story was.

***

Ryan returned to the kitchen, looking dejected. He slumped into a vacant chair at the head of the table.

"That's the lieutenant's spot," Haggarty was quick to point out.

"Of course it is," he muttered. Then he rose and took the open seat across the table from Chloe. *At least the view is better down here.*

"Bad news?" she asked.

"Not yet."

Haggarty said, "He's probably being transferred to another firehouse now that we're at full capacity again."

Nagle looked his way. "Sorry about my rotator cuff healing." Then he smirked. "Sorry. Not sorry."

"I get why you think that. Low man on the totem pole and everything, but no. You're stuck with me." Then he focused on Chloe. "Does that mean you're off Ambulance 1?"

"Yeah." She seemed to be suppressing a smile. "I'll be fightin' fires with the rest of you."

Some of the guys glanced at each other but didn't comment.

"We're lucky, guys," Ryan said. "I didn't think this girl could make it through training. A lot of us didn't, but she proved everyone wrong. She's strong and fast. She'll be an asset."

They nodded. He couldn't tell if they were really agreeing or just shutting him up. It didn't matter. She'd prove herself.

Haggarty shrugged. "Not to mention, she's little. I'll bet she can get into tight spots." He glanced around at the others and some of them grinned, as if there was an inside joke.

Finally, the stew was ready and Nagle took the first bowl for himself. Haggarty took the second bowl, and the rest lined up to grab whatever random bowl was next in the pile. Chloe got into the middle of the line and Ryan, not having much of an appetite after the news, took the last bowl.

When everyone was seated, Nagle said, "What are you waiting for? Dig in."

Ryan scooped up a spoonful and identified most of the ingredients. Carrots, potatoes, onions, meat… Why was Chloe waiting?

The guys began eating, but everyone's eyes were on Chloe. Ryan couldn't imagine what was going on until he had his first bite…and it bit back! Hot sauce. The ingredient many people in this part of the world didn't tolerate well. Of course, Phoenixes were fire birds and loved the stuff. Ryan would add it to everything if he could.

Chloe took a bite and her eyebrows raised. To her credit, she didn't spit it out or make a face. She smiled!

"This is delicious," she said. She took several more bites, then looked around the table at the surprised expressions. "What? It's not what I'm used to, but Mulligan stew can be made with anything you have left over. Usually it's kind of bland. This is much better. Thanks, Nagle."

The guys just went back to gingerly sipping their portions.

Haggarty received a few pointed stares. Apparently he had something to do with the extra "flavor."

When Ryan and Chloe had finished their bowls with lip-smacking compliments and tummy rubs, some of the guys got up and poured what was left of their stew in the garbage.

"Let's order a pizza," one of them suggested.

"Yeah. Haggarty's paying," Nagle added.

Several grumpy firefighters exited the kitchen. Haggarty pointed to the rookies and said, "You two have KP duty."

Chloe looked to Ryan. "Can you translate?"

"We get to do the dishes," he explained.

"Ah. Of course. Whoever cooks doesn't have to clean. That was the rule in my house too. I did a lot of dishes. Do you want to wash or dry?"

"Since there's a dishwasher, how about if you scrape, then I'll rinse and load it?"

She rolled her eyes. "I forgot about the dishwasher. There's not enough work for two of us, then. How about if I just do it all?"

"Nope. I won't hear of it."

She shrugged. "Sure'n I don't mind the help, but…"

He stood so close to her she stopped talking. He wanted to kiss her, but not in a public area where anyone could walk in.

She backed up a step. "Okay then. Let's get this chore out of the way and see if there's any pizza left."

He didn't want pizza, but he'd sure like to have *her* for dessert.

A moment later Haggarty walked back in. He stopped suddenly and eyed the other two.

"Am I interrupting something?"

Ryan took a step back. "Not at all."

A sly smile tugged Haggarty's lips. "I know the stove was on a while ago, but I could swear the heat in here suddenly spiked."

Chloe turned her back to him and began scraping and rinsing the bowls.

Ryan took his cue from her and tried ignoring the jerk who was implying…what? That there was intense sexual chemistry between them? He'd better squash that quick. He no longer wanted Chloe transferred, but he didn't want to leave either. She needed him here.

"Yeah. I see it now," Haggarty persisted. "You two have the hots for each other."

Chloe whirled around. "We do not. We've merely struck a truce. Something I'd like to do to everyone here."

Haggarty leaned back and laughed. "Oh really? You'd like to *do* everyone here?"

Ryan balled his fists and began walking toward him.

Chloe stepped into his path. "Ignore him. He's not worth gettin' your knickers in a twist. Sure'n he's baitin' us." She whirled on Haggarty. "And you… Stop arsin' around."

Ryan leaned in and whispered, "I think the term you're looking for is *horsing* around."

She folded her arms. "Not when the fecker is bein' an arse."

Haggarty roared laughing, but Chloe turned away from him and simply resumed doing the dishes.

She was upset all right. The Irish accent was back in full force. But if she could play it cool, so could he.

The two of them returned to their task, and as soon as Haggarty realized he wasn't going to get a rise out of them, he left the kitchen softly chanting an old ditty, "Ryan and Chloe, sittin' in a tree…"

She let out a loud sigh and returned her focus to Ryan. "So why did you look so upset after speaking to the lieutenant?"

"My grandfather's in Boston General Hospital. Apparently all the Fierros can't leave their posts at once or the city would burn to the ground."

"Ah, so you have to wait your turn?"

"Maybe I won't be getting a turn. We're all hoping they won't keep him long. Jayce is the closest since he works in District 3, and he's with him now. My parents are there and…well, I can't help wishing I could be there too."

Ryan hoped he wasn't overplaying his distress. His grandfather could always rise from the ashes, but getting a body out of the morgue to light on fire could be tricky.

"So are you all on the same shift?"

"Pretty much. My mother likes to have Sunday dinner with the whole family as often as we're available. My youngest brother is still in school and lives at home, so he's expected *every* Sunday."

"I'm sorry to hear about your grandda," Chloe said as she covered his hand with hers.

He glanced down and realized he was gripping the edge of the sink a little too tightly. His knuckles were turning white and he'd have a hard time explaining how the stainless steel got dented.

He quickly loosened his grip and grabbed a towel to dry his hands. That stopped Chloe from continuing to show her sensitive side in case anyone was watching. Until the guys accepted her as an equal, she really needed to keep up the "tough girl" act…if indeed it was an act.

Finally, their stretch of twenty-four-hour shifts ended. They'd had several calls that didn't involve actual fires, including a car accident that required the jaws of life, but at least the work had kept everyone busy. Ryan had had his turn visiting his grandfather and returned to work a little more relaxed, but distant. Chloe was relieved to return to her own family and have a break from her "brotherhood."

Over dinner with Rory and Amber, she'd told them about responding to car crashes, smoke alarms, a gas leak in a high-rise building, and a few drunk teenagers who decided it might be a good idea to have a big bonfire in an alley. Her group had even been called in to back up a structure fire in another district, but the fire had been pretty much contained by the time they'd arrived.

"You sound excited about the work you're doin'," Rory said.

She smiled. It hadn't been overwhelmingly exciting yet, but she knew the day would come when her mettle would be tested.

"I know I've only known you for a year and a half, Chloe," Amber said, "but I can see a change in you. You're more relaxed and focused. I think this job must be good for you."

Her hazing was all part of the "fun," but her brother wouldn't understand—so she'd left that part out.

"I almost wish we had blocks of wooden three-decker homes, like the Jamaica Plain, Dorchester, and Roxbury neighborhoods have. But no. As much as I'm itching to fight real fires, I'd hate to see families out on the sidewalk, grieving their losses."

The doorbell rang.

"Are you expectin' anyone?" Chloe asked.

Rory rose and grinned. "As a matter of fact, we are."

Oh no. She knew that expression. He was up to something, and it better not involve Ryan. As much as she'd finally admitted to herself that she liked the guy, she needed time off from him—from everyone at the station. The energy they'd expended hiding their sexual tension was exhausting.

"Relax, guys. I'll get it," Amber said before she evaporated.

Chloe sucked in a breath. "Won't she get into trouble if Mother Nature knows she's using her muse powers as a way of travel when she doesn't have to?"

"Nah. Gaia loves her modern muses. And Amber is the muse of air travel, after all." He grinned. "Don't worry. She's careful. She materializes in the coat closet where no one can see her suddenly appear."

"The closet, huh? No one thinks it's strange that she's comin' out of the closet…in a literal sense, I mean."

Rory chuckled. "I knew what you meant. She plans to say she was cleanin' it a bit, if anyone asks. So far, no one has."

Chloe heard heavy footsteps on the stairs. A lot of them. Now she was truly puzzled. Her brother wouldn't have invited her whole work group for dessert, would he?

Into the kitchen walked her three Ulster cousins. Conlan, Eagan, and her least favorite—Aiden.

Oh joy.

She pasted a smile on her face and followed Rory to shake their hands. She was surprised when Aiden grasped her in a big hug.

"Welcome," Rory said.

"Thanks fer havin' us, Cousin," Conlan said. "I knew you wanted us to come for Christmas, but that's a busy time of year back home."

"Indeed," he said. "Though there's never a bad time for whiskey makin', is there?"

They all chuckled.

"Anyway, the American Thanksgiving sounded like a lovely holiday, and when Amber told us about how it was for families and friends comin' together to count their blessin's... Well, we could hardly refuse. Are you sure you have room for us?"

Rory laughed. "We do. As much as we still intend to open this place as a bed and breakfast, we've been puttin' it off...enjoyin' a little time alone."

"With your sister, it seems," Aiden pointed out.

"I live next door," Chloe said. "I come when I'm invited."

Eagan slapped her on the back. "An' it's been ages since I've seen you, luv. How's she cuttin'?"

"Survivin'," she answered.

Amber clapped her hands together. "Well, you must be exhausted from your trip. Let me show you to your rooms. Just one more flight up. Would you like to use the elevator this time?"

"No need," said Aiden. He shimmered, transformed into his dragon form, grabbed the suitcase with his clothes, and flew up the stairs.

"Show-off," Chloe muttered under her breath.

Conlan laughed. "That he is. Lead the way, Amber. Eagan and I aren't too tired to amble up another flight of stairs."

They picked up their suitcases and followed their hostess up the stairs the "human" way. As soon as they were out of sight, Chloe frantically whispered in Rory's ear.

"Why did you invite them to Boston? You know Mother Nature spends a lot of time here. If she catches 'em shiftin' into dragon form, she'll be furious."

"I'm sure Amber will speak to them about it. She knows the goddess better than all of us."

Suddenly a small whirlwind formed in the opening to the dining room. When the swirling stopped, Mother Nature, in all her glory, stood there with her hands on her hips.

"Did I hear someone call my name?"

"Ah...no?" Rory attempted.

"Maybe I should rephrase that," the Goddess of All said. "I heard my name. What do you want?"

"We didn't mean to bother you, Goddess. Truly. We were just mentionin' how you honor Boston with your mighty presence..."

She waved a hand. "Cut the blarney, dragon. That Irish charm doesn't work on me."

Chloe knew for a fact the touchy deity was able to be placated with flattery, so she tried her hand. She simply had to be better at it than her brother was.

"Gaia. We *are* honored by your presence. If we mistakenly called to you when we were mentionin' your name in a positive way, we apologize—wholeheartedly. We know how busy you are. Now, if you need to return to any—"

"No, thanks. I think I'll stay right where I am for a few minutes," she said. A chair materialized under her butt as she sat.

Chloe exchanged a look with Rory that could only be interpreted as "Oh, shite. What do we do now?"

"Why don't you make yerself comfortable in the dining room, Goddess?" asked Rory.

Gaia rose and the chair disappeared. She strode to the dining room, took a seat at the head of the long table, and asked, "Is Amber around?"

"Indeed she is." Rory grabbed a stack of plates

from the sideboard. "Some new guests just arrived and she's helpin' them settle in. Would you like to join us for pie?"

The goddess ignored his invitation. "It's about time you had some paranormal guests. I thought for a minute that my plan of keeping you all in one place wasn't working."

Plan? Working? Chloe knew the goddess had gifted Amber and Rory with the building, but she'd thought it was a reward for Amber because she took the job of a modern muse. The goddess badly needed someone to take care of things the ancients couldn't do. As a former flight attendant, Amber had proven invaluable when helping floundering pilots stay calm and land safely in any number of situations.

Gaia looked directly at Chloe. "Yes. The building was a reward for my new muse, but it was your brother's idea to turn it into a bed-and-breakfast for visiting paranormals. I merely encouraged the idea since it served my purposes."

"I see," Chloe said. "Can I pour you a cup of tea, Gaia?"

"Don't trouble yourself." She pointed to a spot on the tablecloth in front of her and a steaming cup of tea appeared. She took a sip and said, "Mmm… Darjeeling straight from my hills of northern India. Delicious."

I guess she's not going to offer us a cup.

"Sit down, little dragon. I'm perfectly capable of sharing—when I want to." Full tea cups appeared in front of her and Rory. "While I'm at it…" She snapped her fingers and four more cups appeared around the table.

How did she know there were four more? Chloe stopped her thought mid-sentence. *Duh, the Goddess of All knows where her children are.*

"Not always, little dragon. Now, what kind of pie do you have?"

Amber appeared in the doorway. "Gaia! What a pleasant surprise." She strode over to her and kissed her on both cheeks. "What kind of pie would you like? I can pop out and get it for you."

Mother Nature narrowed her eyes. "I hope you don't use your powers to 'pop out' to the bakery willy-nilly, Muse of Air Travel. As you know I would be furious if you were seen reappearing anywhere."

"Of course not, Gaia. I'm completely aware of your number one rule, and I wouldn't tip off any humans. My reappearance would take place around the corner from Mike's. That side street is quiet right now."

Her uneven brows rose. "Mike's? In the North End?"

Amber grinned. "Is there another?"

"Damn. Now my mouth is watering for a strawberry cannoli."

"I'll get an assortment," Amber said.

"Don't bother. I'll stop by on my way home. Listen. I need to speak to your guests."

Amber looked surprised but nodded. "Right away, Goddess."

As Chloe and Rory exchanged curious glances, Mother Nature said, "What?"

"Is there somethin' we should know about our cousins' visit?" Rory asked.

She shrugged. "I guess we'll all find out at once, won't we?"

Soon the cousins tromped into the dining room and Rory invited them to sit anywhere they liked. Aiden and

Egan sat far down on one side while Conlan took a spot next to Mother Nature at the head of the table.

Gaia faced Conlan and smiled. "Do you know who I am?"

"No, luv, but I'd like to change that."

Chloe watched as he turned on the Irish charm like a faucet.

"I wouldn't mind knowin' a beautiful lass such as you." He held out his hand.

When Mother Nature grasped his hand, he turned hers and brought it to his lips, placing a light kiss on her knuckles.

Chloe held her breath. Either the goddess was going to interpret the gesture as one of respect and be pleased, or all hell could break loose.

"Me name is Conlan Arish. It's lovely to meet you…"

"I'm Mother Nature," she said.

Conlan dropped her hand. His eyes rounded as he stared at their guest deity, speechless.

"I'll bet you get that a lot," Chloe said.

Mother Nature just chuckled. "Yeah. It never gets old." She turned her gaze to the other two men at the far end of the table. "And you are?"

"Aiden Arish, mum. And this is me brother, Eagan, the youngest. You've met the eldest and head of our clan. That'd be Conlan."

Her expression darkened. "You will not call me mom—or ma'am. Got it?"

Aiden simply nodded. Then he asked, "What would you like to be called? Yer Grace?"

She laughed. "Gaia or Goddess will work." As soon

as everyone had been served pie and tea, she said, "Now I'd like to get down to business."

Conlan had recovered by that time. "What type of business are you in, uh...Gaia?"

She chuckled and shook her head. "I'm Mother Freakin' Nature. That makes me CEO of the Universe."

He slapped himself upside the head. "Naturally. My apologies."

She waved away the comment. "Forget it. I need to ask you a couple of questions."

"Of course, Goddess," Conlan said. "Anythin'."

"What is the purpose of your trip and how long are you planning to stay in Boston?"

Chloe glanced at Amber and whispered, "Is she the paranormal TSA or something?"

Amber gave a slight shrug and turned her attention back to the head of the table.

"We're here to visit our family and celebrate the American Thanksgivin'. We'll be stayin' for about a week."

Mother Nature's brows knit. "Family? I thought you were from Ulster?"

"Indeed we are, Goddess," Conlan said. "We were born in the same castle in Erin as our cousins here. Then, thanks to a little tiff between our parents, me brothers and I moved up to the North."

It was all Chloe could do to keep from bursting out in laughter at the words "little tiff." Conlan had downplayed the bloody Battle of Ballyhoo just a *wee bit*. His father had tried to assassinate and overthrow his own brother—in other words, her uncle had tried to take her father's throne. It was a wonder they weren't mortal enemies…especially when they weren't very mortal. A grudge like that could last for millennia.

"I know all about it, Chloe," Gaia said. "At least the history. What I don't understand, or trust, is this…" She indicated the entire family around the table with her palms up.

Rory cleared his throat. "Goddess. We've put our petty concerns behind us. Our parents' ambitions to rule Ireland as kings is no longer relevant. And to be sure, it was never our concern in the first place. We were but children at the time."

She folded her arms and looked at Chloe and Aiden in turn. "So what was the reason these two were brawling on the castle lawn the summer before last?"

Chloe smirked. She couldn't help it. It looked like Aiden was trying to hide a smile too.

"Sorry, Goddess," she said. "We had a disagreement over some family heirlooms. The whole matter has been put to rest."

"How?" Mother Nature demanded.

"We shared," Rory stated simply.

Gaia's brows rose. "Shared?"

"Yes, Goddess," Conlan said. "Rory is the leader of his clan as I am leader of mine. We talked out the misunderstandin' and decided to split the ancient treasure. All we wanted was to be treated equally."

Something shimmered in the corner of the Goddess's eye. At last she clasped her hands over her heart. "My babies learned to share! No mother could be prouder." Birds broke into song.

"Where did the feckin' birds come from?" Chloe muttered.

Mother Nature raised one eyebrow and stared at Chloe. "Really? I'm celebrating a miracle and you want to disrespect my songbirds?"

Suddenly the ribbet of frogs and chirp of crickets joined the chorus.

Chapter 9

A WONDERFUL THANKSGIVING HAD TAKEN PLACE without too much family drama. Actually, the Ulster cousins had decided they'd like to contribute the turkey. Chloe imagined if Amber knew they were coming home with a live one, she'd have asked them to buy the cranberries.

Amber couldn't kill the bird, so they'd had a pet turkey for a while. Finally it was time for the turkey to return to the farm and for Chloe to return to work at the fire station. Chloe strolled into the kitchen and walked right into an argument between Ryan and some guy she'd never seen before.

"Hire a pet sitter for once."

"I did. I hired the Fierro family. Jayce took my cats and volunteered the rest of you. Gabe has my dog. Noah wanted the rabbits…"

"So, you just assumed you could stick me with your African gray."

She was just about to turn and leave when she spotted a beautiful bird. The feathers were a soft silver color. It was larger and shaped differently than a mourning dove, and it had the sweetest face. "Hello. What's your name?"

"Gwendolyn," the bird answered.

Chloe gasped. "She speaks!"

The guy whirled around, apparently unaware that Chloe had come in. "Yes. She's an African gray parrot.

They're the breed with the largest vocabulary. I haven't had time to train her to say much."

"In other words, Chloe, she'll just screech and squawk most of the time," Ryan said.

"Oh, but she's beautiful. I'd love to take her home, but I'm here for the next few days."

"That's great," the guy said. "I'm only going to be gone for a belated holiday weekend. My family gets together between Thanksgiving and Christmas and celebrates everything at once. You can understand why I *have to* go. She doesn't need a lot of care. She stays in her cage…"

"And poops in it," Ryan added, "which you'll need to clean up, plus the birdseed that lands everywhere."

"There's a newspaper on the bottom that you can pull out and change here." The guy tapped what looked like a thin drawer that ran the width of the cage.

Chloe took another look at the bird's hopeful face. "Does she bite?"

"Not unless you poke or startle her." The guy stuck out his hand. "I'm Private McCall, by the way."

"Oh! You're a firefighter?"

"Yes, ma'am. I work with Scrooge's brother, Gabe." He pointed over his shoulder with his thumb, indicating Ryan.

She smiled. "Scrooge?" That wasn't a name she'd want Ryan to get stuck with. He'd been generous with his time and help. He just didn't want to take care of this bird, for some unknown reason. "I'll do it," she said.

Ryan groaned.

"That's great! If she bothers you, just cover her cage with this." McCall handed her a black fabric cover with gray stripes on it. "She'll quiet right down. You won't even know she's there."

Ryan shook his head and stalked out of the kitchen.

Chloe received instructions on the amount of bird-seed needed and how to refill the water bottle.

She cooed to Gwendolyn and the bird answered her with "Pretty lady." That did it. She was officially in love.

"I may not want to give her back," she said with a smile.

McCall grinned too. "I feel a lot better knowing she's in good hands."

"So where are you going for Thanksgiving that you can't take your pets?"

"I'm from California originally. Most of the family is still there."

"California. I've never been there, but I'd like to go someday. It must be interesting to live near Hollywood and all that."

"I live closer to Oregon than Hollywood."

"Oh. So I guess you're used to colder weather."

"Yeah, but that area gets a lot more rain than snow." He stuck his hands in his jacket pockets. "I should get going. Where would you like to keep Gwendolyn? I'll take her cage and stand if you'll just grab her seed." He pointed to a large bag of birdseed on the kitchen counter.

"Sure. I can keep her in my room while I'm here. If she makes too much noise and keeps the guys up—"

"She won't," he said. "But yeah. You could keep her in an office or the training room. Just don't put her any-where cold, like the basement, or where there are fumes, like the garage."

"Don't worry about a thing. I'll take very good care of her. If the guys complain, my brother may be willin'…

although maybe not. He runs a bed-and-breakfast.
You're sure she won't squawk all night?"

"Positive. Just cover her cage." He kissed her
cheek and took the bird and stand into the hall just as
Haggarty and the lieutenant strolled in. They halted,
eyebrows raised.

"I didn't know you had a boyfriend, Arish," Haggarty
said.

"I don't." She didn't have time for chitchat. McCall
was headed toward the stairs and he'd need to know
which room was hers. She grabbed the seed and strode
after him.

"That's not what it looked like to me," she heard
Haggarty say. "What did it look like to you, Lieutenant?"

She didn't hear his answer, and she didn't want to.
She simply wanted to get the bird up to her room. She'd
cover her if anyone was sleeping. It could be days before
anyone knew the beautiful African gray was there.

With any luck.

Ryan returned to the kitchen. He never had gotten the
cup of coffee he'd gone there for in the first place.

Haggarty and Streeter glanced up at him.

"Did you know Chloe and McCall are seeing each
other?" Haggarty asked him with a sly smile.

*If Haggarty thinks he's going to get a rise out of me,
he has another thing coming.* Ryan returned his smirk.
"If by that you mean they have eyeballs and are probably looking at each other when they talk, then yeah. I
guess they're 'seeing' each other." He used air quotes to
rub in the sarcasm.

"He kissed her."

Shit. How should he respond to that news? Not with the jealousy that suddenly surged through him. That would set tongues wagging. He simply shrugged.

"You don't seem to care. So, if he's not asking her out right now, you wouldn't mind if I do?" Haggarty asked.

Ryan leaned back and burst out laughing. He hadn't had a good belly laugh like that in a while.

Haggarty was frowning. "What's so funny? Oh, you mean because I've given her a hard time? Some chicks dig that, and if not she'll be flattered anyway."

Ryan had to struggle to get his mirth under control. When he could finally speak, he said, "Go right ahead. I'd just like to watch when she shoots you down."

He reared back, looking offended. "What makes you think she'll shoot me down?"

Think fast. You can't say "because she hates your guts." "I overheard her being asked out by one of our fellow trainees. I think she said something about hell freezing over before she dates a firefighter."

"Yeah. Okay. I can see why she might not want to do that."

The lieutenant, who'd been quiet up to that point, looked relieved. "I'm glad she thinks it's a bad idea."

"Why's that?" Haggarty asked.

"Because it is."

"Well, I just came in for a cup of coffee," Ryan said. "Thanks for the, um, interesting conversation."

"Hey, you won't say anything to Arish, right?" Haggarty narrowed his eyes.

"Of course not. What am I, twelve?" Ryan grabbed

his coffee and left the kitchen. He took determined strides to the third-floor stairway—and Chloe.

---~~~---

Ryan stepped inside Chloe's room and closed the door. "Did you know Haggarty was thinking of asking you out?"

She almost dropped the bird's dirty newspaper. "What did you say?"

Ryan folded his arms and leaned against her closed door, smirking. "I said Haggarty wants to ask you out."

"On a date or to meet a firing squad?"

Ryan chuckled and scratched his head. "I know, huh? I was as shocked as you are."

"Are you sure you're talkin' about feckin' Haggarty? The feckin' thorn in my rib since I got here?"

"Positive. He asked if you were seeing McCall first."

She crumpled up the old newspaper and tossed it in the wastebasket. "Idjit. He saw McCall give me that unasked-for, unwelcome kiss on the cheek for takin' care of Gwendolyn."

"That's what I thought too. But there's something you should know about American men."

"And what's that?"

"Sometimes the more they seem to hate you, the more they like you."

She rolled her eyes as she peeled off a couple of new layers of newspaper. "Irish lads can be like that, but they usually outgrow it. One laddie actually tried to put gum in my hair once."

Ryan groaned. "What happened to him?"

A sly smile crossed her face. "Let's just say the gum

landed on the end of his nose, and then his nose landed in the dirt."

Ryan laughed.

She laid the clean newspaper in the bottom of Gwendolyn's cage and continued puzzling out the information she'd been given. "But *men* do this here in America? I'd have thought they'd grow out of that behavior quick when they finally realize what they want us females for. Or do your women sleep with them even if they're treated badly?"

Ryan plopped down onto her bed. "Some do. I've never understood that, but it happens."

"Sheesh." Chloe wagged her head. "Feckin' Haggarty. So what did you tell him?"

"I made up a little white lie. I said I'd overheard you turn down a date with a fellow trainee of ours. And then for good measure I added that you'd said hell would freeze over before you'd date a firefighter."

She walked over to him, grabbed him underneath the arms, and hauled him onto his feet. "That sounds like somethin' I'd say."

He grinned. "Maybe this isn't the best timing, but I got two tickets to a Celtics game. Do you still want to go?"

"Ha. If you were considerin' it a date, then 'tis poor timin' indeed. But if you saved me from havin' to turn down a feckin' date with feckin' Haggarty, then you did me a major favor. I'd be happy to accompany you to this Celtics game if I have the night free."

"I picked one of our days off next week and avoided Friday. I think that's when you play at the tearoom, right?"

"This crazy schedule may mess up some sessions, but I plan to be there whenever I can. My sister Shannon will fill in for me if I can't be there."

"Our tickets are for Wednesday."

"About a week before Christmas then."

"Yeah. Is that doable?"

Her eyebrows raised. "Doable?"

He smiled. "Yeah. It means, can you do that?"

"Ah. In that case, yes. I'm doable."

He grinned at her but didn't say anything.

"What?"

"Nothing. You're just…adorkable." With that, he swooped in and gave her a quick kiss, then opened the door and sauntered away, whistling.

"Feckin' men…" she muttered.

"Feckin' Haggarty!" Gwendolyn announced.

"Shite!" Chloe threw the cover over the cage. "You will forget those words if you want your next meal, birdie. If not, he'll probably have Nagle make parrot for dinner."

⁓

The following Tuesday, Ryan grabbed Chloe in the hallway and pulled her into one of the vacant offices, shutting the door.

"What's goin' on?" she demanded.

He grinned as he pulled two tickets out of his pocket. "Are you ready to be introduced to an American sport with an Irish flair?"

"Drinkin' whiskey and brawlin'?"

He laughed. "Probably not. How about beer and basketball?"

"I guess it sounds okay. A little tame though." A slow smile crept across her lips.

He couldn't help himself. He hadn't kissed her in days. He swooped in and captured her delectable mouth. She responded instantly, wrapping her arms around his neck and meeting his tongue with hers.

Perhaps she'd missed his kisses as much as he'd missed hers. But they had to be careful. Chances are the lieutenant would tell the captain, and then…who knew what would happen? If one of them wasn't transferred right away, they'd at least be operating under a high level of scrutiny.

Ryan had tried to casually ask about couples on the same shift at the most recent family Sunday dinner.

There was precious little information since in-house females were rare, but Jayce had said he knew of a couple in another city. Apparently they had been split and were now working in different groups. It was a pain trying to get together, so they eventually broke up. Or maybe they'd broken up and then one of them had to change groups. Jayce wasn't sure.

Ryan's father had reminisced about one of the earliest female firefighters. She was already married and became a firefighter after helping her husband study for his exams. Apparently what her husband was doing to help people made an impression on her. She wound up retiring as a chief…and they stayed together.

None of that had really helped. It seemed like things could go either way. He wondered if the couple who'd split up would have reconciled if they'd continued to work side by side.

He'd dropped the subject as soon as his brothers

started getting suspicious. When Noah came right out and asked if he was interested in the new female probie in his firehouse, he'd laughed. Then he told the same lie he'd told to Haggarty—about her declaring she wouldn't date a firefighter until hell froze over. She hadn't seemed to mind his saying it the first time, so he figured he'd be in the clear if it ever got back to her.

Miguel and Jayce gave each other a look, as if they had been talking beforehand and were thinking the same thing. Sometimes the Fierros seemed to have a psychic shorthand. They weren't telepaths. They just had some sort of nonverbal communication where a significant glance conveyed something specific and was usually interpreted correctly.

The only look he received that he could interpret was one of sympathy from Miguel's wife.

Had they been feeling sorry for him? That would truly suck. He wished he could tell them about his relationship with Chloe, but he didn't know what it was yet.

He didn't want to spook her by asking her out on a date. At this point, it was enough just to spend time with her. Her smile, which used to be seen so rarely, seemed to appear just for him as soon as he walked into any room. He couldn't help returning it too.

No wonder the guys suspected their attraction. He had to figure out a way to make this thing work—whatever it was.

———∿∿∿———

"So how are we gettin' to this game?" Chloe asked. "Together? Or should I meet you there?"

Ryan chuckled. "I'd better take you since you've never been to the Garden. The place is huge."

"You're not worried about anyone seein' us together?"

"The odds are pretty slim."

Chloe had been trying to figure out if this was a date or just a couple of buddies enjoying a game together. Either way, if he planned to pick her up, she wanted him to keep thinking she lived at Rory and Amber's place. Her apartment in the building next door was right across the hall from the city's only paranormal club. An accidental fang sighting near her apartment would be hard to explain.

"Okay. Well, you know where I live. What time should I be ready?"

He glanced at the tickets. "The game is at seven thirty. Would you like to grab a bite to eat beforehand?"

She sighed inwardly. Again, the invitation could go either way. "A bite to eat" could be a casual date or just buddies filling their bellies. Well, she'd *put the ball back in his court*. From her quick research on the game of basketball, she'd finally made sense of another American expression.

"What would you like to do?" she asked.

He shrugged.

At last she lost her patience. "Oh, I give up! Is this a date or isn't it? It makes no difference to me either way. I just want to know."

He laughed. "I was trying to figure that out myself."

"Good lord. We're a couple of pathetic friends, aren't we?"

Ryan moved closer and whispered, "I don't think friends kiss with tongue."

At last she had her answer. This *was* a date. Now she just had to figure out how she felt about that.

Aw, hell. She was *delighted*.

Chapter 10

"I DON'T SEE A GARDEN," CHLOE SAID AS SHE GLANCED around the steel, glass, and concrete structure. Their bleacher seats were a few rows from the hardwood. "Even the restaurant didn't have a hint of green."

Ryan laughed. "The name goes way back. I don't know if it ever had anything to do with flowers. This isn't the same building that used to be called The Boston Garden. That thing was condemned and this new one was rebuilt on the same spot."

"So why is it called the TD Garden?" Chloe asked. "Does that stand for something, like 'Total Dude's Garden'?"

He grinned, but at least he didn't laugh at her. "No. It was named after a bank."

"A bank? What does banking have to do with basketball?"

"Well, I'm not sure how to answer that. I'd have to say 'nothing and everything.' Most arenas and stadiums are named after whoever put up the most money to build it."

"Oh." She couldn't help sounding disappointed. Modern America seemed to worship nothing but the almighty dollar. She wondered what Mother Nature would think of this "garden."

Ryan gazed at her. "Were you expecting a botanical garden or something? We have one of those too. Just not here."

She smiled. "No. I didn't have any real expectations. I'm just interested in seeing this new game of yours."

"New game?" He laughed. "Are you one of those Europeans who think everything in America is modern just because we've only been a country for two hundred and fifty years or so?"

She snorted. She quickly covered her nostril in case she accidentally blew out a stream of smoke. He certainly didn't know that most of what existed in Ireland was modern to her.

St. Patrick had tried to evict all reptiles from Ireland in the fourth century. Her race had managed to survive in caves off the western coast, so they existed even before that. No one knew when the original dragons appeared. She supposed she could ask Mother Nature sometime, but chances are she'd get some kind of snarky or bored response.

A few minutes into the game, Chloe was catching on…although there was nothing more Irish about it than the team's name and shamrock emblem on their uniforms. The game wasn't very complicated.

But there was one thing that made her cringe—okay, there were two things. The way they mispronounced Celtics with a soft C, and the painting on the floor of a little man spinning a basketball on the end of his finger. *He* reminded her of Shamus—the leprechaun who blamed her family for stealing a pot of gold. And then all the leprechauns kicked the remaining Arish dragons out of Ireland over the misunderstanding…and that's how she'd wound up in Boston in the first place. Well, actually the second place. The first place they'd landed was Iceland, but the language was so difficult she had been relieved when they'd decided to move to Boston shortly after that. They'd learned English when the rest of Ireland had to.

Then she glanced up at Ryan. If that hadn't happened, she'd never have met this handsome firefighter. And she'd never have been kissed like the world could end at any moment.

She took another gander at the leprechaun painted on the floor a few rows in front of her and was able to crack a smile.

Ryan tipped up her chin with his finger. "What is it?"

"Oh, nothing. My mind was just wandering."

Suddenly the guy behind Ryan tapped his shoulder. "Hey, look!" He pointed to the large screen overhead in the middle of the arena. Large flashing letters spelled out *Kiss Cam*.

"Oh no," Ryan groaned.

"Kiss her, kiss her, kiss her," the crowd chanted.

Shite. "Can everyone see that? Even the people watching at home on TV?" she asked.

"Yep. And the only way to make it stop is if I kiss you."

When she glanced up at the giant peeping Tom, it didn't seem to be moving away and the crowd was obviously not satisfied. They began booing.

Ryan cupped the back of her head and moved in. The crowd began chanting again, and after he had kissed her for several toe-curling seconds, the crowd cheered.

"And that was the kiss cam," Ryan said, grinning.

"I feckin' figured that out for meself. So, do you think anyone we know saw that?"

"Unless every firefighter in the district went to the fridge for a beer at that exact moment, I think it's a guarantee."

"Shite. We're screwed. Forgive me for this."

"For what?"

She pulled back and slapped his face, hard.

———∿∿∿———

Ryan stuffed his hands in his pockets and strolled beside Chloe on their way out of the arena.

"I know I said it before, but I'm sorry for slappin' you," she said.

He smiled. "Actually, that was smart. We sure don't look like we're dating now."

After a brief hesitation, she gazed up at him with something unfamiliar in her eyes. Sadness? Remorse? Whatever it was, he didn't care for it. Not on her.

"Do you forgive me?" she asked.

He hooked her arm and halted. "Here's how much I forgive you." He swooped in and kissed her, long and slow.

She ran her fingers through his hair, returning his kiss. The fervor built and the rest of the world fell away. Distantly he heard catcalls and comments like, "Oh, *now* she kisses him!" and "Make up your mind, girl!"

When he heard the inevitable "Get a room" comment, he broke the kiss. Between panting breaths he whispered, "I think that might be a good idea."

"What idea?" She was breathing hard too.

He whispered right in her ear, "Getting a room."

When he leaned back to gauge her expression, he had no trouble interpreting it. Her mouth hung open and her eyes rounded.

Shit. I shocked her.

He was just about to apologize when she nodded. "Yes," she whispered. "Let's."

———ⁿⁿⁿ———

Was she really going to do this? Sleep with Ryan?

Part of her wanted to run, suspecting the inevitable heartbreak would be worse if they acted on their feelings for each other. *No.* She couldn't assume his feelings. Their natural impulses were taking over, that's all.

As they found the nearest hotel and checked in, the war in her head continued. What if she was no good in bed? Would he tell the "brotherhood"? Should she let him know this would be her first time?

Oh, shite. I've no idea what I'm doin'.

She bit her lip and hung her head as they entered the elevator.

"What's wrong? Are you having second thoughts?"

She barely heard him over her internal debate. "Uh, no. I'm just...nervous, I guess."

He rubbed her back and said, "We don't have to do this if you don't want to."

"It's not a matter of wantin'."

His look of confusion made her realize he might call it off if she didn't do something encouraging. She had avoided men for a long time. A loooooooong time. Why this guy was different she couldn't quite figure out. But for some damn reason, she wanted to know him, completely.

She grabbed the back of his head and yanked him down for a hard kiss.

When she let him up for air, he grinned. "I guess you're okay with this, then."

She smiled back and nodded.

They found their room and he quickly used the key

card. A stupid stray thought entered her mind as he took a step back to allow her to go first. *Isn't he going to carry me over the threshold?* She almost rolled her eyes at herself. *Wrong milestone, idjit.*

She almost felt like she needed to be carried, as her legs seemed to liquefy. *Stupid legs! Work!*

"Are you—"

"Yes, I'm sure," she said before he could misinterpret her hesitation.

She marched into the room and eyed the bed. It was huge. Nerves were getting the better of her again. If things didn't go well... *Stop thinking that way, Chloe! This could be the most wonderful experience of your ridiculously long life.*

She unzipped her jacket and let it fall to the floor, then strolled over and sat on the edge of the bed. Smiling, she patted the space beside her.

Ryan followed her lead.

She began to unbutton his shirt, but her fingers were trembling. She hoped he wouldn't notice.

He let her continue, leaned over, and kissed her as she fumbled. To his credit, he didn't try to hurry or help her.

A pleasurable sensation shot through her as he found her breast and massaged it through her sweater. He was gentle, yet there was no mistaking what he wanted.

Suddenly, she needed their clothes *off*. Immediately. She broke the kiss, quickly finished unbuttoning his shirt, and yanked it out of his jeans. As soon as she'd peeled it off him and tossed it who-knows-where, she whipped off her sweater and threw it in the same direction.

"Anxious, are you?" he teased.

She grabbed his belt buckle. In seconds the belt

went the way of everything else, and she yanked his
fly open.

"Whoa. I'm glad you're excited, but stop before you
injure me and spoil our fun. Let me take over from here."

"Oh." She felt dumb, but she used the awkward
moment to undo her own jeans and slip them off. Now
they were in their underwear. For some reason, she
wasn't ready to go completely nude. Not yet.

He seemed to sense that and simply caressed her
face and kissed her. Their tongues met and swirled. She
relaxed into his arms and let nature take over.

Before long, he lowered her to the bed and leaned
over her, resuming their long, tender kiss. She lost track
of time, then lost track of everything except his talented
mouth. She'd never tasted a man before and loved the
uniqueness of it. Or maybe she just loved *him*. She
couldn't picture doing this with anyone else.

He rolled toward the middle of the bed and she found
herself on top of him. He was letting her take the lead.
Now...what to do?

She leaned back and gazed into his eyes. She saw
some kind of soft, white glow. *Could it be?* Was that
enough to match her diamond?

When she thought about the exact match of Shannon's
sapphire to Finn's eyes and Rory's gem to Amber's
eyes, she sighed. *Probably not.* Still, she wanted to cling
to the possibility.

She needed to see and feel all of him. Her pulse
doubled with the thrill of anticipation.

She sat up, straddling him, and unhooked her bra.
She wasn't big in that area, but at least she was propor-
tionate. She'd seen some bizarre figures—probably the

result of surgery. When she flung the garment away, he grinned appreciatively.

"Like what you see?"

"Very much." He reached for her, but she grabbed his hands.

"Your turn." Climbing off him, she smiled wickedly.

He didn't hesitate. As soon as he whipped off his briefs, she almost gasped. Despite the bulge, Chloe hadn't expected...*that*. His arousal was impressive to say the least, not that she had a lot to compare it to.

She rolled onto her back and shimmied out of her thong.

He groaned.

Oh no! "Is something wrong?"

"Not a thing, sweetheart. I'm just blown away by the view."

Lying on her side, she indulged one of her curiosities. She ran her fingers through his springy chest hair, then circled his nipple. He smiled and reached for her breast.

His touch created such bliss inside her, she could have let him rub her breasts all night. Then he cupped one and ran the roughened pad of his thumb back and forth over it. She arched and moaned.

Good Lord, so this is what all the fuss is about. And they had barely begun!

Ryan wanted to make this experience special. Not just because he needed the itch scratched—badly—but because he sensed a vulnerability in her he'd never seen before. She was trusting him with more than her body.

He kissed her again and his tongue slid over her teeth.

He wondered if she'd allow him to indulge in a little oral sex, something he was very good at. If she was moaning from the attention to her breasts, he couldn't imagine her response if he went down on her.

Finally—finally—she ran her fingers over his cock. Her touch was so tentative, he figured she'd need some encouragement. "That's it, sweetheart. Wrap your hand around it."

She did and even gave him a squeeze. When he moaned, she dropped him as if she'd caused him bodily harm.

"I'm sorry! Did I hurt you?" she asked.

"Far from it. You make me feel good when you touch me. Very good."

"Oh." She reached for him again and this time, she cupped his balls. "Does this feel good?"

"So good."

She became a little bolder and rubbed figure eights around them. He sighed appreciatively. When she grasped his shaft again, he murmured more encouragement. "That's it, princess. Now move your hand up and down."

While she was occupied and driving him crazy, he ran his hand down her abdomen and teased her inner thighs. She shivered, but her skin was blazing hot. She parted her thighs without him asking. He wanted to laugh at the guys who'd thought she was frigid.

He tested her wetness and was pleased to see she was ready for him…but he had more to give her. Much more.

He zeroed in on her sensitive bundle and she cried out, arching off the mattress. She dropped his erection. Good thing or she might have pulled it off.

"Do you want me to stop?"

She swallowed. "Hell no. Don't stop."

He chuckled and rubbed her clit as she moaned.

"That's it, luv. Let me take over. Just feel."

As he sped up his massage, she gathered the sheets in a death grip and moaned louder and louder. At last her legs vibrated wildly and she let out a series of screams that would have had the whole fire department rushing to her room if they'd tried this at the station. Their band of brothers might tease the heck out of her, but when one of their own was threatened, they'd stop at nothing to save him—or her.

Good God, I hope no one calls hotel security.

At last, she settled down and he withdrew his finger. Her eyes were glassy and she was gasping for air.

"Holy feck," she swore between deep breaths.

He had no idea she was such a screamer, but to him it was applause. He'd have to think of places he could take her with no one nearby. Maybe instead of buying a condo, he'd buy a yacht.

Then he remembered her reaction to the fishing boat. Oh well. That was out. He'd just have to make sure whatever condo he bought was totally soundproof.

"I..." She panted. "I..." At last she took a deep breath and said, "I want to make you feel like that too."

Sweeter words were never spoken.

He swallowed. "You can get me close to that, if you don't object to taking my cock in your mouth."

She hesitated, then nodded furiously.

"Or, if you object—"

"No! No objection." She quickly slid down the bed until she was eye level with his throbbing erection.

"I've never..." She took a deep breath. "Just tell me what to do."

She's never given a blow job? He didn't know whether to feel flattered or worried. "Are you sure? I mean...you don't have to do this."

"I know. I want to learn. Just don't expect much the first time."

Oh man. Well, she seemed completely willing, and he knew that whatever she did would feel damn good, so why not? "Just take me in your mouth and suck. No teeth, though!"

She did exactly as he asked. The pleasurable sensation shot through him as he lay back and groaned.

She let him pop out of her mouth. "Am I not doin' it right?"

"You're doing great. Can you keep going?"

She grinned. "I can if you can."

"Just do what comes naturally. I'll stop you if anything hurts."

In seconds she had him worried that he might lose control.

Once she got into it, she rather enjoyed her new skill. It was obvious how much pleasure she was giving him. She experimented with little licks and nips that elicited excited gasps. When he told her to stop, she almost pouted.

"I didn't hurt you, did I?"

"Not at all." He grabbed her under her arms and hauled her back up to his face, then rolled her onto her back and kissed her, deeply. When he came up for air, he said, "You are the most surprising woman I've ever met."

"Why? Because I did that blow job thing?"

He laughed. "That was like a delicious ice cream sundae. Just part of a whole bowlful of surprises."

"So, I'm like ice cream?"

"Yup. Plus the hot fudge sauce that surprises the tongue."

She grinned. "What else is in an ice cream sundae?"

He couldn't believe she'd never had one. He filed that information away for later. They'd definitely have to go to an ice cream parlor soon.

"Well, there's whipped cream," he said.

Her smile widened. "Oh. I've heard of some interesting things that can be done with whipped cream."

How was it she'd heard of whipped cream in the bedroom, but not an ice cream sundae? Oh well. That was part of the puzzle that was Chloe Arish.

"So, is there anything else?" she asked.

"Oh yeah. Over the whipped cream, it's covered with chopped walnuts."

"Are you calling me nuts?"

He laughed. "Well…"

She shoved him, but she was still smiling.

"What else?"

Oh no. Don't say it, Fierro. Don't say it… "And a cherry on top." *Damn it. I said it!* Without waiting to explain that one, he quickly added, "There's more dessert coming. Are you ready for it?"

He touched her intimately, inserting his fingers into her heat. She parted her thighs, doing what came naturally. It was a good thing Mother Nature gave her instincts.

Having lived in a cave with a brother and sister most of her long life, she naturally had zero exposure to sex. And living in heavily Roman Catholic Ireland didn't help fill in the blanks.

"Yes, you certainly are ready." He rolled up onto his knees and positioned himself between her legs. "Give me one second."

He rooted around under the mattress and came up with the packet he must have deposited there. After he tore it open, he placed a rubbery disc over the tip of his penis and unrolled it. Her curiosity was piqued, but she'd ask about that part later. Right now she was too engrossed in what was happening to stop him with questions.

He lowered himself over her, braced on his elbows. "Bend your knees, sweetheart."

She did as he asked, and felt an odd sensation, but it wasn't at all unpleasant. "Are you okay?" he paused and gazed into her eyes.

"I'm fine. Are you?"

He chuckled. "I'm great. But you need to know something... If you've never done this before, there might be a momentary stab of pain. I'll do what I can to minimize it. As soon as it passes, you'll feel wonderful. Do you trust me?"

She wasn't afraid of a little pain. "Completely."

"Okay. Hold on."

She grasped him around the neck and he drove into her. He was right about the sharp stab of pain, but she'd endured much worse.

He stilled and stared into her eyes, as if searching for something.

"Ah, that was nuthin'," she said.

He broke into a slow smile. "Okay. Here comes the fun part."

He rocked into and out of her sensitive channel, and she loved the way it felt.

The whole movement became like a dance. As soon as she realized that, she again followed her body's instincts and began dancing with him. He pressed into her, and she lifted her hips to meet him. He pulled away and she let her hips fall, but not so far as to lose him.

As he picked up the pace, she continued to match his rhythm. A pleasurable sensation grew within her. Before she knew it, the same wonderful feeling she'd had from his fingers returned and seemed to be building...then cresting.

As if letting go of the handle bars and riding a bike down a hill with no hands or feet, she flew, feeling completely free. She screamed in joy as she might on any amusement park ride. She also felt as out of control and helpless as she would on a ride that someone else was operating.

That someone was Ryan, and he seemed to be working hard to keep the ride going. His eyes were closed and beads of sweat popped out on his forehead. At last his mouth fell open and he groaned, shuddering and jerking.

"Good God," he said on a gasping breath.

Her eyes felt wet. When he opened his and stared at her, his expression quickly became one of concern. "Are you all right? Did I hurt you?"

She grinned and said, "That was incredible. I've never been less hurt in my life."

Chapter 11

"I'M SORRY ABOUT THE FECKIN' BIRD."

He chuckled and slung an arm over her shoulder as they entered the elevator. "It's probably a good thing we had to check on him. Otherwise we might have stayed in bed for three days and forgotten to eat."

She glanced up at him with an impish grin. "That doesn't sound so bad."

God, this woman surprised him! He'd taken her virginity, and all she'd wanted to do was give it to him again...and again. Before the elevator doors opened, he swooped in for a quick kiss. "From the lobby on, we're just friends. Coworkers who partied together after the game. Right?"

"Sounds right to me."

Where had this woman been all his life? Melanie hadn't crossed his mind for days, but when the unbidden thought intruded, all he felt was, *Thanks for leaving me, Mel. If you hadn't, I'd never be with Chloe now.*

"So is McCall coming back soon?"

"Yeah, he was supposed to be back yesterday, but texted and said he had to take care of one thing first, then missed his flight."

Ryan was amused. Maybe he had a girl in California that needed a little loving before he left. He hoped it was something like that. He almost chuckled as he noticed the change in his mood. Ordinarily he'd have been cursing his name. Now Chloe would have to tell the guys on Group 2 why a bird was in her room and he thought it was kind of funny.

As soon as they hit the street, Ryan removed his arm from Chloe and felt the loss of heat immediately. He stuffed his hands in his pockets to keep from wrapping his arm around her again and saying "to hell with it" if they got caught.

"So, was this a one-time thing?" he asked.

Her wide eyes betrayed her shock. "I hope not. Is that what you wanted?"

"No!" He gentled his voice. "I mean, no. It isn't. I just wasn't sure how you were feeling about it."

"Oh. I feel fine about it, but I know hotels in the city aren't cheap. Can we go to your place? I mean, I know you live with your parents, but you said it was in a separate part of the house. How would they feel about—"

"No. We can't go there."

She was quiet for a while. How could he explain? *You can't scream in a houseful of first responders?* At last, he settled on, "My family would welcome you a little too enthusiastically. My mother would insist you come for Sunday dinners. My brothers would tell everyone and soon the whole city would know. One of us would be transferred before the next shift rotation."

"Oh! I understand. Neither of us wants that."

"Absolutely. I'd miss seeing your beautiful face."

She rewarded him with a beaming smile.

"I guess we can't go to your place either. Your brother and sister-in-law seem to like me, but they might not if they think I'm killing you."

She halted, reddened, and put a hand over her mouth.

"Hey." He stopped and faced her. "Don't worry about it. I'm glad to know you had fun."

"Fun?" Her smile disappeared.

"Now what did I do?"

"You call feeling like I died and went to heaven 'fun'? Like I left my body and my spirit soared free, fun?"

"Well…yeah. What would you call it?"

She looked away and stayed silent for a few uncomfortable moments.

At last she nodded. "I guess it *was* fun. I don't know how else to describe it, but it seemed like more."

Uh oh…

———

Chloe spent the entire morning humming and cleaning her apartment. In the afternoon she went shopping to fill her pathetically empty refrigerator and pantry. She had tried to imagine what a man like Ryan would like to eat, and shopped accordingly. Meat and potatoes she'd guessed. She wasn't much of a cook, but she could bake a potato and broil a steak.

Now she just needed to call him and invite him to dinner. Yes, she lived in paranormal central, but hopefully she could get him in the door and up to her apartment without him seeing anything "weird." All the paranormals knew the rules and they kept their identities under wraps while humans were around.

Still, it might be worth mentioning the possibility of "noise" next door and asking the members to ignore it.

Chloe almost skipped across the hall. She breezed into the club and saw very little activity. Drake, the only dragon she knew outside of her Irish clan, was playing pool with Kurt, the bald wizard. Rumor had it that Kurt was completely human, but also completely trustworthy. His wife was a vampire, but not an easygoing one like the couple managing her building.

They looked up from their game.

"Chloe!" Drake exclaimed as he laid down his stick. He strode around the table and gave her a big hug.

"How's it going, Drake? How are Bliss and that baby of yours?" she asked.

"Ah," he chuckled. "Nuts, as you'd expect. I snuck off to have a few minutes of peace." He turned toward his buddy who'd strolled over. "You remember Kurt, don't you?"

"Of course. What's new in your world, Kurt?"

"Not a lot, but that's a good thing." He grinned. "Life is either calm or calamity for me. Ruxandra is out hunting—or shopping, I'm never sure which." He laughed.

"Nice. Well, I just came over to ask you a favor and to pass on the message to anyone who may come in after you."

"Oh. Sure. What is it?" Drake asked.

"Um…" She could feel her cheeks heat as she hesitated. *How do I phrase something like this?* "I may have a gentleman over later. If there's a lot of noise… that is to say, if you hear me soundin' as if I need assistance, well…"

Drake laughed. "I think I know what you're trying to say."

"Oh, thank the Goddess!"

Both guys grinned.

"So, you won't come chargin' over, tryin' to break down me door?"

"We'll mind our own business unless you call for help. How's that?"

"Mind your business no matter what I say, all right?"

Kurt raised his eyebrows. "Are you sure you'll be all right? I mean, I don't know what your gentleman is capable of. Do you?"

"Good question," Drake added. "What kind of paranormal powers does he have?"

"None. That's why I don't need anyone's help—at all."

The two guys glanced at each other with raised eyebrows. "He's a human—with no powers at all?" Kurt asked. "Or is he like me and able to use magic to freeze time, situations...*or manipulate people?*"

"Human. Please don't ask me for any other identifying details." Chloe had to keep Drake out of it. He was a District 3 firefighter and since there were Fierros nearly everywhere in the city, he probably knew one of Ryan's relatives...or more than one.

"Okay. You know the rule about keeping our paranormal identities hidden," Drake said. "So I assume you won't be bringing him over here for a tour of the club."

"You assume right," she said.

"What time is he coming over?"

"I don't know if he *is* coming over yet. I haven't invited him."

"Ah. You waited to scope out the circumstances. Good move," Kurt said.

Drake picked up his pool cue. "You might want to warn the managers above you. Vampires hear everything."

"Shite. I hadn't thought of that." She sighed. This might be more trouble than it was worth. How could she be sure every resident didn't have hearing like that? Did

she have to make sure everyone in the building knew her
business so they wouldn't interfere?

"Feck. I may not have thought this through enough.
Forget what I said, guys. I need to figure out a way to
deal with this building's paranormal residents as well as
the club members. Feck, feck, feck."

Drake chuckled. "I guess you won't be doing much
'fecking,' at least not tonight."

Before her cheeks became completely red, she turned
on her heel and marched across the hall. She heard
chuckles behind her, even though she'd closed the door.

Yeah. Not a good idea to meet him here.

Ryan just wanted to hear her voice. He was on his way
to dinner with two of his brothers, so he couldn't invite
her along...yet. Maybe someday they could declare
themselves an item and continue working together.
Apparently there weren't any hard-and-fast rules, and
each captain could handle it any way they saw fit. He
needed to scope out the situation at *their* firehouse—
without setting off any warning bells.

He clicked her number in his contact list and continued walking toward the Prudential Center. For some
damn reason, his brothers wanted to have a "nice" dinner
at a glassed-in atrium there. He'd be fine with burgers at
one of the casual places on Lansdown Street.

She picked up on the third ring.

"How's it hangin', Ryan?"

He laughed. "It's hanging its head. I think it misses you."

She broke out in giggles.

He wouldn't have thought she was a giggler, but

the sound was about the most delightful thing he'd ever heard.

Ryan must have been sporting a goofy grin. People passing him were staring. "I just wanted to ask how your day was." *And I can't stop thinking about you.*

"It was productive, but not very exciting. I did laundry, shopping, and cleaned my apartment. Please tell me you had a more interesting day than that."

"About the same."

"So, where are you?" she asked. "I hear traffic noise."

"Just walking toward the Pru. I'm supposed to meet my bothers Miguel and Jayce for dinner."

"Dinner at the Pru, huh? At the Top of the Hub?"

He laughed. "No. They wanted to go a little upscale, but not *that* fancy. The last time I wore a suit was—I can't even remember."

She lowered her voice to a sultry tone. "So, what are you wearing?"

He laughed. "Nothing that would turn you on. Dockers and a sweater. The restaurant is someplace with a glassed-in atrium. They keep it business casual in case people look in, I guess. Can't bring the place down by dressing too sloppy."

"That sounds nice."

He was faced with an awkward silence. Not something that usually happened with her. "Well, I just wanted to ask about your day. I'm almost to the restaurant now."

"Okay. I'll let you go—but only because I have to."

"Talk to you soon."

"Yeah. Maybe you can take a picture of your dinner and show me later."

He chuckled. *Ah…back to our usual teasing. What a relief.*

It was time to end the conversation, but what should he say? If he were talking to Melanie, he'd have to reassure her with "Love you," and wait for her "Love you too," but it was way too early for that.

"Well, see ya."

She hesitated. "Yeah. Later," she finally said, then hung up.

He spotted Miguel waiting, leaning against a pole. Then he looked closer and saw his sister-in-law. *Huh. He didn't say anything about bringing Sandra.*

Oh well. He liked her, but she'd probably have to put up with a lot of shop talk. That's really all he had in common with Miguel. Jayce, on the other hand, was his buddy.

"Hey," he said as he approached.

"Hey yourself," Sandra said.

Miguel got to the point as usual. "Our guests are waiting. Let's go in."

"Guests?" He eyed his brother, but there was no more information forthcoming. Maybe he'd invited some friends—or Jayce did. Jayce had a lot of friends.

When he approached the long table, he spotted Jayce with two women. *Looks like I'll have to come up with more than shop talk tonight.*

"Why don't you sit here, across from my friend, Gail," Sandra said.

Uh-oh. This is looking like a fix-up. He slowly took the seat next to Sandra, across from the grinning redhead. *Not. Good.* Not that he had anything against redheads. It was just that a certain blonde was ruining him for all other women.

"So, I'll bet you're wondering why I called you all here tonight," Jayce joked.

Ryan raised his brows. "I am."

Miguel leaned across Sandra so he could make eye contact. "We saw you get socked in the face on the kiss cam. Who was the blonde? Someone you knew, or did you kiss a total stranger?"

Ryan groaned and dropped his head in his hands. *Fool. They felt sorry for me.* "So I was invited on a group date? Am I being fixed up with...what was your name again? Gail?"

"You answer our question first," Jayce said.

"Yeah. I know her, but I had no business kissing her. She's a coworker. And it was only a slap. It's not like she 'socked' me."

His brothers nodded. "Yeah. I figured you probably deserved it, but the ladies were adamant that you shouldn't have been slapped, no matter what you did."

"So, you, Miguel, Sandra, and your date—sorry, I didn't catch your name..." he said to the beauty next to Jayce.

"Diana."

A Roman goddess. Figures. "So, were you four at the game?" Ryan asked.

Miguel said, "Yeah. We were."

"Why didn't you talk to me there?"

Miguel stared at the menu. "We didn't want to get involved."

Ryan barked a laugh and folded his arms. "So, you didn't get involved by setting me up on a blind date?"

Sandra frowned. "You're being rude to my friend, Ryan. Behave."

"And by 'behave,' you mean that I should just ignore my policy of not accepting blind dates and ignore the fact that you didn't respect my wishes."

She fidgeted, as if uncomfortable in her seat. "Well, no. But you could be civil. Talk to her. Enjoy the evening."

He gazed across the table. Gail had the most pathetic look of hurt on her face. Before she burst into tears, he had to do something.

He reached across the table and took her hand. "I'm sorry, Gail. I didn't mean to be rude to you." *I was just upset with these other assholes.*

"It's okay," she said meekly.

He gave her hand a squeeze before he let go and smiled at her.

Jayce jumped in and talked about the game itself. With the attention off him, Ryan was able to relax a bit. He'd made it pretty clear that he didn't want or need a blind date. If Gail wanted his number afterward, he'd have to make up some kind of polite excuse not to give it to her.

With a fake smile painted on his face, he spent the next few seconds wracking his brain for what that excuse might be. *I have a gross venereal disease?* Oh yeah. That would spread like wild fire. *I'm gay?* Nope. It might work with strangers, but his brothers knew him too well.

He couldn't help wishing he could just tell everyone about his relationship with Chloe. In fact, he was wishing so hard, he could have sworn he saw her outside the atrium window.

Oh shit. It is *Chloe!* Gail may have appeared upset earlier, but she had nothing on the feral look in Chloe's eyes. Shock turned to murderous rage right before she took off running.

Ryan shot to his feet, threw his napkin on the table and took off after Chloe.

"Ryan!" Sandra exclaimed.

Miguel's voice called after him, "What the hell?"

He didn't care what anyone thought at that moment. Anyone but Chloe. Where did she go?

He caught sight of her charging toward Exeter Street, a couple of blocks from the fire station where they both worked, but she was running away from it, thank God.

"Chloe!" He charged after her, dodging both foot traffic and cars on Boylston Street. She turned and caught sight of him, then sped up. *Shit*. She was the fastest runner in training, and he'd have a helluva time catching up to her. *But catch her, I will.*

———

Chloe had hoped Ryan had a doppelganger or that one of his brothers was an identical twin, but when he called her name, her worst fears came true. A knife twisted in her gut when she spotted him through the glass, and now she felt physically ill.

Just as he rounded the corner of Exeter Street, he called her name again and really sped up. She had to do something drastic.

She dodged down one of the public alleys. She didn't see anyone, so she ran behind a dumpster and shifted as quickly as she could. She flew to the rooftops and landed just as he charged down the alley yelling her name.

She peeked over the edge of the brownstone she'd landed on and saw him slow down at the next corner. He turned left, then right, and glanced behind him, shading his eyes from the streetlamp, as if peering straight down the alley.

"*Damn* it!" he swore. The cold air outside turned his breaths into columns of fog.

She'd lost him. Chloe slumped down away from the roof's edge, and felt a big dragon tear starting at the corner of her eye. *Oh, feck no. I am* not *cryin' over some two-timin' bastard.*

Yeah. Tell yerself that again. The tear slid down her cheek.

Her grandmother was right. There was no man on this earth for her. No true love in her future. She had just begun to hope the prediction was wrong. But instead, Chloe was wrong to hope.

Ryan stuffed his hands in his pockets and looked up at the Beacon Street brownstone. Lights shone on the second floor, but nowhere else. He remembered the kitchen and office being on the second floor, so they might be preparing dinner.

If Chloe had gone straight home, he'd have to get past her brother. The guy was big, and he probably wouldn't like him anymore. Although maybe Chloe didn't spill her guts to her brother as he pictured. She didn't seem like the kind who would.

He marched up the steps, determined to at least *try* to speak to her. If she were as angry as he imagined she must be, he'd be in more danger with *her* than with her brother. Still, it wasn't his fault. He had to make her see that.

He rang the bell and waited a few moments. Amber stepped out of a door in the hallway and smiled when she recognized him through the glass.

"Come in, Ryan," she said as she swung the door open wide.

So far, so good. Chloe had either said nothing or hadn't come home yet.

Amber shivered, so he stepped inside the foyer and let her close the big wooden door behind him.

"Hi, Amber. Is Chloe home?"

Amber's brows raised. "Um. I don't think so. Let me check. Would you like to come upstairs and have a cup of coffee with Rory while you wait?"

What should he do? Have coffee with the big brother who could punch his lights out, or maybe gain sympathy by explaining what happened to her family first? "Uh, sure. If it's no trouble. Don't make a fresh pot just for me."

"No trouble at all. I can whip up coffee or tea in one of those individual cup thingies. It'll only take a sec."

"Thanks." He followed her up the stairs.

In the kitchen, Rory sat at a granite island, sipping a cup of tea. He hopped off the stool and strolled over to Ryan with his hand extended. "Ryan! How's it goin'?"

Ryan returned the firm handshake, then hung his head. "Not so well, I'm afraid. I need to see Chloe...to explain something."

"Ah, you've had a misunderstandin'. Well, that happens. Have a seat. What can I get you? Coffee? Tea?"

"Uh, Amber offered me some coffee. I hope it's not too much trouble."

"No trouble a'tall. I'll get it."

"I'm going to see if she's home," Amber said. Ryan thought he caught a strange look pass between them before she gave Rory a peck on the lips and went upstairs.

The coffee only took a couple of minutes, and Rory asked him what he took in it. Black was easiest, so that's how Ryan asked for it. The bitter taste seemed appropriate to his mood.

When Rory set the cup in front of him, he settled on the next stool. There was one other seat, so Amber or Chloe could join them. Hopefully, Chloe.

"What's happened, if you don't mind me askin'? You can say it's none of me business, but where me sister is concerned, I might disagree."

"It's a simple misunderstanding, like you thought. Chloe saw something that wasn't at all what she thought it was. She ran off before I could explain it to her."

Rory raised one eyebrow. "What did she see? Were you huggin' or kissin' another woman?" He narrowed his eyes. "Was it your sister?"

"No. Of course not. I don't have any sisters."

Rory snorted. "Consider yerself lucky." He fell silent and stared at the island.

The silence was killing Ryan, so he figured he could divulge a little more. "I was supposed to have dinner with two of my brothers. That's all I was told. When I showed up, my sister-in-law was there with one of her female friends and my other brother brought a date. It didn't take long to figure out I'd been tricked into a blind date. I never would have gone if I had known. Believe me."

Rory leaned back and scrutinized his face. "So what did Chloe see?"

"Just the six of us sitting at a table in the Atrium restaurant."

"You weren't holdin' hands with the woman, nor putting your arm around her?"

"I wasn't touching her! Well, not at that moment. She was sitting across the table and I held her hand for a few seconds. That's all. I don't know what Chloe saw."

"Why were you holdin' the woman's hand?"

"Because I was apologizing. She looked like she was about to cry when I said I wanted nothing to do with a blind date. It wasn't personal, but she didn't know that. I had to explain that my policy was never to go on blind dates, at all. My family tricked me."

Rory chuckled.

Whew. Maybe he'd escape with his life after all—if Chloe didn't kill him.

"Did you try goin' after Chloe?"

"Of course."

Amber was gone awhile. She'd had plenty of time to check and return if Chloe *wasn't* there. Maybe they were having some girl talk. He could only hope that Amber would encourage her to hear him out.

"So, you're sayin' me sister jumped to a wrong conclusion and outran you?"

"Uh. Yeah. That about sums it up."

Rory smirked. "That sounds like Chloe all right."

Ryan glanced at the empty stairs. The longer he waited the more uncomfortable he became. At least Rory wasn't pushing for any details about the extent of their personal relationship.

"So, have you told her you love her yet?"

Shit.

Chapter 12

AMBER HAD POPPED INTO CHLOE'S APARTMENT IN the building next door. She heard sniffles coming from the bedroom. *Damn.* Knowing Chloe as well as she did, she figured the female dragon almost never cried.

She approached the bedroom door with trepidation and knocked softly.

"Go away," Chloe shouted.

"Chloe, it's Amber. Talk to me."

"No. Leave me alone."

Amber took a deep breath. Being a muse, there wasn't much the woman could do to her. If she shifted into dragon form and blasted her with fire, Amber could disappear. She might get singed, but she'd heal with a snap of her fingers.

"I want to respect your wishes, but I can't leave you like this. We have three choices. We can either shout through the door, I can come in without your permission, or you can treat me like a friend and open the door."

Apparently, Chloe was considering the options, because she didn't answer right away.

At last, the door opened and a very defeated-looking woman stood there. Her shoulders were sloped, her head angled down, and her hands hung by her sides. Amber barely recognized her boyfriend's sister.

"Chloe…"

Amber waited until she looked up at her with

red-rimmed eyes. "Oh, honey." She strode forward and grasped her in a big hug. Chloe barely returned the gesture, as if she didn't have the strength to hug her back. When she finally grasped her, she let the dam burst and sobbed onto Amber's shoulder.

When her tears finally abated, she mumbled, "It's my own fault."

Amber rubbed her back. "Being mad at ourselves is usually worse than being mad at other people. We tend to judge ourselves pretty harshly." She hoped she was speaking the truth. At least it was true for her, but she and Chloe differed in how they reacted to adversity.

"I'm mad at Ryan and meself, both. We're both feckin' idjits." Then she chuckled.

Was that an inappropriate laugh, or am I not getting the joke? She hoped she was just dense and that Chloe wasn't going off her rocker. "Come and sit down. Tell me what happened."

Chloe allowed herself to be led by the hand to her couch. It was facing the fireplace, so Amber lit the candles there. Fortunately, she didn't have to leave Chloe's side and merely pointing her finger took care of it. The firelight seemed to comfort her and she relaxed a bit.

Amber waited until Chloe was ready to share whatever she needed to.

"I slept with Ryan. Last night. Tonight, I saw him with another woman." She snorted and a curl of smoke exited her nose.

"What did he have to say for himself?"

"I don't know. I left. He'd probably just tell me a pack of feckin' lies anyway."

"Probably? That means he might also tell you the truth."

"I doubt it."

Amber didn't know how much to reveal about Ryan's visit. Should she tell Chloe he was next door, asking to speak to her? Christ, the woman shouldn't be lied to... even if only lying by omission. She took a deep breath. "He's next door, talking to Rory right now."

Chloe stiffened.

"He wants to speak to you," Amber added. "It might be better if he did."

"Shite." She shot to her feet and squared her shoulders. "I'd rather hear what he has to say firsthand instead of through me well-meanin' brother, who might try to soften it."

Amber rose and took her hand. "You're wise and brave, Chloe. You can do this."

"Wait a minute. Is there anythin' you can do about me face? I don't want him to see me all red and puffy from cryin'."

Amber smiled and drew an oval in the air, right in front of Chloe's beautiful face. Her eyes and skin became as clear as they were yesterday. "Ready?"

Chloe nodded. "Let's go."

Amber transported the two of them to the third floor of the B and B. Chloe rocked a bit on landing, but that was par for the course. As a former flight attendant, Amber was used to keeping her balance while flying through the air.

She gave Chloe a smile and picked a piece of lint off her green sweater. Doing a quick perusal, she didn't see anything else to fix. "There. You're good to go."

———

Chloe marched downstairs, determined to hear this "explanation" from Ryan's own lips. She trusted Rory had used his horse-shite detector—he would have tossed Ryan onto the sidewalk if he'd tried to lie.

They were still there. Ryan rose immediately and said, "Chloe…"

There was a certain softness in his voice that she hadn't heard before. Was it remorse?

Rory gazed at Amber and cocked his head toward the stairs. She nodded and the two of them left the others alone.

Ryan stepped toward her and she took a step back.

"Chloe, please hear me out. I think you owe me that."

Her eyebrows shot up. "Owe you?"

He scrubbed a hand over his face. "Forget I said that. Just listen, okay?"

She folded her arms and waited.

"My brothers caught the slap you gave me on the kiss cam. I didn't know they saw that, and I certainly didn't know they felt sorry for me and would try to fix me up with someone. Chloe, I had nothing to do with it."

"Are you sayin' you didn't know you were on a blind date?"

"I knew after a few minutes. I thought it was weird that my sister-in-law was there, and Jayce had brought a date. The extra woman was introduced as a friend of Sandra's…my sister-in-law."

"You were smilin', like this dinner was the best thing that ever happened to you."

"No, Chloe. *You're* the best thing that's ever

happened to me. I had to plaster that smile on my face because I was trying not to cause a scene. I wanted to pummel my family for tricking me."

She wasn't sure she'd heard him right. Did he say that *she* was the best thing that had ever happened to him?

"Say something."

She couldn't. A lump in her throat prevented her from speaking.

"Okay. I'll say something. I would *never* knowingly hurt you. I'm sincerely sorry if this situation caused you any pain. I'll tell my family about us and let them know that slap was staged. I'll explain it was because we didn't want to be split up on different shifts or transferred to different firehouses. I love being with you...even just being around you. I'll ask them not to say anything, but if they do, I'll beg the captain to keep us together."

He took a tentative step toward her. "I'm crazy about you." This time she didn't retreat. He took another, then another. When he reached her, he gathered her into his arms.

His warmth and the sincerity of his apology eventually got to her and she melted into him. She tipped up her chin to see his face. His eyes said he meant every word. He leaned in slowly for a kiss, but gave her enough time to stop him.

Stopping him was the last thing on her mind.

His lips touched hers. He applied light pressure and slid them back and forth. She responded and opened her mouth. His tongue slipped into her mouth and found hers. When she curled her tongue around his, he cupped the back of her head and deepened the kiss.

Her hands automatically reached up and slid over his

shoulders. She ran her fingers through the dark hair at the nape of his neck. His drugging kiss could erase not only the last two hours, but the last thousand years. All that existed was the two of them.

Rory yelled down from upstairs. "Have you told her you love her yet?"

Ryan broke the kiss and hung his head. Then he looked up the stairway and loudly answered, "I was waiting for a happier moment."

Chloe startled. *He loves me?*

"Oh!" Rory shouted. "Sorry." His snickers said he wasn't sorry at all.

Ryan turned his gaze back to Chloe, and she stroked his jaw. "Is it true?"

"Yes. Like I said, I was waiting for a happier moment, but yes."

Tears shimmered in her eyes. "There is no happier moment than this."

He smiled and captured her lips again.

Then she realized how vulnerable she was. They both were. When love is given, a heart can be broken—especially if betrayal is involved. She pushed his chest and pulled back, just enough so she could speak. "Wait."

He froze.

"I think it's only fair that you know what will happen if you ever do cheat on me."

"You'll never have to worry—"

She clapped her hand over his mouth. "Like I said. I should warn you."

He pulled her hand down and kissed her palm. "I know, I know… You'll kick my arse all the way to the street and leave me in the gutter where I belong."

She grinned. "Something like that."

"Consider me warned." He grinned back at her. "Fortunately, that will never, ever, happen. Just do me a favor…"

"What?"

"If you think you see or hear something suspicious, tell me. Right away. I want a chance to explain *before* you upset a dinner party with homicidal threats."

"Ah, you know me well." She tipped up her chin and they resumed their kiss. Before long, passion took over and grew until she was afraid she might burst into flames.

Ryan broke the kiss and whispered, "Hey, let's get a room."

———~~~———

Rory and Amber were still enjoying their extended vacation, holding off on advertising their B and B. She was sitting on his lap in the large first floor living room while they watched a movie on the big-screen TV.

A knock at the door surprised them.

"Are we expectin' anyone, luv?" Rory asked.

"Not that I know of." Amber strolled to the door and smiled, recognizing someone through the glass inset. She opened the door wide and exclaimed, "Aiden! What brings you here? I thought the Christmas season was your busiest."

"'Tis, but I have somethin' important to discuss with your Rory, and the others said they could spare me."

By now Rory was joining them in the foyer. He clasped his cousin's hand in welcome and drew him into a man-hug, pounding him on the back.

Aiden carried a paper bag in his free hand but did his best to return the friendly gesture.

"What have you there?" Rory asked, eyeing the paper bag.

"A bottle of our finest Ulster Arish whiskey, of course," Aiden said as he drew the bottle sporting his family's coat of arms—three gold dragons—from the bag and presented it to his elder cousin.

"Ah! And a welcome guest you are." Rory winked. "Can you take his coat, Amber? I'll carry your bags to your room. Same one as last time all right?"

"That will be fine, indeed. But I'll take me bags and use the lift this time." He grinned.

Rory chuckled. "Good to know you remember our rules. No shiftin' and flyin' around the house."

Aiden laughed. "Yes. I remember." He hefted his suitcase from the stoop and headed for the elevator.

"As soon as you're settled, meet me at the bar. I'll just open this fine gift now, if I'm not supposed to wait for Christmas."

"It's meant to be opened and enjoyed any time you want it, Cousin. And if you want more, I have a whole distillery full of it back at home."

What could be so important as to take a man away from his whiskey-makin' business at the busiest time of year? Rory laughed to cover his anxiety. "Let's hope I don't need it so."

He wasn't alone for long. Amber returned from the hall closet as soon as Aiden was in the elevator.

"What could be so important?" she whispered, knowing that dragons had sensitive hearing.

"I was wonderin' that meself. We'll play the gracious

host to him, and it will come out in good time." Rory held out a glass of whiskey, straight up. "Would you like some?"

Amber wrinkled her nose. "No, thanks. Unless there's ice and sparkling water in it, that's too strong for me."

"Ah, but it's smooth as silk," he said, encouraging her to take a sip.

"Okay. I'll try it." She took a generous mouthful and swallowed. Then her eyes nearly bugged out of her head. "Yech!" She sputtered and fanned her mouth as if it were on fire.

Rory laughed. "Ye're supposed to take small sips. It should just warm your throat goin' down. Not burn you."

"Sheesh. You could have told me that before I scorched my esophagus."

He took the glass from her and set it on the bar. Then he stepped into her space and gathered her into his arms for a long, deep kiss. Whiskey never tasted as perfect as it did when he sucked on her tongue.

"Ahem."

Rory pulled away reluctantly, and Aiden stood there wearing a grin.

"Forgive me for interruptin'."

"Ah, you caught me," Rory said. "I was just tasting your fine whiskey. Again."

Amber rolled her eyes. "Have a seat, Aiden. I'll be right back."

Aiden took the armchair and Rory poured two fingers for him. No need to ask him if he knew how to drink it.

When he'd poured his own as well, he took the glasses over to the coffee table. "Would you mind settin' a couple of those coasters down, Aiden?" He nodded once toward the pile of them on the end table. "Amber's peculiar about keepin' the furniture pristine."

"Peculiar, am I?" Amber came around the corner with an ice bucket and plate of cookies.

Rory gave a nervous chuckle.

"I understand why she wants to, Cousin. *Someday* you're openin' a new business here."

"Oh…burn," Amber said.

"We've been talkin' about a January first openin', so as to have the taxes all in one year."

"And I think we could open just a bit earlier for the New Year's Eve goers," Amber added as she set the ice bucket on the bar. "Taxes, shmaxes."

"Ye're not the one who's goin' to fill out all the complicated paperwork."

"That's what tax consultants are for."

Aiden was patiently listening to their discussion. "By the way, I was wonderin'… If you're supposed to cater to paranormal visitors, how will you advertise?"

"Ah, that's the rub," Rory said. "All we can safely do is rely on word of mouth. I'm thinkin' we'll put a note on the bulletin board at the paranormal club next door. Members can tell their out-of-town relatives."

"Well, we don't need to decide right now, so let's not ignore our guest," Amber said.

"Ye're right, luv. Forgive us, Cousin. How are Conlan and Eagan?"

"They're right as rain. Busily supervisin' the new staff, makin' sure orders go out quickly… Keepin' well. Thanks fer askin'." His posture and expression changed, but it was hard to say why. "And how's Chloe?"

"You just missed her. She and her new fella were here a few moments ago."

His face fell. "She has a man in her life? Is it serious?"

Rory nodded, confused. Why would he be disappointed to hear that?

Aiden cleared his throat. "It's just, well… I guess it doesn't matter now."

"What doesn't? If you have any concerns, it matters."

Aiden fidgeted uncomfortably.

"Out with it, Cousin. We're family. You can tell us what's on your mind."

Amber had set the cookies on the coffee table and was about to sit down, but she paused. "I can leave you two alone, if it's personal family stuff."

"You're family too," Aiden said. "No need to leave."

"If you're sure," she said hesitantly. He nodded and she nestled into the space beside Rory on the couch.

His arm automatically wrapped around her. "So, about Chloe? Should she be here for this?"

"Nay!" He slumped back in his chair and sipped his whiskey.

"All right. I know you two haven't always been friendly, but if it's something that concerns the family…"

"Forgive me, Cousin. I mean, Prince," Aiden corrected himself and offered a slight bow of his head.

"Jaysus, if you're using me formal title, somethin' must be desperately wrong."

"Not at all, Cousin. I'm sorry to cause you any undue concern."

Rory scratched his head. "The only thing you're causin' me is confusion."

"I know it. Here's the thing. I was thinkin'… I mean,

we—me brothers and I—were discussin' the fate of our species one day."

"Ah. I see the importance now. And what did you talk about?"

"Well, as you know, a dragon can only have children with another dragon. And dragons are as rare a breed as there is on this earth."

"You speak the truth."

"Aye. And with wee Shannon already wed, to a *human*, that leaves only Chloe to procreate the next generation."

Rory didn't care for the way Aiden almost spat the word "human." After all, he was mated to a former human too, but he wouldn't address that now. His more immediate concern was for Chloe. "Again. You speak true. Now speak plain and tell me what you and your brothers have in mind to do about that."

"Well, obviously one of us needs to volunteer to mate with Chloe. Conlan realizes that as the oldest and leader of the Ulster clan, if he were to wed her, he'd be made king upon your death, and we don't want anyone worryin' about a repeat of what happened with our fathers."

Rory's brows shot up. "You think one of you would try to kill me to take the castle, title, and land—what's left of it?"

Amber's hand shot up. "I vote for no."

"It's all right, luv," Aiden said and chuckled. "No one's goin' to try to assassinate Rory. We like the big lug." He grinned.

Amber relaxed, but only slightly. "I don't understand."

"I'll try to make it simple. Rory is king as far as anyone knows. His parents, like ours, disappeared long ago and without knowin' where they are—or *if* they are—no one can be certain that the king and queen still live. That's why Rory is called crown prince and is still next in line for the throne."

Rory laughed out loud. "King of a crumblin' castle and caretaker's cottage. I don't think the good people of Ballyhoo or the Irish government would consider letting me rule anythin' more than what I already own."

"I still don't understand," Amber said.

Rory explained. "When I die, Chloe will be next in line. She is a princess now, and unless we find out what happened to our parents, she'll probably stay a princess." He looked to Aiden. "Did you think she'd call herself queen if I don't call meself king?"

"No. But she'd rule Ballyhoo and what's left of your clan. In other words, Shannon and Finn." Then he leaned forward and clasped his hands. "But wouldn't it be grand if we could unite our clans? Conlan has already said he'd abdicate his position as clan leader due to the worry. Then with age being the deciding factor, Chloe would rule. She's a few months older than I am…"

Amber scratched her head. "Doesn't the next male become king? That's what they do in England. The only reason Queen Elizabeth is the queen is because she didn't have any brothers."

Aiden gasped, and Rory pinched the bridge of his nose.

"I beg your pardon, Amber," Aiden was quick to say. "I didn't mean to react so. It's just that you brought up the English… But never mind. You see, long ago, we lived in a matriarchal society. The eldest, male or female, would rule the rest.

"So that's why I'm proposin' that Chloe and I could marry and—"

"Whoa!" Rory held up one hand. "I think you're for-gettin' somethin'."

Aiden crossed his arms. "The boyfriend?"

"That and somethin' else," Rory said.

"And what might that be?"

"Chloe hates you."

Aiden reared back. "She hates me? Sure'n we've had our differences, but *hate* is the wrong word, Cousin."

"She attacked you on our front lawn, and the two of you looked like you were fightin' to the death."

Aiden chuckled. "Oh, that. Nay. She's *attracted to me* and pushes me away, because that's what she does." He paused for a moment and said, "At least that's what she did in the past. I was surprised to hear she was seein' someone. I was beginnin' to think she was gay."

"And you'd marry her even if she was?"

"To save the species? Of course I would."

"And how do you propose to, well, propose? She'll laugh you into next week."

"Not if her crown prince *orders* her to marry me."

Rory's jaw went slack, and he forgot to breathe for a moment. Soon he recovered enough to kick his brain into gear.

On the one hand, he could do that. He could order her to marry a dragon and shag every five years until the species had been repopulated. However, he'd never do that to Chloe. His beloved sister would truly hate him for the rest of his life, and he couldn't bear the thought of that. On the other hand, the Ulster clan was right about her being the last hope for the species. But Aiden? Of all his three cousins?

"Why do you want to volunteer for this, Aiden?"

"Because the attraction goes both ways. You don't have to worry. She'll grow to love me. I know our love would be passionate and our lives would never be boring. And I swear to you, I would never hurt a hair on her head."

"It's not her hair I'm worried about."

Apparently, he took that personally. Rory and Amber indulged Aiden while he ranted. Rory had expected him to wear himself out, but he continued pacing and swearing across their living room floor, going strong.

At last, Rory rose, held up one palm, and said, "Stop. Me poor ears can't take any more."

"But don't you understand? Chloe marrying me is the last hope for our race. You're her king. You need to think of what's best for your people. You *must* order her to procreate."

Rory laughed. "First of all, I'm not sure I'm king. I haven't heard about the demise of me father and mother. Until I do, I'm just a prince, and a limited one at that."

"What do you mean by 'limited'?"

Rory snorted a light curl of smoke. "Have you seen me castle? It's in ruins. And me subjects? They consist of two sisters. Finn doesn't give a fig about me royal status. He was born a free Irishman just nineteen years ago."

"What about the Ulster Arishes? You could be crown prince of us all. My marrying Chloe would unite our clans again. I'd restore the castle as a gift to you and me bride. Isn't it time?"

"Our truce has held without uniting clans. I'm not sure we're meant to."

"How can you say that?"

Rory rose. "First, our markings are different. You and your brothers have dyed the orange streaks in your hair, but I know the color doesn't match our red ones."

"Perhaps our children will have reddish-orange markings. The two colors would blend rather than compete."

Rory was the one pacing now. "Perhaps you're right, but I can't—rather, I *won't*—order me sister to marry you."

"You'd rather condemn our species to extinction than have me as a brother-in-law, is that it?"

Rory stopped and sighed. "That is not it. I'd welcome you as a brother, but me sister would eat you alive and make herself a widow before she'd let you touch her. It's for your own safety."

This time Aiden snorted. "You know she wouldn't. And I'd be so good to her, she'd grow to love me. Mark me words."

Like hell. "She'd hate both of us forever. If you don't realize that, you don't know me sister a'tall."

Aiden balled his fists and his lips thinned. Steam poured out of his nostrils.

Amber jumped in, probably fearing that steam would be blasting out of his ears at any moment. "I'm sure you're angry. It's never easy to be rejected, but you can't take this terribly personally. Chloe fell in love with another firefighter before you ever thought about marrying her. Maybe you could find another dragon…"

He crossed his arms. "Where?"

She shrugged. "I don't know. I'm sure there has to be one somewhere."

Rory grasped the chance to present a new option, since the other one was awful. "You should talk to Drake.

Find the missin' branch of our family tree. Mayhaps there's a whole enclave in the Scottish Highlands where his family came from."

"Terrific!" Amber said. "I can fly you to his apartment right now if you like."

"Not so fast. I know you're tryin' to get rid of me, but I'm not ready to go just yet."

Amber strolled over to him and clasped his shoulder. "Yes you are." Then the two of them disappeared.

Chapter 13

RYAN ROLLED OVER WITH CHLOE IN HIS ARMS. HE liked the way she moved over him when she was on top. She played his body like she played her music.

She'd had plenty of experience with instruments and almost no experience with the other—um—instrument, although he wouldn't have guessed it. Instinct must be showing her the way. Of course, his groans of pleasure probably guided her as well.

Her own sensations were evident by the way she threw her head back and moaned as she rode him…like now.

God, I love this woman.

Because she was so adventurous, he thought he might try some flavored lube next time. She didn't need it, for sure. Her hot, wet channel was plenty lubricated, but it might make the experience of sucking his cock more pleasurable. She insisted that she liked to do it, but he couldn't help wondering if that were true. Melanie had grudgingly done it when he'd asked, and soon he'd stopped asking.

He'd thought Melanie leaving him was devastating. Now he was grateful she had. Meeting Chloe really was the best thing that had ever happened to him.

She ground her pelvis against him with each thrust until her inner muscles spasmed hard. She bucked and tried to hold back the scream she obviously wanted to let out.

"Go ahead, baby. Scream if you want to."

She whimpered and moaned, but eventually gave in to a series of louder animalistic cries. So much for trying to be quiet. Suddenly his own orgasm hit. He let out a groan and she milked him as he surfed an incredible high, and he rode his release all the way to the last aftershock.

At last, Chloe stilled, then toppled off him onto the mattress. He gathered her panting body into his arms and kissed her forehead.

"That was incredible," she said between deep breaths.

"Yes, it was." He cradled her head in his hand and stroked her back while she recovered. They stayed like that, basking in the afterglow for several minutes. He wondered if he should tell her how he felt...if he should say those three little words, packed with such enormous meaning.

This would certainly qualify as the happier time he'd been waiting for. He was just about to speak when a soft snore met his ears.

Amber had transported Aiden to the room he used when he was visiting. Apparently she wanted to speak to him alone.

"We need to talk to Drake Cameron," she said.

"The only other dragon in this city?" he asked. "For Chloe? I thought he was already married."

"Not for *that*," Amber exclaimed. "Bliss would kill anyone who touched her man—dragon or not. I just know he searched for female dragons already. We should find out what he may have learned."

Aiden sighed. "It wouldn't hurt to ask. Maybe there's someone else out there."

"I'm glad you're being reasonable." She muttered "at last" under her breath, but he heard it clearly.

"So, where does Drake Cameron live? Can I get there from here?"

She grinned. "I can get anyone to anywhere. Let me go speak to him. Meanwhile, why don't you unpack?"

Impatiently, Aiden did as she suggested, then returned to the parlor where Rory was still sipping his whiskey.

Aiden didn't even have a chance to say hello. Amber and Drake strode out of the closet and Rory jumped to his feet.

"Drake," Rory exclaimed. "Grand it is to see you. Can I pour you a taste of me cousin's fine Irish whiskey?"

"Sorry, Rory. I'm going on duty in a few minutes, otherwise I'd be glad to join you."

"Ah. Some other time, then."

"I can get a cup of tea for you, Drake," Amber said. "It won't take any time at all."

"That would be great. Thanks."

She disappeared into the closet again and Aiden eyed Drake. The firefighter sported his dragon clan's yellow streaked widow's peak without trying to hide it. Aiden and his brothers had covered theirs since hair dye was invented, thinking they'd need to blend in.

"You remember Drake, don't you, Aiden?" Rory asked.

"Actually, I've never had the pleasure of meetin' him before now."

"Oh! My apologies. Aiden Arish, meet Drake Cameron, and vice versa."

Amber returned with Drake's tea just as they were shaking hands. Then all four of them sat down in the living room.

"I hate to skip the pleasantries, but Amber didn't have much time to explain things to you. Since you're due somewhere else soon, would you like the short version?" Aiden asked.

"Actually, she filled me in pretty thoroughly."

"Ah, that's right. A muse can manipulate time a bit. So, what can you tell us about your hunt for a female dragon before you met the love of your life?"

Drake groaned. "You don't want anything to do with the only willing one I found. That ended in disaster. There are the Asian dragons, but they wouldn't even consider me."

"Why not? Are they racist?"

Drake laughed. "It probably had more to do with my not-so-dear departed uncle."

Rory nodded. Aiden didn't know who he was referring to, but he caught the undercurrent of resentment. Since Drake's time was limited and he had more important questions for him, Aiden decided to skip the details.

"It sounds like you found no one suitable," Rory said.

"That's the gist of it."

"So Chloe is our only option to continue the species?" Aiden said hopefully.

"I'm not saying that at all…only that *I* couldn't find anyone but the psycho Gaia had to banish to Siberia."

Now there's a story I'd like to hear at some point.

"You know, we have a missin' branch of our family tree," Rory reminded him.

"Uncle Faelan?" Aiden asked.

"The very same."

"Wait," Drake said. "My grandfather's name was Faelan Harris. Now there's a coincidence, eh?"

Rory and Aiden stared at him with rounded eyes. *Could we be related?*

"Did you have any sisters?" Rory asked.

"No," Drake said and sighed. "And if you didn't pick up on my slight accent, I came from Nova Scotia, but I was born in Scotland—I think."

"What do you mean, you think?"

"Well, I wasn't there. I mean…I *was,* but I sure don't remember it. I was told my mother was in Scotland when I was born."

"Tell us more," Rory said. "About your grandda, I mean."

"He was supposedly the last dragon. When St. George slayed him, my grandmother was pregnant. She fled to the Scottish highlands and hid in the deserted mountains there."

"Did she happen to remarry?" Aiden asked.

"The timeline doesn't fit," Rory said. "Our uncle was the youngest and there's already a generation between."

"True. But it's still possible that we're related. My grandmother found another dragon also hiding out in the Scottish Highlands. He was younger and she married him—informally, of course."

"Jaysus," Rory breathed. "We may have found the missin' branch."

⌐∿∿⌐

Ryan and Chloe returned to work, but purposely staggered their arrival times. The weather had been frigid and blustery, and the Charles River was beginning to freeze over. They had no sooner taken over for the previous shift when a call came in.

Ice rescue: Under the Mass Avenue Bridge. Engine 33 and Ambulance 1, respond.

Chloe and Ryan reached the pole almost at the same time, but Ryan held back to let her go first. She didn't hesitate. Chloe ran to her gear and suited up quickly.

"What kind of fucking moron thought that going out onto the ice this early was a good idea?" Haggarty grumbled before he jumped into the ambulance with Nagle.

"I guess we'll see," Lieutenant Streeter responded in a clipped tone as he barreled into Engine 33's front seat. "It's been cold as hell for a couple of weeks, but yeah. Not smart."

When they arrived, a young boy clung to the edge of the jagged hole he'd fallen through. His lips were blue, his eyes glazed, and his teeth were chattering.

"Shit," Haggarty mumbled under his breath. "It's a kid."

The lieutenant stood between the shore and his firefighters. "That ice won't hold us and I don't know if the kid can grab the life preserver without going under." He spoke quietly so the boy couldn't hear him.

"I can reach him," Chloe volunteered.

"Hell no," Ryan practically shouted.

"Stuff your protectiveness, Fierro. I'm the logical choice." Her small, light size would finally come in handy. This was her chance to prove her worth.

He glared at her as Haggarty retrieved the rope and tied it around her waist.

"You'll want to lie down as flat as you can and crawl. It'll distribute your weight across—"

"We were taught ice rescues in trainin'," she snapped. "Just let me get out there."

The kid's eyes were beginning to close, signaling hypothermia setting in.

She grabbed the life preserver the lieutenant handed her and wasted no time lying on the ice and inching her way to the lad as quickly as she could. His grip was slipping and she reached his wrist just as he let go.

"I've got you. Stay with me, lad," she said reassuringly. She slipped the doughnut-shaped life preserver over his head and under his free arm. Looking back over her shoulder, she yelled, "Pull!"

Ryan held the other end of the rope and pulled so hard the two of them flew across the ice to safety. It was a good thing she had a tight grip on the kid.

Nagle had a blanket ready and wrapped the boy up tight. Haggarty handed her another blanket and nodded. "Good work, Arish."

There was no sarcasm in his tone, and if she wasn't mistaken, the look he gave her conveyed respect.

"Thank you," she said. Her teeth began chattering. She looked over at the boy. "Where are your parents, hon?"

He didn't answer. He was probably too cold to think straight.

Nagle cradled him close to his body and took him to the open doors at the back of the ambulance.

Haggarty said, "The hospital will locate them, Arish. He needs medical attention right away. Get into the front seat where it's relatively warm."

"But I'm soaked."

Haggarty smirked. "I didn't say to sit in *my* seat."

He glanced at the lieutenant. "Okay if I take her with us?"

"Absolutely. Get her checked out too. I think Fierro may have yanked her arm out of the socket." He frowned at Ryan.

Haggarty chuckled and said, "Let's go, Chloe."

She smiled at Ryan and climbed into the passenger seat.

On the way to the hospital, Haggarty glance over at her a couple of times. "How are you doing?"

"I'm fine."

"Really?"

"Yeah. Why wouldn't I be? I wasn't on the ice more than five minutes."

After a short pause he said, "I'm sorry for giving you such a hard time."

She wasn't sure she'd heard him correctly. "Did you just apologize?"

He chuckled. "Yeah. I was an asshole, but I'm capable of admitting it."

"Hmmm…" was the only response she could think of.

"Well?"

"Well what?"

"Do you accept my apology?"

"Oh. Of course!" She smiled. "Apology accepted." After a few moments she couldn't help but ask, "Does this mean you'll treat me kindly in the future?"

He grinned but looked straight ahead. "No promises…but I'll try."

Aiden wanted to take Chloe for a walk and explain his feelings for her. He was sure she'd understand. Even if she didn't react well at first, she'd come around. Rory had already told him he wanted to stay in Boston with Amber, even if it meant abdicating the throne.

That meant Chloe could return to Ireland as queen. She'd probably insist on the title of crown princess, but he'd change that too.

It was hard to wait until she was off duty. Four twenty-four-hour shifts on and a day off, then one shift on and four days off? "Who ever heard of such a daft schedule?" *Oh well. She won't work at all after we're wed*.

Yule came and went with little more than a cup of eggnog and a small exchange of gifts.

Amber gave Rory a plush crimson robe. She winked, saying he might need one as soon as they began admitting guests. Aiden didn't need the visual of his cousin strutting around in the nude.

Rory gave Amber a diamond ring. Aiden didn't know if it was supposed to signify an engagement or not, and he didn't want to make either of them uncomfortable by asking. He hoped to be a brother-in-law, not just a cousin, at some point. Preferably very soon.

At last Chloe breezed through the door into the living room and said, "Merry belated—Christ!" Her eyes widened. "Aiden?"

"Ah, there she is. Merry Christmas and blessed Yule, luv…and soon a very happy New Year," he said with a wide smile as he advanced toward his confused female cousin with his arms open wide.

Chloe approached him slowly. "Glad tidings, Cousin," she said and allowed him to hug her, briefly. Too briefly. Oh well, that would change too. She'd soon realize how important it was for the two of them to procreate and rule the castle in Ballyhoo together.

"How was your work?" Rory asked.

Amber interrupted. "Before that, can I get you some eggnog? I spiked it with some Arish Irish Whiskey." She winked.

"Perfect. Thank you kindly." As Amber strode off to the bar, Chloe turned to her brother and answered his question. "Work was excitin'!" Her face became more and more animated as she recounted the story of an ice rescue.

Shite. This job of hers sounds dangerous. She'll have to leave it at once in order to protect the royal bloodline.

She went on about how some bloke named Haggarty had been giving her a hard time until she proved herself.

"Why should you have to prove anythin' to anyone?" Aiden asked. "Ye're a princess, after all."

Chloe laughed. "Yeah. That and five dollars will get me a cup of coffee at Starbucks. Even at home I wouldn't tell anyone I was a princess. Or if I did, they'd assume I was descended from a long-forgotten king— which I am."

"Ah, 'tis a sad thing, indeed. You should be livin' a life of privilege and leisure."

Chloe snorted, and a curl of smoke escaped her nostril. "You don't know me well, Cousin, else you'd know I could never sit around and do nothin' all day."

Someday you'll be too busy raisin' our dragon babies to worry about that.

After she finished her eggnog, Aiden said, "I was hopin' you'd take a walk with me, Chloe."

"It's feckin' freezin' out there."

He shrugged. "We come with our own source of heat." When she still looked reluctant, he said, "Did you know that Gaia gave our ancestors fire after she saw them freezing their arses off in the mountain caves?"

She leaned back and looked as if her attention had been piqued. "No. I didn't. How did you learn that?"

"Drake mentioned it. I had to do something while I was waitin' for you, so I spent as much time with him as his job would allow."

"Ah. Why didn't you just come and visit me? My firehouse is even a bit closer."

"I—uh…I wanted a bit of privacy. I have somethin' important to ask you."

She glanced nervously at Rory. He didn't give anything away. In fact, he just shrugged, as if he had no idea what Aiden was talking about. It's true he hadn't told Rory he was going to propose tonight. And the clan leader may have thought he'd talked him out of it. To be honest, his cousin's reluctance almost made him more determined.

"I—I guess I can spend a few minutes with you. I was invited to Sunday dinner at my boyfriend's home tomorrow, so I figured I'd spend tonight with my own family."

"How fortunate that I'm part of your family." *And all she'll be doing tomorrow is saying good-bye to the boyfriend and packing her bags*.

Amber stood. "Shall I get your coat, Chloe?"

"I can get it. Is it in the hall closet?"

Amber grinned. "In a manner of speaking…let me get both of your coats. I'll be back in a flash."

While they waited, Chloe looked everywhere except at Aiden. When Amber returned with their winter

jackets, she seemed relieved and shrugged into hers
without waiting for him to help her. He could see he'd
have to teach her a bit about manners too, but all of that
could wait. The important thing was to get them married. She had an Ulster birth certificate just like he did.
No need to worry about international logistics.

When they were both bundled up, he held the door
open for her and she strode through. She opened the
second door, the one to the outside, and held it for him.
He jogged forward and took the door handle. "Let me
get that for you, luv."

She looked at him strangely as she passed, then
walked into the howling wind. Apparently she wasn't
used to being around a gentleman.

"Where did you want to go walkin', ousin?" she asked.

"I don't know the area as well as you do. I like these
picturesque residential streets, but are there some that
are less noisy and more private?"

She tipped her head and then her face lit up. "Yes.
There's a cute little area near the theatre district called
Bay Village. It's tucked away and quiet there."

"Perfect."

She set off at a brisk pace and he kept up, trying to
make small talk until they reached the area she spoke
of. He filled her in on the health of his brothers and
asked after her sister, Shannon. It sounded as if Shannon
was happy living in the caretaker's cottage on the castle
grounds in Ballyhoo.

That would be fine. He'd like to move his bride to
the family's ancient castle at some point, but from what
he'd seen several months ago, it needed work to make it
livable first. They could stay at the local B and B until

it was ready. She'd be impressed when he restored it to its former glory.

Finally, she slowed her pace when they came upon a place named Church Street. He noticed a church nearby, but it didn't appear to be on the street named for it. However, there was a tiny park on one corner with a couple of benches. A decorated pine tree made the place look festive—almost romantic.

"How's this?" she asked.

"Perfect," he said.

She sat on one of the benches and he plopped down next to her.

"You have me mind spinnin' with curiosity. What's so private you had to talk here instead of in me brother's comfortable home?"

He slipped an arm around her shoulder. She leaned away and frowned, as if he were out of his mind.

"Are you warm enough, luv?"

"I'm fine." She cocked her head. "So, get to it. What is this about, Aiden?"

He thought he'd better make his case, quickly, but there were a few details that led up to his question and he had to start with those.

"You know how verra verra few dragons there are in this world?"

"I don't, really. No."

"Well, as far as any of us knows, other than the Asian dragons, there are the six Arishes, and Drake Cameron. He thinks he is the last of his clan. He mentioned one female, but said she was 'batshit crazy' and banished to Siberia. Can you think of any others?"

"I know of none, personally, but I think we had an

uncle who left the Arish clan right before the battle of Ballyhoo began. Isn't that right?"

"I believe so, yes. As it turns out, we may know what happened to him after all. Drake said his grandmother came upon a young male dragon in the Scottish highlands centuries ago."

"Ah! That may have been him, then."

"Mayhaps. She sort-of adopted him, so he was considered the brother of Drake's mother. His uncle, in other words."

"Ah. That's wonderful, but what has this to do with us now?"

"Maybe nothing. Both his mother and uncle are dead now. I just wanted to point out how few options we have."

"Options for what?"

He tried to take her hand, but she tucked it into her pocket. *Have faith. She'll come around.*

"As you know, Gaia only made female dragons fertile once every five years. It was supposed to control the population, because of our long lifespans. If you don't mind me askin', where might you be in your cycle now?"

"I do mind you askin', because it's none of your bloody business!"

"All right. Don't get your knickers in a twist."

"Leave me knickers out of this."

He took a deep breath and tried to calm her with a smile. She just continued to frown at him. "Well, I'll get back to what I was sayin', then. Unfortunately, that cycle, along with bloody battles and knights provin' their bravery, has almost wiped us out. Our existence hangs in the balance, Chloe."

She remained quiet, and just blinked at him a couple of times.

"A female dragon can only produce offspring with a male dragon. Shannon is already married to a human. Rory abdicated the throne by leavin' Ireland permanently. And Conlan doesn't want to worry your brother by outrankin' you, because he's the next eldest. Eagan has a lass he's serious about. So, they left it up to me."

"Huh?" She stared at him blankly.

"It's us or no one, Chloe. I'm askin' you to marry me and have me dragon babies."

Her mouth dropped open, and he thought she was going to agree with his logic, but instead she was gasping.

As soon as she could form words, she shouted, "Are you out of your feckin' mind?" Then she leaned back and let out a belly laugh that went on too long to pretend he wasn't insulted.

"Chloe. You can stop laughin' anytime, if you please."

She clutched her belly, laughing harder.

Just as he was about to get firm with her, a man wearing a black hoodie stepped around the corner and demanded, "Hand over your wallets and you won't get hurt."

That got Chloe to shut up. Aiden rose, holding her in place with a hand on her shoulder, then inserted himself between her and the stranger.

"Go along, little man. You don't know what you're up against here."

The guy pulled a long knife out of his sweatshirt and said, "No. I don't think *you* know what you're—"

"Be quiet," Aiden hissed. This guy had the nerve to butt into their private conversation just as he was proposing and try to rob them too? Oh, *hell* no.

Aiden's eyes began to glow, signaling an impending shift.

"No!" Chloe yelled. "You can't do that here…"

The guy's jaw dropped, but he didn't back away.

Aiden's skin turned to shimmering scales, and his clothes magically disappeared as he shifted into his dragon form. Then he rose off the ground, towering over the guy.

The perp dropped his knife but didn't look like he was about to leave, so Aiden decided to prove to Chloe once and for all that he would do anything to protect her from danger…and that he'd make a great dragon father.

He opened his jaws wide, crashed down over the guy's trembling body, and bit him in half. The man's bottom half swayed and toppled over onto the sidewalk. As he chewed the crunchy bones, he wished he had some ketchup.

He was mildly aware of Chloe frantically whispering behind him. "Killin' and shiftin' in front of humans is strictly forbidden. What the feck were you thinkin'?"

He swallowed and shifted back to his human form. "That was a very disappointing dinner. If you want the other half, I'll go find you some salt and pepper, while you roast…"

She reared back and punched him, *hard*. He heard his nose crunch, and a shot of pain nearly blinded him. Blood poured out of his nasal cavity.

"Hey! What was that for?" he cried out toward her retreating back.

"For bein' a feckin' moron." She marched off with steam pouring out of her nostrils.

He'd give her some time to settle down. He was already healing as he strolled back to the B and B.

Chapter 14

RYAN HOPED CHLOE WOULD LIKE HIS BIG, BOISTEROUS, sometimes insane family. *Like* might be too much to hope for. He'd settle for tolerate. Bringing her home to Sunday dinner was a risk he'd have to take. He had to show them she was his girlfriend and the slap was just for show. Then he had to convince them all to keep their traps shut at work. No small feat.

Hopefully none of them would trigger her Irish temper, or if they did, she'd be able to smile through it and yell at him later.

"So, this is the slugger," Mr. Fierro said as soon as everyone was seated.

Ryan palmed his eyes. Before he had a chance to admonish his father, Chloe laughed. "You saw that, did you?"

"I think my whole family saw it, sweetheart," Ryan said. Then he raised his voice to address everyone. "She did it for show. We work together and I don't want to risk a transfer. She knew that and had to make it look like we were coworkers and nothing more."

"Aw…you can come to my firehouse, Chloe," Jayce said. "We'd be happy to have you, and you already know Drake."

"Thank you kindly, Jayce. But I don't want to be transferred either."

"You mean you don't get enough of this big lug's

ugly face on those twenty-four-hour shifts?" Miguel
said. "I can't imagine working with my wife." He shuddered, and Sandra, who'd been quiet up to that point, hit
his arm. He just laughed.

"What is it about my boys getting socked by their
girls?" Mrs. Fierro said. "Is it because I raised them to
never hit back? You know you can get away with it, but
is that fair?"

"Maybe it's because they deserve it," Sandra said,
smirking.

Most of the family laughed. His mother didn't.

"It's okay, Ma. We're men, and we can take it," Ryan
reminded her.

"I still don't like it," she said.

Chloe fidgeted. "I swear it was only for show, Mrs.
Fierro. I'd never hit your son in anger."

His mother nodded. "I understand. I just hope you
don't break his lovely, straight nose…or his heart."

Chloe's eyes widened. He wondered about her reaction. Should he have told her about Melanie? He hoped
no one would bring up his ex-fiancée before he had a
chance to fill her in.

"We're just glad he's finally dating again," Miguel
said. "And you can beat him up all you want. We've had
our share of boxing matches."

"Yeah," Mr. Fierro added. "To the point that I was
thinking of building a regulation ring in the basement."

Everyone laughed—except for his mother, again.
Thank God Gabe changed the subject by mentioning pet
sitting and how Chloe took in McCall's bird.

"That was nice of you," Mrs. Fierro said.

Then Gabe blew it by saying, "Yeah. Apparently

his parrot learned some colorful new expressions." He winked at Chloe. "Don't worry. I won't tell 'feckin' Haggarty.'"

She groaned.

Jayce snorted in disgust. "Has that prick been giving you a hard time?"

She smiled. "Not anymore. I think I finally proved to him that I can be useful."

Ryan quickly jumped in and told everyone about the ice rescue and how the kid would have been a goner without her bravery. He even mentioned her dislike of large bodies of water.

At last his mother smiled and seemed impressed too.

"I guess we won't be taking you fishing, then," Jayce said.

She made a face.

"I hope you don't have anything against fish," Mrs. Fierro said. "You wouldn't get to enjoy my paella."

Murmurs of "Mmm…" sounded around the table.

"It's to die for," Sandra said. "If you and Ryan wind up married or living together, you'll have to learn to make it."

Ryan coughed. "Let's not jump the gun here. We've just begun dating."

"Yeah," Mr. Fierro chimed in. "She hasn't had a chance to get sick of all his bad habits yet."

"What bad habits?" Ryan asked, offended.

His father just grinned, then stuffed his face with more manicotti.

Mrs. Fierro rolled her eyes. "First you call him ugly, then you accuse him of bad habits. That's no way to impress his date."

"I know he's teasin', Mrs. Fierro. Irish families tease a lot too. I see it for what it is—a form of affection."

His mother nodded.

"Besides, we've seen each other's bad sides already. Mostly during training," Ryan added.

"Oh? What's Chloe's bad side like?" she asked.

Shit. I pitched that one right over the plate. I should have known Ma would swing.

Unfortunately everyone waited in uncharacteristic silence. He had to say something. "Well, she's distracting," he said. "I can't keep my eyes off her."

The family's reactions were mixed…either groans or laughter. His mother smiled.

"Good save, Brother," Miguel said with admiration.

Luca piped up. "He had to learn that skill with Melanie. She was way too sensitive for this bunch."

Crap.

—⁓—

On their walk back to her place, Chloe had to ask, "So who's Melanie?" She assumed Luca was referring to an old girlfriend, but Ryan had changed the subject so abruptly she never got any information other than her own warning bells going off.

He sighed. "I should have told you about her before this, but I didn't really know how to tell you I was engaged."

"*Was?*"

"Yeah. It ended about a year and a half ago. She never liked the idea of my becoming a firefighter. After I got home from Afghanistan, I went for a college degree in business but soon realized I'd be bored stiff in an office. She insisted that I try working in a cubicle for the rest of my life, and I just couldn't do it."

"So you broke it off to follow in your family's footsteps."

"*She* broke it off. And as far as my family goes, they understood completely. We have a talent for serving the public—bravely."

"I'm sure you do. I wasn't questioning that choice. Jaysus. I made that decision myself. I guess I was being a 'Captain Obvious.' Sorry."

He snickered.

Did I butcher that saying too? She was pretty sure she'd gotten that one right.

"So, you're okay with my leaving corporate America to fight dangerous fires?"

"Why wouldn't I be? Hypocrisy, thy name is not Chloe."

He laughed. "You really are adorable."

"Well, I'd say I'm sorry things didn't work out for the two of you, but to be truthful, I'm not sorry a'tall." She smiled up at him.

He took her hand. "Me neither."

Shite. He had come clean. He had introduced her to his family. Now she was the only one with a secret, but it was a doozy.

When they reached the B and B she thought, *Maybe there's one thing I can let him know…* and she kept walking.

"Where are you going? I thought I was taking you to your place."

"You are. I don't live at the B and B."

"You don't? Where do you live?"

She stopped at the next building and pointed to the front steps. "Here."

"Oh. Right next door, then."

"Yup."

"Why did you let me think you lived with your brother?"

She shrugged, embarrassed to admit the truth, but she'd come this far… "I wasn't sure I could trust you."

He just stared at her.

"And, some of my neighbors can be a little weird."

"Ah." He smiled. "That I understand. I was nervous about you meeting my not-always-normal family."

If only he knew how normal they are compared to the supernatural bunch who live in or visit my apartment building.

So now that she'd been honest about her address, was she willing to take him upstairs? It was the middle of the afternoon. Most of the club members visited at night. *It should be safe.*

"Do you want to see my apartment?"

He hesitated. "Do you trust me now?"

"I trust you with my life—literally, and on a daily basis."

What might he see? Most of the time it was pretty sedate, so she hoped it would stay that way. "All I ask is that you speak only to me about anything out of the ordinary here. I can probably explain…" *I hope.*

"I'm intrigued."

Oh Lord and Lady. I hope I haven't made a mistake.

He followed her up the concrete steps and she used her key to enter both the outer and inner doors. Then she quickly strode to the elevator. "It's only on the second floor, but I'd rather ride, if you don't mind." *Maybe if we're in the elevator he'll be less apt to see something.*

Gwyneth had told her about a bird fight that had happened in the stairwell a couple of years ago, but she'd gotten rid of her owl that wanted to eat the raven and falcon shifters.

Oh dear Goddess…please let nothing weird happen today.

When they stepped out of the elevator, she noticed the chandelier swinging by itself. *Oh, shite. The ghost must be saying hello.* She grabbed Ryan's hand and dragged him to her door. Opening it quickly, she pulled him inside and slammed the door behind him.

He cocked his head. "You seem anxious."

She breathed a sigh of relief when he appeared not to have noticed the chandelier. Grinning, she said, "We're finally alone."

He stepped into her space and tipped up her chin. "Yes, we are." When he captured her lips in a heated kiss, she practically melted into his arms.

He finally broke the kiss and nuzzled her neck. "Where's your bedroom?"

"Don't you want the whole tour?"

He glanced around the apartment and she felt silly when she realized he could see everything *except* the bedroom from their vantage point.

"There's more?"

"Well, ah, no. Let me take your coat."

He pulled off his jacket and handed it to her. She hung it in the hall closet and followed it with her own.

Holding his hand, she jogged past the open kitchen, took a left at the bathroom door, which stayed open when no one was using it, and pulled him into her one and only bedroom. "Here 'tis. There's a walk-in closet over there, of course." She pointed to the closed door on the opposite side of the room. "Now you've had the tour."

He grinned at her. "Nice place."

The only decorating she had done was to hang the Irish flag over her headboard. She shrugged. "I don't spend a lot of time here, so that's why you don't see a lot of knickknacks and such."

"It's nice this way. I'm kind of Spartan, myself."

"Are you now?"

"When I finally have the money saved, I'd like to buy a condo in one of those high-rises with an ocean view."

She whistled. "You may be savin' up fer the rest of your life."

He laughed. "Maybe, but I don't need a lot of space. Something this size or smaller would suit me just fine. As long as my mother doesn't try to fill it with junk, I'll be happy."

She slipped her arms around his neck. "Speakin' of bein' happy…"

He smiled. "Yeah?"

"Are you? With me, I mean. Do you miss what you had with Mel—"

He clapped his hand over her mouth. "Don't think for a minute that I compare you to Melanie. What you and I have is better…much more honest and real than I ever had with her."

Her mood plummeted. *Honest and real?* If only she could be. That was another reason she never had relationships. They might go along fine for a while, but eventually she'd have to tell the guy she was barren. And if things really got serious, she might need to explain why no amount of artificial insemination would help.

It was probably too much to hope Ryan didn't want any kids, and it was too soon to discuss it. Even if he didn't think he needed a lot of room now, that could all change if he wanted to have a family later.

He seemed to be studying her, and she quickly put the smile back on her face.

Might as well enjoy him while I can. She crooked her index finger at him and backed up. He grinned and followed. When the back of her knees hit the mattress, he tackled her.

They fell onto the bed in a desperate tangle of arms and legs. Their mouths met in a hard kiss, and then with open mouths as if they intended to devour each other.

An unintentional moan escaped her. First she was on top, then he was. Soon it seemed as if they were swirled together like chocolate and vanilla soft serve ice cream.

Their heat built as they rolled back and forth. At last, Ryan broke the kiss and said, "We need to get these clothes off."

"God yes," she breathed.

She grabbed his belt buckle and undid it. He had noticed her demure black dress had a zipper in the back, so he slid that open, making a rasping sound. Or was that his zipper, which she was opening at the same time? No matter. They twisted and pulled until everything landed somewhere on the floor.

At last, skin to skin, she slid her toes up his calf and down again. He rolled her onto her back and began kissing a path from her neck to her collarbone, and then to her breasts. He cupped one breast as he suckled the other.

She arched and moaned when the deep sensation coursing through her caused a visceral reaction. It was as if her womb clenched in anticipation. She wanted nothing more than to be filled with him.

He switched to the other breast and created the same need. Her hand had wrapped itself around his cock long before she realized it. She stroked and squeezed him until he leaned back and groaned.

She scooted down the bed and took his stiff rod into her mouth. He gasped as she sucked and then moaned when she applied increasing pressure. She couldn't help reveling in her womanly power, but just to be sure it wasn't too much, she paused to ask.

He assured her that what she was doing was absolutely perfect. She happily resumed pleasuring him, never dreaming it could be so fulfilling—for *her*.

Eventually, he pulled out of her mouth and sighed. "That was incredible, but it's your turn now."

"Oh. I get a turn too?"

He chuckled. "Of course you do. A *big* one." He pulled her up on the bed and slid down her body, then caressed her ribs and hips.

She laughed, but quickly reminded herself not to scream. With all the sensitive ears in the place, something like that could prompt an embarrassing invasion of privacy.

His talented mouth began teasing her labia.

Maybe if she cried out her *pleasure*, the paranormals would realize someone was just having sex and would leave her alone. *Yeah, and that wouldn't be embarrassing either,* she thought sarcastically.

Soon his tongue found her most sensitive area and swirled around it, not quite touching. Oh, why didn't she realize this would happen the minute they were alone together?

He inserted first one finger, then two, into her pussy

as his tongue zeroed in on her clit. *Oh God. Oh Goddess. Oh God...*

The sensation built and built until she teetered on the brink of what promised to be a perfect storm of an orgasm.

"Oh, Ryan... You're so... I can't help... RY-ANNNNN!" She crashed over the edge and rode the wave, realizing she couldn't stop if she wanted to.

She vibrated, jerked, and bucked as if she were lying on the epicenter of an earthquake. Her screams erupted as quick repeating blasts.

A crash in the distance penetrated through the fog of her climax-addled brain. Eventually she floated back to earth and opened her eyes...catching sight of red hair and one blue eye peeking around her bedroom door frame!

"It's okay, y'all," the redhead called out. "Chloe's just in bed with some naked guy."

"Is she okay?" a male voice asked.

"She ain't dead...unless he's killing her with his tongue."

Chloe gasped and bolted upright.

"He must be a damn god," an unknown female voice said.

Another male voice added, "I thought they were shooting a slasher film."

Jaysus!

The red-haired woman, whom Chloe now recognized as the witch Gwyneth from the third floor, quickly shut the door. Chloe gaped at Ryan. He hadn't moved except to lift his chin and give her a broad smile.

"Oh. My. God!" she cried as she bounded out of bed

and snatched up her panties. When she had them on, she threw Ryan's clothes at him and hissed, "Get dressed."

"Isn't it a little late for that?" He was simply lounging on his side, with his head resting in his palm and his elbow propping him up.

"I—I…" She didn't actually know how to answer that and just sputtered to an anticlimactic sigh.

Flopping back on the bed, she covered her mouth and tried to stifle a giggle. It was no use. Her giggles turned into laughter, and Ryan didn't help by laughing along with her.

She flipped herself over and slapped his leg. "Stop that. We should be ashamed."

"Of what? Having sex?"

"Yes. I mean, no! Maybe. At least I should apologize for worryin' me neighbors."

"I guess they don't hear you scream like a banshee very often, then?"

"Stop it," she giggled and shoved his knee. It was hard to be mad when he was grinning from ear to ear like that. "You're just proud they all know you're great in the sack. You'll probably strut out of here like a rooster."

He grabbed under her arms and pulled her back up to his face. Kissing her deeply helped calm her down a bit, but nothing would stop her from blushing when she saw any of her neighbors again.

"I think I'll have to move."

Chapter 15

Ryan sat at Chloe's kitchen table, sipping his coffee. "How long do you want me to hide out here?"

"Just until every one of the neighbors either goes to bed or moves across the country."

Ryan grinned.

"Why? Do you have someplace you need to be?" she asked.

"Not for a while. I told Jayce I might be over tonight to watch the game, but we never made any solid plans."

"Well, don't let me keep you." Chloe tapped her coffee cup.

"So now you want to rush me out the door? I feel so used."

She smirked. "Stop it." Then her luscious lips turned up into a grin.

They just sat there, grinning like idiots for the longest time.

At last she broke the silence. "Do you want kids?"

"Huh?"

"Kids. Rug rats. Ankle biters. Do you want any? I'm not makin' any plans. I'm just curious."

"Oh. Yeah, eventually…" He studied her for a moment. She was just casually sipping her coffee, like her question was no big deal. Now curious, he had to ask. "Do you want kids?"

She set down her coffee cup. "I can't have them. Does that make a difference to you?"

"Oh." *What should I say?* "Is this a trap?"

"Huh?" Now it was her turn to look confused. "How could it be—oh. I get it. You think there's a right and a wrong answer. No. I don't play those games. When I ask a question, I want an honest answer."

Thank God. "That's what I thought, but you'd be surprised. Sometimes girls can seem very straightforward and down-to-earth, and then one day they set a trap—and stupid guys like me fall right into it."

She chuckled. "Nope. I don't think I'll be doin' that. If I want to know how my butt looks in a pair of jeans, I'll use one of those three-way mirrors."

"Whew." He made a gesture of wiping sweat from his brow.

After a brief hesitation, he wondered if he was supposed to comment any more on the question of children. His not having any might become an issue with his family.

He'd been told by his father that he wanted Ryan to be the next family leader. It wasn't a formal position, like head of a mafia family, but the large Fierro clan took it seriously. Ryan might *seem to be* right smack in the middle of the birth order, but appearances could be deceiving—especially in a family of phoenixes.

The only benefit that came with the position was inheriting the family's brownstone. That was no small thing. They'd kept it in the family since the eighteen hundreds when it was built. Family meetings took place there, and so far having a central hub had worked well for all involved. The home acted as a multigenerational (multimillion-dollar) investment, a crash pad to extended Fierro families visiting Boston, and a paranormal hospital/safe house if necessary.

Fierros who shared the shifter gene could never be treated in a conventional hospital. Their "recovery" from fatal incidents had to be handled by those who knew what a phoenix was and how they reincarnated.

The bird *did rise* from the ashes of its former self. Then the individual had to remain in bird form while recovering—which included growing up all over again. Birds aged much faster than humans, so in a matter of weeks they'd be teens and soon in their prime again. The Fierro phoenix changed back when they were ready to pick up where they'd left off. It sometimes required a move to another city with no mention of the individual's previous demise, but most often, they could make up some excuse that involved "taking a sabbatical."

Chloe finished her coffee and took her mug to the sink. Casually, she asked, "So would you want to adopt or remain childless if you wound up with someone like me? I'm not sayin' we'll wind up together, I'm just wonderin', you know…hypothetically."

He scratched his head. "To be honest, I've never given it much thought." *Hell, I've never given it* any *thought!* "What about you? You've probably thought about it since you know you can't have children of your own."

She nodded slowly and returned to her chair. "I've thought about it in passin'. To be sure, if things were different, I'd probably carry a child to term in me own womb, but I'm not sure about adoption. I guess I could go either way. It might be nice not to worry about baby-sitters and waiting for school vacations to go anywhere, not to mention the state of the world we live in. Who wants to keep a kid inside all day, just because some predator might be out to snatch him or her?"

He set down his mug. "I know what you mean. Although as my parents had more and more of us, they worried less and less. We were boys, and a rough-and-tumble bunch at that. If anyone picked on one of us, he'd be swarmed by so many Fierros he'd soon realize they'd gotten in over their heads." He laughed remembering how Jayce, Miguel, Gabe, and he took on a couple of bullies who thought they'd give Noah a hard time. Yeah, they paid back all the lunch money they'd taken—with interest.

Chloe excused herself for a moment and went to the bathroom. That left Ryan to ruminate on the topic of kids. Pros and cons.

He'd always assumed he'd have some, although not as many as his parents did. Maybe he'd stop at three or four. Seven was a bit much. He'd known plenty of Irish families that had more than that. One family had eleven kids. It seemed Mrs. Flaherty was pregnant every other year and at one time had kids from ages zero to twenty.

The whole point had become moot when Melanie left him. He had put off telling her what she was getting into until his father insisted it was time. It was at one of those family Sunday dinners where he received the love and support, as well as the arm twisting, he needed.

Sandra had tried to help. She'd had to go through the "talk" before marrying Miguel, and she'd managed to swallow and digest the news—if not the rest of her dinner.

But Melanie's reaction had been harsh. At first she'd

laughed. She had been sure they were putting her on. When they'd insisted they were completely serious, she'd accused them of coming up with a far-fetched story to scare her off. They'd tried to reassure her that they loved her and would gladly give her time to adjust to the news, offering to answer any questions she had… but she'd just freaked out and ran.

Ryan had thought she'd come back. His mother and Sandra had said that if she really loved him, she would. She'd stuck by him when he went to Afghanistan. Apparently, she hadn't loved him enough to live with this particular family secret…even though it would mean he couldn't be killed in a fire—at least not permanently. That was the part that had sold Sandra.

But Melanie hadn't been happy about his wanting to fight fires for the rest of his life. He'd figured she'd get used to the idea, as many women did. But she'd said she never would, and at last he'd believed her when she mailed back his ring. She couldn't even face him long enough to hand it to him. Eventually he'd tracked her down just to ask her to keep their family secret in confidence.

She'd assured him that she'd never tell a soul, because they'd make her see a shrink…not because she cared for the welfare of his family or the man she supposedly loved. And then she'd acted terrified of him.

He thought about the responsive woman who moaned under him last night. The one who gave as good as she got. He smiled as he pictured Chloe cussing him out for "keepin' a feckin' secret" from her, but he couldn't picture her being afraid of him—ever.

When she came out of the bathroom, she said, "Ah, you're still here?"

He raised his brows. "Was I supposed to leave?"

"No. I just figured my bringin' up the subject of children might have you running out of here on your two cold feet."

He laughed. "Nah. You gotta do better than that if you're trying to scare me away."

She smiled, then the expression on her face grew a little sad.

"Are you okay?"

"Yes. I'm right as rain. Of course, some people don't like rain and don't think it's right when it falls on their big plans."

He nodded. "But rain can be a beautiful thing too. Without it, our world would dry up and turn to dust. People would cease to exist."

In his head he took the metaphor a step further. Without Chloe in his life things would indeed look depressing. He wouldn't feel nearly as fresh, renewed, and alive as he did now whenever he laid eyes on her.

He stepped into her space and tipped up her chin with one finger. Then he kissed her tenderly, almost sweetly. It was as if he knew she needed reassurance of his feelings, not his passion this time. His desire was never in question.

Finally it was time for their shift rotation. A long four days at the station might be a hardship on firefighters with families, but not for Chloe. Now that she was accepted by her firefighter "brotherhood," she felt like part of a large family. She found herself talking about them in her off hours, with either Rory and Amber or Ryan.

The guys had even attended some of the Arish folk band sessions at the tea house. Most were impressed enough with her talent to suggest she play for them at work. She declined, but couldn't help being secretly pleased.

Nagle poked his head around her bedroom doorjamb. She'd left it open to welcome anyone who cared to visit. Now *that* was a milestone.

"Hey, Chloe," he said.

She set down the magazine and sat up against her single headboard. "Nagle! How's it goin'?"

"Pretty good. I was wondering if you had any Irish recipes you'd like me to try."

She couldn't help but be surprised. Especially since the guys teased that the Irish weren't exactly known for their cooking. "Why?"

He shrugged. "I just thought I might be able to make something more authentic for St. Patrick's Day than corned beef and cabbage. I was told that's not even a true Irish dinner."

She snorted and quickly covered her nose to prevent any smoke from giving her away.

"I take it you don't like corned beef and cabbage?"

"I don't like St. Patrick's Day." If only he knew how much the Arish dragons hated that day. Being reminded of how their ancestors had to flee and hide in a cave, while making it look like they fell over the cliffs and into the sea… It was a humiliating disaster. She wouldn't even be here if not for the quick thinking on the part of her grandparents.

"Oh? Are you from Northern Ireland, then?"

Feck. If she told the truth, it would make her birth

certificate a lie. If she lied, they'd believe she was indeed from Ulster and it would grate on her nerves. Thank the goddess Aiden had finally gone home. Although his parting words were something to the effect of her eventually coming around to the truth of her duty. That made her throw up in her mouth a little bit.

She sighed. "I'm no cook, but Irish soda bread is a fairly traditional Irish recipe I can recommend. Potatoes in any form are a staple." She couldn't help teasing him just a bit. "Why not make that delicious stew you made to welcome me. I loved it. But if you leave out the yummy hot sauce, it would be a sight more Irish—and I'll bet the rest of the guys would even eat it."

He gave her a sheepish grin. "Sorry about that. It wasn't my idea."

"I'm sure. What's that sayin' about too many cooks spoilin' the stew?"

He laughed. "Fits the situation to a T. Let me make it the way it should have been made. We can make some Irish soda bread to serve with it—hopefully we won't have to leave it half-baked."

Chloe didn't need to ask why. If they got called in on a job, that was the end of whatever was happening in the kitchen. Stoves and ovens were shut off and whatever was cooking had to wait. Nagle preferred making dishes that didn't require precise timing.

"St. Patrick's Day is a couple of months away. Why would you want to make that now?"

"For practice, mostly. If it sucks, I can toss it and make something else."

She raised her eyebrows.

"Or if it's good, but can't be left unfinished for a few

hours, I can make some ahead of time and store it in the big freezer."

She nodded. "That makes sense. But if you do it right, there's no way you'll throw it away."

He smiled. "That's why I need your help. It can be frozen, right?"

"As long as it's sealed against air and freezer burn, it should be fine."

He looked thoughtful. "Freezer burn. Sounds like an oxymoron, but in this weather a firefighter can freeze his ass off and burn his face at the same time."

Suddenly, the tones rang out followed by, "Structure Fire. 780 Boylston Street. Nineteenth floor. Engine 33, Ladder 15, and Ambulance 1 respond."

A second later a loud explosion was heard from the street.

"Shit," Nagle muttered. As they were running down the hallway, he shouted over his shoulder, "Welcome to every firefighter's worst nightmare, Arish."

—⁕—

Ryan had been playing ping-pong in the basement. He raced up the stairs, beating Haggarty and Streeter to their turnout gear in the garage. As they suited up, he glanced at the pole and sure enough, Chloe was the first one down.

"That's the Pru apartments, right, Lieutenant?" Ryan asked.

"Yep. Luxury high-rise."

"Was that explosion from the building, then?" Chloe asked.

"More than likely," was all Streeter had time to say before they all charged to their various vehicles.

Ryan held the door open and Chloe leaped in. He followed along with a couple of other privates who usually kept to themselves. Fortunately when it came to fighting fires, everyone worked together and, for the most part, smoothly.

The engines were rolling past the sidewalk a few moments later, and anxious-looking pedestrians gazed at the firefighters with a combination of awe and dread. Smoke pouring into the sky was visible for miles. He wouldn't be surprised to see one or more of his family members at this motherfuckin' fire.

Chloe sat across from him, just staring out the window. He couldn't help wondering what she was thinking. They'd never fought a high-rise fire like this before. Nineteenth floor? That meant they could be carrying heavy equipment up nineteen flights of stairs, and possibly carrying bodies down that many—or more, depending on how quickly they could extinguish the flames.

What seemed like a minute later, Lieutenant Streeter was announcing into his radio, "Engine 33 and Ladder 15 are on scene with heavy smoke showing from the upper floors of a high-rise."

The District Chief took over and said, "Car 4 is on scene and assuming command."

The dispatcher acknowledged the command info and ended their transmission with, "Ten-four."

As the firefighters grabbed all the gear they'd need, they glanced up at the fully engulfed apartment on the nineteenth floor. Suddenly another explosion boomed and the windows of the apartment on the twentieth floor blew out.

"Shite!" Chloe yelled and ducked into the building's lobby. She grabbed Ryan's arm and yanked him inside as glass and debris rained down.

The captain barked out orders, but this time they were being told to use the elevator on the other side of the building. Chloe looked up at him with wide eyes.

Lieutenant Streeter announced, "We'll go to the sixteenth floor and walk up from there." Focusing on Chloe, he continued, "Otherwise it's a long hike up nineteen floors with sixty pounds of gear on plus another fifty or more of equipment."

Six of them crowded into an elevator with extra SCBA cylinders, and a high-rise pack—folded lengths of hose to attach to the standpipe system of the building. Ryan knew they'd find those in the stairwell. The trick was to get as close as possible to the fire, but not too close. Back drafts were a frighteningly real hazard.

As the doors were closing, Ryan saw people reaching the ground floor via the stairs and pouring out onto the sidewalk. It must have been a long climb down for some, but they didn't look the least bit tired. Most looked frightened, especially those carrying small children or pets in their arms.

When they reached the sixteenth floor and rushed to the stairs, a few stragglers were still descending.

"Is anyone else up there?" the lieutenant shouted to a long-haired guy carrying a guitar and a couple of framed gold records.

"Not as far as I know."

A young woman in front of him said, "We're from the twenty-first floor. We don't know who's still on any of the other floors."

"Arish, Fierro…see if the floors above nineteen are clear," Streeter ordered.

"Firefighters coming up," Chloe yelled. "Move to your right!" She had already begun charging skyward, and it was all Ryan could do to keep up with her.

Damn, she's fast. If he didn't know better, he'd think she had some kind of paranormal abilities. It had to be the adrenaline making her almost fly.

They passed one group of people, probably slowed down by the elderly woman clutching a small suitcase. *Did people really stop to pack when their building blew up?* It looked like a maid and butler were with her, so they may not have felt it was "their place" to hurry her along.

"What floor are you from?" Ryan asked.

"Twenty-five. It's the penthouse, and no—there's no one else up there, I live alone," the woman announced, as if she were miffed that he would have to ask.

The staff exchanged glances and the butler behind her rolled his eyes. Ryan imagined them thinking, "What are we? Chopped liver?"

Whatever. They were there to save rich and poor alike.

———

"Shall we start with twenty-four?" Chloe asked. She could have just told him that's what she wanted to do. She hoped she wasn't turning into one of those women who deferred to the man all the time.

Ryan nodded. They reached the floor quickly and began pounding on doors. So far it seemed as if everyone had made it out. Of course, it was nine in the morning, so a lot of people had probably left for work.

The twenty-third floor produced the same result. Twenty-two followed suit. Twenty-one was next. They split at the center stairs and each took their half of the hallway. This time Ryan's pounding and yelling was followed by a weak sound. It may have been someone who was immobilized.

The place was one floor above the apartment they'd last seen catch fire. At this point their fellow firefighters were probably knocking down that blaze. Black smoke was filling the hallway, completely obliterating any light from the window at the end of the hall.

Chloe wouldn't have heard the sound if she didn't have supernatural hearing. She wouldn't have seen what was happening either. She was on the opposite side of the corridor. Ryan had heard the noise though. He tried the door handle, but it was locked.

He dropped to the floor and was just about to kick in the sheetrock beside the door when Chloe noticed the wall bulging, and the black smoke seemed to be puffing back and forth.

"Stop!"

But she was too late. His powerful kick introduced oxygen into a tightly closed space. An explosion of superheated smoke—a back draft—was imminent and Ryan lay in front of it.

"No!" Chloe charged toward him, hoping to yank him out of the way in time. She was fireproof and would survive, but Ryan...

In the blast that immediately followed, windows shattered, the floor collapsed, and a raging fire ensued. Chloe had to shift into her dragon form immediately. She didn't give a crap if anyone saw her alternate form or not. This was why she'd become a firefighter. She, Drake, and any other dragon willing to go through the rigorous training involved could do the impossible.

A ripping sound said her turnout gear may have torn when she didn't shimmer it off fast enough. *Feck it.* A millisecond later, she had spread her wings and was hovering over the inferno.

Chloe feared the absolute worst but prayed for a miracle. Peering through the smoke to the floor below, she located a foot poking out from a pile of debris. Ryan's faint groan was the most beautiful sound she'd ever heard.

She flew to his side and began tossing everything off his dirt-smudged face. His protective head gear had been knocked off and his eyes had narrowed to mere slits. He looked as if he would pass out any second, and if he did, she would consider it a blessing. Not only would he be spared any pain, but he wouldn't catch her in her dragon form.

Too late. His eyes rounded, and he stared at her moments before he lost consciousness. She grabbed him with her tiny but strong arms and tried yanking him out from under the debris, but he was stuck on something.

She burrowed beneath as much of the rubble as she could and came upon the problem. Ryan was impaled through the stomach on a shaft of rebar. And he was not just unconscious…he was dying.

Chloe yelped. She knew not to remove the rod. He'd bleed out in seconds. But what could she do?

She cried for help in her dragon voice. Her fellow firefighters were probably scrambling down the stairs to save their own lives, but at least they'd know someone was there. Who or whatever had made the noise in the apartment couldn't have survived the blast.

Chloe shook his shoulders. "Don't you feckin' die!" When he took his last breath, she covered his mouth with hers as best she could without biting his face or breathing fire and blew some oxygen into him. She didn't think CPR would save him, but she had to try.

She blew another breath in and started chest compressions. Blood gushed out of the wound in his stomach. It was no use and she knew it, but she continued anyway. The fire raged on and soon she was trying to fight it off and bring her only love back to life at the same time.

The fire won. She sobbed big dragon tears beside Ryan's lifeless body as they were engulfed in flames. She knew she should get out, but she couldn't leave him. She held his charred hand, told him over and over that she loved him in her croaking voice, and watched as his body turned to ash. She hung her head and said a prayer for his brave soul.

Suddenly the pile of ash began to shift. It wasn't the kind of movement caused by a swirling fire.

What was that? After nothing happened for another second, she thought, *I must have imagined it*. Maybe her brains were fried. She rose and realized she'd have to find a way to shift back and explain why she wasn't dead.

The pile stirred again.

Feck. I did see something move! As she grappled for a logical explanation, a bright-white object rose slowly. Soon the shape of a bird about the size of a hawk emerged from the pile of ash. She stood fixed in place, staring in awe.

Beneath the gray ash, yellow and orange feathers appeared as the bird flapped its wings and hovered in front of her. Its eyes glowed white hot and glittered—like *diamonds*.

Then the creature turned and flew out the giant hole in the side of the building.

Chapter 16

CHLOE LAY ON HER BED AT THE FIRE STATION, HER arm covering her eyes. Her mind was a whirl of depressing facts, but she was *not* going to cry.

The hospital staff had marveled at how well she'd survived the fire and released her. The only explanation she could think of to give the chief was that the blast had thrown her clear. Then she (conveniently) lost consciousness.

How does Drake do this? As much as she'd wanted this job—more than she'd wanted anything her whole long life—she had to question if she shouldn't just forget it and go back to Ireland.

Chloe hated that idea, but she had to acknowledge Aiden was right about one thing. She was the only hope for preserving the Arish clan and possibly the whole species. She was to be queen *if* their parents were dead and *if* Rory abdicated to stay in America with Amber.

Conlan, the only Arish older than she, might try to usurp the Erin clan's claim to the castle…even though their branch had scuttled off to Ulster in disgrace. But he'd agreed not to if she returned as queen.

Like it or not, she was next in line, and *queens* did what was good for their people, not themselves. Even if their "people" consisted of a tiny handful of dragons.

Feck, feck, feck!

None of this made sense. She'd finally found her true

love only to lose him…maybe. She guessed. Hell, she didn't know. Was he some kind of paranormal bird or had she seen his spirit fly off to Summerland? She didn't know anything anymore.

It was true that the cousins could cause trouble for Shannon, Chloe's softhearted sister and her mortal, human husband. Keeping the Ballyhoo castle with the Erin Arish clan was of paramount importance. Their father had sacrificed too much to just give it to their Ulster cousins.

She sighed. Maybe, even if Ryan was alive, she'd be doing him a favor by leaving. He wanted something she couldn't give him. Children. She had already accepted a childless lifestyle and was quite content with her lot. But now…

Why did this have to fall on my shoulders?

She was worried enough about having children with a first cousin. Would dragons be subjected to the same risks of inbreeding as humans were? No one seemed to know. Could a damaged dragon be worse than no heir at all?

"Jaysus. I'm gettin' a splittin' headache."

Haggarty must have passed by her room just as she muttered those words. He poked his head in. "I'm sorry about your headache. After what happened to Fierro, it's no wonder. I know you two were…close."

She sat up and snorted. A slight curl of smoke exited her nostril and she waved it away quickly so it dissipated and Haggarty didn't notice. He probably thought she was waving away his comment.

"Are you okay?"

Her shoulders slumped. "To be sure. Right as rain."

Haggarty invited himself in and pulled the desk chair over. "Talk to me."

She stared at him. How could she begin to tell him what was wrong? It was better to say nothing than to open a door that couldn't be slammed shut.

"Chloe, I know you're tough as nails, and I may not be the most sensitive guy in the world, but you need to talk to someone. If not me, then someone else. Otherwise, they'll probably send you to the department shrink."

"Crap."

"Yeah. And you could be suspended if they think you're not coping well," Haggarty said.

She hung her head. In a low voice she admitted, "I've been thinkin' that mayhaps goin' home to Ireland could be in my future."

"You mean for a visit?"

She couldn't get the words past the lump in her throat, so she just shook her head.

"Wait a minute…" Haggarty exclaimed. "You mean to tell me you're going to quit? Oh, *hell* no. I won't let you. You're one of the best firefighters I've ever seen. If I have to throw my body over yours until you come to your senses, I will."

He would too. She had to smile.

The captain poked his head around the doorjamb. "Chloe, can I see you in my office, please?"

His tone sounded sympathetic, but she knew he'd want an explanation for her survival and every last detail about what happened to Ryan. Steeling herself to tell a fantastic lie if she had to, she stood up slowly.

"I'm worried," Mr. Fierro whispered as his family fussed over the phoenix that was their Ryan.

Miguel nodded. "I know. He isn't responding the way he did the last time this happened."

Jayce sat next to his brother on the rec room couch. "He wasn't a man in love last time. Hell, he was just a kid. He was about seven, right, Dad?"

"Yeah." The Fierro elder reflected on the last time they'd "lost" this particular son. Ryan had used lighter fluid on a charcoal barbecue that was taking too long to catch. A stupid mistake. A smoking charcoal was actually masking the fire, not that a kid would know that. Even the kid of a firefighter.

The flame followed the stream of fluid back and exploded the entire can, resulting in serious burns over eighty percent of Ryan's body. He was put out by Jayce and Gabe, then Mr. Fierro had to make the tough call. Ryan was incinerated and allowed to reincarnate.

He'd stayed home, with the family looking after him as he healed. Mrs. Fierro home-schooled all the boys, which kept authorities from knowing too much. Had he only stayed in phoenix form a few weeks while he aged back to a seven-year-old human, it would have been easier. But, alas. They had to tell some fanciful stories to keep the neighbors from wondering where one kid went and the other baby came from.

None of the Fierros wanted to explain why the family could treat burns better than a modern hospital could, so they were careful, but thank goodness they'd survive if all were lost—like now.

"Do you think we'll have to act as if he's dead—go through the funeral and everything, and then help him start life over somewhere else?" Miguel asked.

Antonio Fierro dropped his head in his hands. "We'll

have to. I can't think of any way he could have survived that back draft."

Ryan squawked and flapped his wings.

"Hush, now," Mrs. Fierro said as she offered him a bowl of mineral water. "Nothing has been decided yet."

Ryan settled but didn't take his beady eyes off his father.

Riiinnng. "Saved by the bell." Their doorbell had been ringing all damn day. He rose. "I'll go tell the media, brotherhood, or whoever the hell is out there to leave us alone. We're grieving."

"Luca's still up there. He can do it."

"Nah. I think they need to hear it from me." He strode to the stairs and jogged to the first floor, ready to give the curious and well-wishers alike a lecture.

———

Fortunately the captain had asked Chloe to take a couple of days off. Well, it wasn't exactly a request. "Go home. Get some rest," were his exact words.

Ordinarily she'd protest and insist she was fit for duty, but to be honest she could use a couple of days to hide from the world and cry. Haggarty had said she was "tough as nails," but right now she felt about as tough as boiled potatoes.

She slipped her key into her lock and was about to schlep into her apartment when the door across the hall opened. Drake stood there.

He strode over and grasped her in a secure, comforting hug.

He didn't have time to say a word. She burst into tears and her knees started shaking.

He just held her tighter. "Let's get you inside and sit down."

She nodded. Her feet barely cooperated, but she made it to her couch with his strong hand under her elbow. Drake returned to her door and shut it gently.

Chloe grabbed a tissue from the box on the coffee table, dried her eyes, and blew her nose. "I—I just don't know what to say. How to feel. I've never... I've never..."

Drake must have understood despite her lack of vocabulary. He sat down beside her and nodded. "I know."

"How?"

"Been there."

She took a deep breath. "For some feckin' reason, I never thought about the possibility of losin' someone I loved to fire. I thought with our secret weapon—dragonhood—we'd be able to prevent any fire-related disasters."

He shook his head. "It's true that we have special abilities, but we're still limited by the laws of physics."

"Huh? What do you mean?"

"Like not being in two places at one time. Like gravity—not being able to hold up a building that's determined to collapse." He softened his voice. "Like the mortality of humans. There's only so much we can do."

She struggled against the tears and lost. He just wrapped an arm around her shoulder and let her cry.

When she could form words again, she said, "How do they do it? I mean, most of them have no special powers at all. They're risking their own lives to *maybe* save someone else's."

He nodded. "I know. Pretty incredible, isn't it?"

Suddenly angry, she ground out between her teeth, "It's nuts, that's what it is. It's crazy."

"So why do you do it?" an unfamiliar female voice said from behind her.

Chloe whipped around. The Goddess of All stood silhouetted in her bay window. Gaia's long, white hair hung loosely over her shoulders, and she wore her usual Grecian robe, belted with a vine.

Stunned, Chloe said, "I do it because I can."

"You can do other things," Mother Nature stated matter-of-factly.

Chloe stared at her a few moments. When no elaboration followed she asked, "Like what?"

Mother Nature shrugged. "It's not up to me to be your career counselor. Didn't you have dreams when you were a little girl?"

Chloe snorted. "Yeah. Like a lot of little girls, I wanted to be a princess. And that dream came true the day I was born."

Mother Nature smiled. "There. You see?"

Chloe frowned. "I see nuthin'. My father's kingdom was in ruins and most of his men were dead before I was old enough to understand why."

"So? What can you do about that now?"

"Not a bloody t'ing, Goddess. Not a bloody t'ing." Her Irish accent came back in such force, she couldn't help realizing it.

"You're not thinking broadly enough." Mother Nature spread her arms wide. "Don't stop at what looks like a dead end. Push through that. Follow your thoughts—but let them run free. No one is *trapped* in their situation. There are always options."

"Oh, to be sure… I could go home to Ballyhoo and take the throne in a crumbling ruin, but my 'subjects' wouldn't recognize my authority. They'd laugh at me if I tried to tell 'em what to do."

"I didn't say they were all *good* options." Mother Nature lowered herself gracefully onto the window seat and folded her arms. "You know…I didn't invent kingdoms and royalty and all that shit. *You* invented that. I mean, the collective you. In other words, everyone who isn't me."

"So, what are you sayin'?"

Gaia shrugged. "I'm not saying anything."

Chloe stared at the floor and muttered, "You got that right."

The goddess's posture straightened and she began to lift up off the seat.

Drake looked over Chloe's head. "Gaia. Please don't take what she's saying right now as disrespect. She's grieving. She needs time."

Mother Nature's posture seemed to relax and she floated back to the bench. "You're right. Very little I could say right now would help. In that case, I'll go."

Neither she nor Drake had a chance to say yea, nay, or see you later. Gaia was gone.

Chloe felt a little better. Why she should was a mystery. Nothing had changed. Just being able to talk about it with an understanding friend was the only difference from earlier that day.

"Is there anything I can do?" Drake asked.

She thought about it for a few minutes. "No. You've already done more than anyone else could have. Actually, I don't know. Maybe you can explain something…"

"Explain what? Death?"

"No. I'm quite feckin' familiar with death. That's why I rarely get close to anyone. They just get to the point of interesting me more than they annoy me, and then they go and die. It sucks."

"Yes it does."

"Is that why you gave up your immortality for Bliss?"

He smiled. "Yes."

He didn't have to say any more. If she'd had a chance to spend a normal life with Ryan and then give up living when he did, she might have to think about it for a millisecond.

"Well, I'm glad Bliss changed her mind and you both became immortal as a result. Was Gaia upset about it?"

Drake chuckled. "Oh, you could say that. But Bliss can dig her way out of trouble just as easily as she gets herself into it."

"How so?"

"She recognizes her worth. She knew Gaia needed her to be a modern muse, and she hammered out an agreement with her until they were both satisfied."

"I assume you were part of that agreement."

Drake nodded. "I was to have my immortality back and she would become the muse of email. As a minor goddess, that gave Bliss immortality too. Gaia wanted her to be the muse of the entire Internet, but I don't think Mother Nature realized what an impossible task that was."

Chloe sat silent for a while.

Drake narrowed his gaze. "Are you okay?"

"I'm just doing what Gaia suggested. Thinking of all the possibilities. I'm no good with the Internet. Is she looking for any other positions?"

Drake cleared his throat. "It's not as if she advertises. In fact, I'm pretty sure the offer has to come from her. If you want to work for her at some point, you'd be better off not insulting her."

Chloe focused on the hardwood floor at her feet and mulled that over. "I don't think I insulted her—yet. Did I?"

"No, but you came close. I only know that because I've seen Bliss walk that line. You remind me of her, in a way."

"I remind you of who? Bliss?"

"Yeah. She has a tendency to spit out what she's thinking before she has a chance to think about the consequences."

"Oh." Chloe pondered that for a moment. "And she became the muse of email? Isn't that one of the risks? People who say things in an email that they later regret?"

Drake smiled. "Exactly. And who better to recognize the potential disaster before it happens?"

"Someone with prior experience," Chloe supplied.

"Yup."

It was true that Chloe didn't have a lot of experience with problems of the modern world. Even if Gaia was looking for help, she might have nothing to offer her.

But at some point, Chloe might make this disaster count for something...somehow. She just had to keep her eyes, ears, and mind open, hoping that someday she'd recognize how this horrible experience might help someone else. It sounded like new age prattle, but it was all she had to hold on to at the moment.

With a sigh, she said, "I think I'll be all right, Drake. I know you have a wife and a baby to get home to..."

"Are you sure? Can I get Rory or Amber over here before I leave?"

She smiled weakly. "I'm not on suicide watch, Drake. I'll be fine. Besides, I think I need a little time to process this, alone."

He patted her shoulder. "I'm just a phone call away if you need me."

"Thanks. You've already helped, more than you realize."

It was all Ryan could do not to shift back and explain to his family that Chloe *had to* know he was alive... and that she'd probably understand. But if he came out of phoenix form, he'd have to be incinerated again and start the aging process all over.

That's what had happened when he was seven. He'd come back too soon, and suddenly baby Gabe had a twin. His parents couldn't stand incinerating an infant, so they hadn't. That's how he became the middle child.

No, it was better if he reincarnated in his adult form as soon as possible and told her himself.

Weeks ago, he had hidden in the trees above his own funeral procession. Chloe had marched in her dress uniform, if you could call it marching. She kept up with the others but she looked like a zombie. She may have been hung over, but he'd never known her to drown her sorrows. He suspected it was simply grief over his "passing."

As he soared above the twinkling lights of the night-time cityscape, his mind wandered.

He'd taken a chance by giving her a good look at himself in his alternate form. He wasn't sure what he'd seen through the smoke, but he was pretty sure Chloe was hiding a paranormal secret identity of her own. If he'd had to name it, he'd say he had been looking at a dragon. But dragons weren't real, were they?

Hell. No one would guess that phoenixes are real either.

He'd managed to get out of the house with Luca's help, mostly at night. He wasn't your usual nondescript brown bird, so he had to be careful. It wouldn't do for some bird watcher to snap a picture of his yellow and orange tail and try to identify the unusual species. Yet, he'd take the chance to watch over Chloe.

When she wasn't on shift, she walked the darkened streets at night, staring at the sidewalk as if she didn't care who might sneak up behind and try to rob her—or worse. And as much as it was forbidden, he'd peck the eyes out of anyone who might hurt her. Would she know who he was?

She'd seen him. He was sure of it.

Would she know he still loved her? Was there a way to let her know? He'd been wracking his maturing brain, trying to come up with a way. It was almost St. Patrick's Day, and before this all happened, she'd let him know she'd rather burn in hell than march in the St. Paddy's Day parade. He should be able to shift into his mature body by then.

Only one thing nagged at him. She'd said she couldn't have children. Was that because she wasn't human? His mother was human but gave birth to shifters. Maybe if a shifter spent most of his or her time as a human, it was enough. He couldn't help wondering if dragons were the same way.

He'd be disappointing his family, especially his parents, if he chose to remain childless. His father was set on Ryan taking over as head of the family, and that included populating the South End brownstone with a family of his own.

In time his father and mother would have to fake their own deaths and move on, so as not to raise eyebrows when they reached a couple hundred years old. Phoenixes could live to be five hundred.

Well, it didn't look as if she was going to come out tonight. Maybe she was finally able to sleep.

Maybe she was moving on...

The thought pained him, but he didn't want her to continue suffering either. He hoped she'd forgive him when he returned.

~~~

On March 17, as Chloe was reading, Haggarty knocked, then poked his head around her bedroom door. He'd been awfully kind and attentive to her since Ryan had passed, left, or whatever he'd done...

She remembered what Ryan had told her about Haggarty wanting to ask her out and prayed he wouldn't. She reinforced her disinterest in dating a firefighter, but they all knew she and Ryan had been a couple. She didn't know how they knew, but they knew.

"Hey, it's almost parade time."

"I told you, I'm staying right where I am."

"Come on. The non-Irish firefighters are filling in for all of us. We even got an extra Fierro in case you changed your mind."

"I won't change me mind."

"Is this just because you're from Ulster?"

What could she say? Certainly not that her species was almost decimated by the "saint" they were celebrating. Her fake Northern Ireland birth certificate was finally coming in handy.

"Yeah."

"Well, wear an orange arm band or something."

She tossed the book on the floor and sat up abruptly. "I'm not marchin' in the feckin' parade and that's my final answer!"

He backed away with his hands up. "Okay, okay. It's a beautiful day though. The first one in a long time. Try to enjoy that much. Open your window or something."

"I'll do that." She narrowed her eyes, hoping he'd get the hint and leave her alone. Fortunately he did.

She sighed and rose. Fresh air did sound good, so she opened her window wide. Leaning on the sill, she noticed there was a light chill despite the sunshine. It could be a spring day in Ireland. But this weather was even more welcome, because of the horrible Boston winter. The frigid cold seeped right through her gloves whenever she climbed the metal ladder. Going back to Ireland was looking better and better.

The ladder engine below started up. The Back Bay firehouse had the "honor" of showing off their rig with Chief O'Brian riding shotgun.

She was relieved when it finally pulled out, leaving her to her book.

An hour later, after rereading the same paragraph three times, she decided it was time to grab a cup of coffee. She had half expected one of the Fierros to make an appearance, just to say hello. Maybe they didn't know what to say to her after that. But that went both ways. She could say a quick hello and then return to her room with her coffee.

She set down her book, rose, and stretched. Before she had a chance to leave, something swooped past her, ruffling her hair. In through her window had flown the beautiful bird that rose from Ryan's ashes. It landed on her bed.

She rushed to the door and shut it. Somehow she just knew this special bird shouldn't be seen by anyone but her. She crept back and sat gingerly beside it.

The bird didn't fly away. She reached out and was about to pat its head when the bird fell over onto its side and grew—and changed. She watched breathlessly as the body lost its feathers and fine dark hair covered its head.

In a matter of seconds, a naked man lay beside her. His legs dangled over one side of the twin bed and his head over the other side. When he levered himself up, she saw Ryan's beautiful face.

She blinked hard. "Ryan?" she whispered.

He pushed himself up and nodded. He tried to speak, but had to stop and clear his throat a couple of times first.

"It's me, Chloe." Gazing down at his nakedness, he grinned. "In the flesh."

She fell on top of him and pinned him to the mattress. As she covered him with kisses, he laughed.

Chapter 17

RYAN AND CHLOE CUDDLED BUT DIDN'T DARE MAKE love in the firehouse. Even though Chloe wanted to figure out how to "keep it down," Ryan wanted to make her scream. He was trying to hold her without getting hard, but it was impossible.

Then he remembered that there were some things they should talk about, which might be like throwing cold water over him. *Perfect timing.*

He propped himself up on his elbow. "So, my love, you know my secret, but I'm not entirely sure I know yours."

"I'll be glad to tell you, but I need to know more about you too. I take it we're both shifters."

"So it would seem." He couldn't help grinning. This conversation with Melanie had gone so wrong. Chloe was taking it entirely differently…but he really did need to know more about what he'd seen. "I'm a phoenix. And you are…"

She stuck her hand out as if introducing herself for the first time. "Chloe Arish. Dragon. Pleased to meet you, phoenix."

He chuckled and shook her hand. "I didn't know dragons existed."

"And I didn't know phoenixes were real. How about that? We both thought the other was a legend."

They shrugged and at the same time said, "Legends had to come from somewhere." Then they laughed.

"I'm happier than you can imagine," Ryan said.

"Why is that?"

"Well, for one, I don't have to hide my family's supernatural secret from you."

She bit her lip. "I take it you had to lie to Melanie. She was human, right?"

"Yes. She was human, but no, I didn't lie. When I proposed and she said yes, I knew I had to tell her the truth. Sandra handled it when Miguel told her, and I expected some kind of disbelief at first, but I thought eventually she'd come to accept me with all my, um... quirks. It's what couples do."

Chloe nodded. "Ideally, yes. I take it she never got to that point."

"She didn't even try. She ran from me. Wouldn't talk to me. I was afraid she was going to call the men in white coats."

"The who?"

Ryan chuckled. "It's an expression, meaning psychiatric hospital staff. She would have asked them to lock me up."

"Oh. Well, that's nasty. I hope she didn't actually do that."

"No. I think she realized that if she reported a shapeshifter, *she'd* be the one locked up."

After a brief silence, Chloe asked, "Didn't you get the Gaia lecture?"

"The what?"

"The lecture that Gaia—Mother Nature—gives to paranormals about revealing their existence to humans, or specifically, *not to*. Remember that staff member who dragged me away from the weight bench at the gym?"

"Yeah…" he said apprehensively.

"That was Gaia in disguise. I got a stern lecture in the ladies' locker room."

"Seriously?" Ryan had thought he'd heard everything about the supernatural. Apparently there were a few gaps in his knowledge. He wondered if the rest of his family knew that Mother Nature herself was monitoring their activities. His father must know. But why would he keep a secret like that from his family?

"I don't get it. I'm not human. Why would she care if you revealed yourself to me?"

Chloe shrugged. "You weren't the only person in the gym. If anyone had seen me lifting that much weight, they'd have whipped out their cameras and YouTubed it to the world."

He loved the way she used a technical term as a verb—that was happening with a whole generation, the generation she was learning "American-speak" from. He had to admit, it was an effective way to communicate. He knew exactly what she meant. He swept some of her silky hair behind her ear. "I love you, you know."

She surprised him by shoving his chest. "Then why did you feckin' leave me? You saw what I was, and I saw you. So why did you put me through two months of hell, thinkin' me brain made up somethin' it wanted to see and that you were actually dead?"

He captured her hand in his and held it to his heart. "I wanted to explain it to you in the worst way. I had hoped my family might hint at it, but I should have known they wouldn't. We treat our secret as seriously as Mother Nature wants us to." *Maybe that's why I never heard about her. Maybe she only shows up when a paranormal is about to screw up.*

"What kept you? Why didn't you explain it to me yerself before now?"

"I had to grow up all over again. If I'd shifted right away, I'd have come back as an infant and I couldn't tell you squat."

Her brow wrinkled as if she didn't quite understand.

"In our bird form, we mature much faster. But once we reincarnate, we'll stay whatever age is parallel in human years. I'd thought about coming back at age seven or eight, just to ask my family to clue you in, but there was no guarantee they would, and then they'd have to incinerate me and let me start all over again until I reached my prime."

Chloe's wide eyes and slightly open mouth just meant she was listening attentively, but he couldn't help wanting to kiss her. Ah, hell. What was stopping him?

He pulled her tight to his chest as he took possession of her lips. Taking advantage of that open mouth, he slipped his tongue in and she responded instantly. She wrapped her arm around him and twined her fingers in his hair.

Kissing her was one of the things he'd missed most. They fit together perfectly and her hot mouth drove him wild.

When they finally broke the kiss, they were both breathing hard.

"I can't get off this feckin' shift rotation fast enough. As soon as we can have some privacy, I'll ask Rory and Amber to take a hike and we can make love in every room of their B and B."

He laughed. "I like the sound of that."

"Me too. I'm still a little confused, but maybe you can explain it again later. Right now all I want to do is kiss you."

He gave her a quick tap on her pert nose. "It's your turn now. What can you tell me about your dragon side? And don't forget to include the part about not being able to have children. Is that because a dragon and a human can't mate for some reason?"

"Ah. Well, here's the thing. We can mate till the cows give their milk for free, but we can't create life. Gaia, in her infinite wisdom, felt the need to keep our numbers down. Probably because we're capable of incineratin' her lovely landscape." She sighed. "At any rate, female dragons are only fertile once every five years and only for one month. If we happen to mate with another dragon during that time, we'll probably have a baby dragon or two."

"Two?"

"Twins have been known to happen. That's what led to a bloody battle between... Ah, shite. You don't want the whole history lesson."

"Sure I do."

Chloe sighed. "Okay, get comfortable."

Ryan reclined on her bed with his hands interlocked behind his neck. "I'm ready."

"You'd better cover yourself or I'm bound to get distracted."

He grabbed her pillow and used it to cover his growing erection.

She grinned. "Thanks. You know how you used to call me 'princess'?"

"I still do…if I find an occasion to use it."

Still smiling, she set a hand on her hip, but couldn't help having a little fun with him. "Well…it's a better nickname than you think. I really *am* a princess."

His brows raised. "Go on…"

"Sure'n you know that Ireland used to be ruled by kings and queens…"

"Sure'n," he said with a cheeky grin.

She ignored the tease. "So, anyway, long, long ago, me grandparents, King Brian and Queen Luigsech, had three sons: Cathesach, Eogan, and Faelan. Me father, Cathesach, was the eldest of twins. Uncle Eogan believed himself to be the eldest, because it was never exactly clear which was which.

"The king asked the attendants in the birthing room which child was his heir. Their nursemaid swore it was Cathesach who was handed to her as soon as the midwife had delivered him. Then she went back to her work and delivered Eogan. So, everyone went with that…until a few years later when she became a little befuddled and began calling one by the other's name.

"Eogan was raised as the second son, but when the two were fully grown, he was slightly taller than me father. So some fool friend of Eogan's saw a chance to elevate his own status and called the birth order into question."

"Sheesh. My father gets us mixed up all the time, and he's sharp as a tack."

She snorted. "It happens to a lot of people." A tiny wisp of smoke left her nostril and this time she didn't attempt to cover it.

"By the way, how old does that make you?" Ryan asked. "I thought Ireland recognized Great Britain's monarchy."

"I should have mentioned I'm an older woman." She winked and gave him a sly smile. "About nine hundred and seventy-five years older."

"Really? Wow. But you're assuming I'm what? Twenty-five? Thirty?"

Suddenly she wondered how long phoenixes had been around. "Ah, how old are you, then?"

He chuckled. "Oh, you're older all right. I'm only about forty. I used to be the oldest, but then I screwed up and barbecued myself when I was a kid. Anyway, I reincarnated before I was supposed to and had to grow up all over again. That's how I wound up as the middle child, instead of the eldest. My brothers know this, but don't tell them *you* know. Not yet, anyway."

"Hell, I don't know which secrets to keep from whom anymore."

"Best to keep everything to yourself for now."

Her posture straightened. "They knew you lived? They knew and they didn't tell me?" Her voice was raising by the second and Ryan shushed her.

"I will not shush. How dare they let me grieve like that? They hugged me after the funeral and let me cry all over them."

"Look, princess... They had to go along with it. If they acted like I was alive, someone would have looked into it. Suspicions would have been raised. Hell, your honesty would have been questioned since you were there."

Her posture deflated. "Ye're right. But now what will you do? Pretend you're the second comin'?"

His expression turned serious. "I don't know yet, Chloe. But whatever plans I make, I want to include you in them."

She gazed at him. There was nothing but sincerity in his eyes. So what was he saying?

A knock at the door was immediately followed by the door opening. Whoever stood behind it didn't believe in waiting for an invitation.

"Shite."

Ryan rolled out of bed and onto the floor in one fluid motion. He had scooted half under her bed by the time she shot to her feet and met the intruder at the door.

"Hey, there, Chloe. We just thought we'd say hello since we're working here today."

"Jayce? And Gabe, is it?"

"Yep. Two of the famous Fierros," Gabe said, trying to sound chipper.

"I think I heard something heavy fall on the floor," Jayce said. "Is everything all right?"

Well now. These two were among the throng who'd allowed her to think her true love was nothing but ash. There had to be some small amount of revenge she could extract from this situation.

"Oh, quite. I just dropped…me dictionary."

"I'll get it," Jayce said as he started inside.

"Leave it. I'll get it later." She opened the door wider. "Come in, come in. I don't have much room to sit, but there's a comfortable armchair in the corner for one of you, and I can bring over the desk chair for the other."

"I'll get it, Chloe," Gabe said.

"Don't be silly. I'm closest to it," she said. "Besides, I certainly don't want to be treated any *differently*.

Certainly not because I was in love with your brother, and you think I'm a fragile little girl."

They laughed.

"No. There's no danger of anyone thinking that, Chloe," Jayce said.

She stopped on her way to the chair and turned slowly. "There's not? Why not? I'm a girl, and I've been in a terrible state since your brother died."

Their faces fell and their expressions became decidedly uncomfortable. Jayce kicked at the old wooden floor. "Of course. I'm sorry."

"Sorry? For what?"

"For not… You know…" He looked to Gabe for help, but his younger brother just shrugged.

She could almost see him trying to gather words back into his mouth and swallow them. "I—I don't know what to say, Chloe."

"I think that's why it took us so long to check on you," Gabe added. "None of us know what to say."

"And why is that?"

She had *almost* had her fun. Pretty soon, she'd let them off the hot seat, but for now…

"I called your mother a couple of times, just to ask how she was doin'. She sounded all right. I figured your mother was gettin' through it, because she had a lot of support. I would have liked some too."

"We figured you were getting through it," Jayce said.

"But you didn't ask. How could you know?"

Gabe began to fidget. "Yeah, well…"

She tipped her head and waited, but Gabe didn't finish his thought. He just tried to get past her to the desk. "Let me get that chair."

She stepped back and when he rounded the end of her bed, he couldn't help noticing the back half of a naked man trying to jam his big frame under it.

"Oh!" he said. "Oh, I didn't realize…"

She batted her eyelashes innocently. "Didn't realize what?"

"That you had company." He pointed to Ryan's ass, wiggling out from under the bed.

She crossed to the door and shut it, waiting for the inevitable moment of recognition. As she turned the lock, Jayce got up from his armchair and followed his brother's gaze. The two of them stared at the form of a man, buck naked, beside Chloe's bed.

When Ryan rose and turned around, Chloe could see they'd had no idea he was here, and "in the flesh" as he'd earlier put it. She grabbed a bath towel off her dresser and tossed it across the bed to her lover.

Their eyes rounded. Gabe whooped and hugged him, briefly. He backed away and let Jayce shake Ryan's hand.

Grinning, he set his hands on his towel-covered hips. "Yup. No dust bunnies under there. You passed inspection, Chloe."

His brothers burst out laughing.

───※───

Mr. and Mrs. Fierro hurried over the wet sidewalk. Antonio Fierro carried a nondescript paper bag filled with clothes for Ryan.

"I didn't expect him to come back for another week," Gabriella Fierro said.

"Well, can you blame him? If I knew you were

grieving for me, I'd come back as early as possible too. Plus I'd be horny as hell by that time."

She blushed and bumped into him on purpose. "Still, wouldn't you think he'd shift at home where all his clothes are?"

"You mean, where *we* are. No. I think he'd shift right where he wanted to shift. So, obviously Chloe means a lot to him. We just don't know how much he told her."

When they reached the Back Bay Fire Station, Mr. Fierro held the door open for his wife and she breezed in. This was his old station house. It looked as if nothing much had changed.

"Well, the fact that she was still conscious and able to call us is a good sign," Gabriella said. "He must have made up a believable story."

"Quiet now. Let me sense where the boys are."

He paused just inside, then smiled. "Top floor. Toward the front on the right.

"I wish I could have done that when the boys were young. It would have saved my lungs when I had to call and call for them to come in."

He strode to the stairs and took them two at a time. His wife hurried after him, trying to keep up, but it was no use.

Mr. Fierro burst through Chloe's door and dropped the paper bag on her bed. Upon seeing his son, alive and healthy, he sighed with relief. Then he asked him, "How much does she know?"

Ryan smiled at Chloe with pride. "Everything. She knows everything."

Mr. Fierro whooped. "And she's still standing!" He grabbed Chloe up in his arms and gave her a huge, impulsive hug. He was impressed when she didn't cry out or act like he was squeezing her to death. Instead, she simply gave as good as she got.

When he'd put her down, he strode around the bed to his son and shook his hand.

Mrs. Fierro finally appeared in the doorway, huffing and puffing. "Thanks, Antonio."

"Sorry, love. I couldn't wait to see our son."

His wife strode around the bed. "Neither could I. It's just that some of us don't have such long, strong legs." She winked at Chloe, as if she'd understand. Mr. Fierro had his doubts. Ryan had said more than once how impressed he was with her ability to keep up with any man.

Gabriella hugged Ryan hard, and he returned the hug more gently. As they stood there, his towel fell off. Chloe closed the door while everyone laughed.

"I guess I should get dressed."

His mother glanced at Chloe, who just smiled and shrugged. Antonio couldn't help but smile.

"I think she's seen it all before," Gabriella said.

"I guess so."

Ryan unrolled the paper bag and slipped on his tighty-whities. Then he pulled the fire department T-shirt over his head. Gabriella Fierro had stacked everything in order of dressing, just like firefighters do. Antonio couldn't help but be proud of his wonderful wife. He also couldn't help noticing the loving looks his son was exchanging with Chloe Arish.

They were a match. He'd bet his beak on it.

———

The tones rang out.

"Damn," Mr. Fierro muttered. "Poor timing."

Chloe couldn't have disagreed more. This was perfect timing. She needed time to forgive the Fierros for letting her cry herself to sleep almost nightly. When it happened at work, she'd had to cover her face with a pillow, so no one could hear her.

Now, she felt the familiar rush of adrenaline as she took off down the hall to the fire pole.

The warm reunion of phoenix and family had left her with an awkward feeling. Like she hadn't just witnessed a miracle. To them, it seemed like Tuesday. Well, all right…more like Christmas when it fell on a Tuesday.

Gabe and Jayce were right behind her and followed her down the pole to the garage. The other firefighters were arriving by the stairs. They'd probably been in the kitchen since it was almost lunch time. They'd be fighting this fire on empty stomachs.

Dispatch was announcing a structure fire and gave the Congress Street address for Harrison Hall.

"Shit," Lieutenant Streeter mumbled.

"What's the matter?" Chloe asked.

"It's one of the oldest buildings in the country. Historical landmark." He turned to the two substitute firefighters. "Jayce, you're on Ladder 15. Gabe, you're with us in Engine 33."

Everyone found their places and the rigs rolled out.

"Is there some kind of special protocol when it comes to historic structures?" Chloe asked the lieutenant.

"Yeah. Put the fire out."

Gabe laughed. Then he looked at Chloe sympathetically and said, "Sorry."

"No. It's perfectly okay," she said. "Ask a silly question, get a shite answer, right?"

Gabe tipped his head.

"Don't worry," the lieutenant said to Gabe. "You get used to it."

Her face heated. *Feckers. I must have screwed up another American saying.*

Well, it wouldn't matter shortly. She'd show the Fierros just how valuable she was in a fire. She was usually the first one in and frequently the last one out.

But so was Ryan. If he took foolish chances, knowing he could always come back if needed to, he tried not to let anyone see it. She realized that now. Knowing how rarely they held empty casket funerals for firefighters who were reduced to ash, she'd guess the phoenixes were *usually* as careful as any mortal.

But she was special too.

Hmmm… To show off or not to show off? That was the question.

No question about it. She'd excel and show Ryan's family how well suited she was for the job they all loved—and how well she'd fit in with them at every Sunday dinner.

Chapter 18

THE SMOKE WAS POURING FROM WINDOWS AT THE back of the building. At first it seemed as if only the second floor was involved, then Chloe saw flames reflected in the window on the third floor as well.

The District 3 chief had beat everyone to the scene and began barking orders as soon as they jumped out of their vehicles. "We expect more firefighters on the scene, but you've gotta get this fire out now. Lieutenant, get your guys on the roof and provide top ventilation to remove toxic gases."

"Yes, sir." Lieutenant Streeter pointed to Chloe and Gabe. "You two go to the roof. Be careful. It may be slippery."

Within minutes, they had two lines working and the aerial hose was laying a master stream on the top floor. Jayce was teamed up with Nagle and another firefighter she didn't know. Their mission was to bring water to the back left corner of the second floor, which they suspected was the seat of the fire.

As the others charged in the back door, Chloe and Gabe climbed the ladder. With sixty pounds of gear and a pickax, a human could only climb so fast. Chloe didn't want to delay, knowing the significance of the building and wondering if tourists were stuck inside.

Plus this was a chance to show a Fierro what she was made of. She scrambled up the ladder faster than a man

could…only Gabe was keeping up with her. Hmmm…
Now she realized the kind of pressure Ryan had been
under to keep up the family's reputation of excellence.

Cops were arriving and keeping people across the
street. Farther down they were blocking off traffic alto-
gether. Flames shot out like angry fingertips, attracting
a crowd. The roof would be ventilated with a saw, but
axes might be needed for shingle removal.

The ladder had been placed with five rungs above the
roofline, and tied off to a chimney to keep it in place.
Below, someone was laying another ladder off to the
right in case the crews needed an alternate escape route.
They worked as if they'd been practicing for this for
years. Chloe realized they had been. No wonder seasoned
firefighters like Haggarty worried about probies making
one wrong move and jeopardizing the whole operation.

Two firefighters from District 3 were already on the
roof and held the K-12 saw. One had marked the two-
foot by four-foot opening. She noticed the other one
wore a lieutenant's insignia.

Even though cold surrounded them, the firefighters
were sweating. Not watching where she was going, she
slipped on the roof that was wet from melting ice and
fire hoses. Righting herself before she fell, she tried to
be more careful as she made her way to the spot that the
firefighters were concentrating on.

The private pulled the cord to start the saw, and
slipped. As he regained his footing, Chloe stopped just
below him to act as a brace if he needed it. He pulled the
cord a second time. When nothing happened, he swore.

"Move over, Chloe," Gabe said. "Let me catch him
if he falls."

"I can do it," she insisted.

Gabe nodded, grabbed the ax, and had half the shingles off when, thank God, on the third try, the machine roared to life. She breathed a sigh of relief knowing they might have had to waste precious time opening the roof with their axes alone.

Quickly the firefighter made the cut on the short side away from his body, then moved and cut the longer side. Soon the roof hole was done. As debris fell downward, the firefighters stepped back. Fire often burst from the vent hole as superheated gases received oxygen. From behind, Chloe braced the private just as the furious flames shot through the opening.

Gabe shot her a smile. She was relieved to be making a positive impression. From what Ryan had told her, his brother would probably report her abilities at their Sunday dinner.

"Everybody, listen up," the District 3 lieutenant said. "The roof is getting spongy. I want everybody off."

Gabe got to the ladder first and as soon as he had his footing, he took the saw from the other firefighter. The private looked at Chloe as if she should be next, but she just said, "Go!" He nodded and preceded her down the ladder.

The lieutenant got a call on his radio and said, "I'll be right there." He took the ladder ahead of Chloe and she followed him down. She was just passing a window, which had been blown out by fire, when she heard crying and a woman yelling, "Help."

"Jaysus. There's somebody still in there!" She peered around the window casing and saw a mother and child huddled against the far wall—trapped on both sides. Through the smoke she could barely see them and knew they might not see her. "Come to the window," Chloe shouted.

She knocked the jagged glass out of the bottom of the window and they inched their way toward her.

She felt weight on the ladder behind her.

"Why did you stop, Arish?" Gabe had climbed back up.

"Two people inside. They're scared as hell. I'm going in."

"Go ahead. I'll take them from out here."

He was treating her as an equal. She had wanted to earn Ryan's family's trust and approval so much, and it looked like that was happening.

Gingerly, Chloe braced her boot on the windowsill. She managed to slide it inside, but her other foot slipped on the rung of the ladder. Gabe grabbed her and pushed her the rest of the way in.

Righting herself, she reached out and grabbed the little girl's hand. She couldn't have been more than four or five years old. The mother gratefully pushed her forward, saying, "Go with the brave firefighter, honey."

Chloe picked her up and said to the girl, "Your mommy is next."

She placed the young one in Gabe's arms and he carried her down. She stopped the mother from climbing out after her with a hand on her shoulder. "He'll be right back and then it'll be your turn."

The woman bit her lower lip and wrung her hands while they waited for Gabe to return.

"Are you doing okay?" Chloe asked.

The mom looked like she was gulping back tears

and nodded. "I panicked and fell. I hit my head on something on the way down and must have been unconscious for a few minutes. When I think of what could have happened…"

Gabe appeared at the window, and both he and Chloe made sure the woman got onto the ladder and her footing was secure.

Chloe was about to climb out the window when she noticed flames licking around the closed door inside. Before she could get out of the way, the door exploded off its hinges and pitched her forward out the window and too far from the ladder.

She would have hit the pavement if Jayce hadn't been there to catch her.

She groaned. "Thanks." *Way to show off, Chloe.*

At the next Fierros Sunday dinner Chloe was an invited guest. Before they sat down Ryan had to ask her an important question, so he hung up her coat quickly and tried to bypass the rest of the family. He enfolded her hand in his and led her directly to the basement stairs.

They had just reached the bottom of the steps when Mrs. Fierro came looking for him. "Ryan!"

Before she saw Chloe, he whispered, "Meet me in the bedroom," and then gave his lover a pat on the ass.

She jumped slightly but turned enough so he could see her grin.

"Oh, there you are!" Mrs. Fierro said.

Ryan halted and began to climb the stairs again. If he met her at the top, maybe she wouldn't come down. "Be right there, Ma."

He needed to talk to Chloe alone and in person. It hadn't been possible for him to go out until everyone had agreed on "the plan" for his reemergence. He wasn't sure she was going to like the decision that had been made on his behalf.

Mrs. Fierro gave him that special smile a mother reserves for a child who has just accomplished something wonderful. "When is your young lady coming?"

"You mean Chloe?"

Mrs. Fierro set a fist on her apron-covered hip. "No, Princess Kate." She rolled her eyes. "Of course I mean Chloe."

"She'll be here any time, Ma. I need to speak with her for a few moments first. Alone."

The understanding smile returned to her face. "I know. This can't be easy for you."

What neither of the women in his life knew was that Ryan had no intention of following the plan if Chloe couldn't accept it. He'd adjust. He'd find a plan B — or C.

"Yeah. I really need to talk to her first."

"I just thought I'd grab you before you did, in case you wanted to give her…" Mrs. Fierro twisted the rings on her left hand back and forth.

"What are you doing? No, Ma. That wasn't the plan."

She gritted her teeth and finally popped off the two rings that had worn grooves in the fourth finger of her left hand. "There." She separated her diamond ring from the other plain gold band and held it out to him. "Pah. I know the plan, but I never thought it was a very good one. Son, men aren't thinking of romance when they're making decisions for someone else."

He gazed at his mother with his mouth open. Reaching for the diamond ring, he said, "But this was your great-grandmother's ring. Are you sure?"

She smoothed his hair back. "I am, if you are."

He nodded, giving her a humble, grateful smile. "I am."

"Then go ahead. Oh. By the way, I know she's down there. Don't keep her waiting." Mrs. Fierro winked.

Ryan laughed. Nothing much got past his mom.

He admired the ring on the way to the basement bedroom. It sparkled as if it were new. He didn't think his mother had polished it, but perhaps she had. The woman was a little scary in her ability to predict the future.

When he opened the door, he saw Chloe admiring his childhood trophies. He'd won some for track and field. A few for bowling. Hopefully she wouldn't ask too many questions. He didn't want to get sidetracked.

"So are we finally alone?" she asked.

"For a little bit." While he strolled over to her, he tucked the ring into his back pocket.

She met him halfway and tipped her face up for a kiss. He enveloped her in his arms and pulled her closer. Taking a moment to gaze at her face, he noted her complete lack of guile. He appreciated the trust they shared, and the nervousness he'd had about their upcoming conversation eased.

His lips descended to hers in what he hoped was a tender kiss. It didn't stay tender very long. She pulled him to her and wound her arms tightly around his neck. He yanked her up against his hard length. Heat built quickly. They were like glowing embers, always a whisper away from bursting into flames.

She opened her mouth and his tongue swept inside.

For several moments, they sought and stroked, tasted and breathed each other.

At last, Ryan pulled back just enough to break the kiss, and the two of them panted for breath. Her hooded green eyes opened and gazed up at him.

"I can't believe you're standing here." She ran her hands over his chest, as if checking to be sure he was solid. "When I thought you were dead, I died too."

He rested his forehead against hers. "I know." Before they got too caught up in the demands of their impatient bodies, he pulled away. "Please sit. I have to tell you something."

She nodded and glanced around the room. Other than his desk chair, the only seat available was on his bed. He sat and patted the spot next to him. "I'll try to behave."

"I guess we'll have to. I almost forgot we were in your parents' house for a minute there."

He grinned. "Yeah. I know what you mean."

She sat down beside him, but left a few gaping inches in between.

He took her hand. "First of all, I love you, Chloe."

"I love you too."

"I know. I mean…I'm pretty sure you do. Otherwise I wouldn't even be talking to you about this."

"About what?"

"The future…and us."

She remained silent. Her innocent eyes blinked up at him, as if she had no idea where he was going with any of this. Maybe she didn't. This kind of thing didn't happen every day.

"I want to stay with you, Chloe. You and my family and the fire service."

She nodded.

"But the city thinks I'm dead. Hell, they even had a funeral for me."

Her expression dimmed. "I guess things are a bit complicated now."

Ya think? "Look. My family is important to me, and I know you love yours…and Boston."

Her eyebrows rose. "So?"

He sighed. "We Fierros protect each other. A family meeting decides what to do in complicated situations. You must have something like that in your family…"

She tipped her head as if thinking. "Not really. We argue. Me brother reminds us he's the boss and then tells us whatever it is he thinks is best for all."

Ryan nodded. "It's sort of the same thing with us."

Chloe snorted. "I doubt it."

"Why is that?"

"Because you're probably willin' to do what you're told."

"And you're not?"

She grinned, but didn't confirm or deny his suspicion.

"Okay. Well, we may be more alike than you realize. My family gave me two choices. Both of them bad. I can go to Brazil, get plastic surgery, and trade identities with my cousin, who wants to quit the fire department. That way I can get a job doing what I love right away, at home, and he'll be paid well for his cooperation."

"Jaysus! That's drastic. What does he think of that?"

"I don't know. I haven't asked him. The only reason they thought of it is that he's not happy in the fire service. Then he can take a new identity and do something else."

"So, how will he fake all the documentation?"

Ryan shrugged. "The family will think of something."

"Well, I don't know what he looks like, but I'm partial to your peculiar face—for some damn reason."

He was insulted until he saw her sly smile. "I meant particular, not peculiar." Then he laughed and took her hand in his. The warmth was exactly what he needed.

Her brow wrinkled. "You said there was some other choice?"

"I can get a fake ID and become someone completely different. Then I'll have to create a whole backstory. Move. Start over. And without plastic surgery, I'd have to wear a damn good disguise and never return to Boston. It sounds like a total pain in the ass."

"Oh, I don't know… It's not so bad."

Suddenly, things fell into place. "Are you saying that's what *you* did?"

She gave a slight shrug. "Well, I couldn't very well say, 'Hello, there. I'm a centuries-old Irish dragon without an existing birth certificate. Would you let me take your citizenship test?'"

He rubbed her fingers with the pad of his thumb. "Is this your real face?"

She smiled. "It's the only one I've ever owned, freckles and all."

"Good." He swooped in for a quick kiss. As always, the magnetic pull made him want to hold her close and topple onto the mattress with her. But he couldn't—yet. With a herculean effort, he pulled away.

"So, what are you goin' to do?" she asked.

He shook his head. "I don't know. I just know I want you with me." He took a deep breath and dropped to one knee. Rooting around in his back pocket, he found his mother's ring and presented it to her. "Chloe…"

Her eyes rounded.

"Will you—"

He didn't have a chance to finish his question. She answered him by grabbing his collar and planting a hard kiss on his mouth.

———

Feeling like she was floating, Chloe followed Ryan up the stairs when his mother called out that dinner was ready. How this family would handle their news was anyone's guess. She'd never been so nervous, and she didn't care for the feeling.

She reminded herself that they might accept her. After all, they were a little *different* too.

Ryan pulled out a chair for her and she sat, scooting up to the table as he pushed her chair forward. Most of the "boys" were taking their usual chairs, but she noticed Luca bringing in an extra one from the kitchen. He took a space that had been set on one corner of the tablecloth. There was another son seated on the other corner. She thought his name was Nico or Noah.

"Our family needs a bigger table," Luca said.

"Not necessarily," Mr. Fierro said. He eyed Ryan as if knowing he wouldn't be around much longer.

When everyone was settled, Ryan cleared his throat. "Um, folks. Chloe and I have an announcement."

The salad bowl and bread basket that were being passed around were set down. The room fell silent. Chloe had her heart in her throat, wondering how Ryan would drop this bombshell, and if the family would blow up.

"Well, speak," Mr. Fierro said.

Ryan took Chloe's left hand and raised it. "I proposed and Chloe accepted." Then he kissed her knuckles.

She held his gaze, so she missed whatever immediate reactions were occurring around the table. Maybe it was a good thing. No one spoke at first, but his smile helped her relax and breathe.

Finally Jayce asked, "Is that Mom's ring?"

"Yes it is," Mrs. Fierro answered before Ryan could.

"I'll let Chloe pick out her own, later," Ryan said. "I don't want you to go without yours, Ma. But thanks for letting me borrow it."

His mother waved her hand. "Borrow, shmorrow. I meant for her to have it. She'll be married to the next Fierro leader, after all."

Mr. Fierro sighed. "I wish you'd told me this might happen. I had no idea. Now our situation is even more complicated."

Chloe was surprised by the elder's words, but maybe that would explain the reaction of the others—or lack of one. "I'm a complication?"

Mr. Fierro chuckled sadly. "I'm sorry, dear girl. I didn't mean it like that. Our Ryan is happier than he's been in ages. And we're happy for him. The situation was already complicated, but we'll figure something out." He shot his wife some kind of disapproving look.

"If the ring should go to someone else, I'm perfectly okay with that. I mean—it's beautiful, and I would treasure it, but if there's some kind of protocol I'd be breaking…"

"Not at all," Mrs. Fierro said. "I can give *my* ring to anyone I choose. It was my mother's and her mother's before that."

Chloe glanced around at the rest of the clan. The only one who seemed to be smiling was Sandra. She immediately reached across Ryan and clasped Chloe's hand, giving it a squeeze.

"Welcome to the family, *Sister*."

Chloe couldn't help being genuinely touched and gave Sandra a soft smile.

Others murmured their congratulations, but the tone seemed tentative. She tried not to take it personally, telling herself they were naturally worried about their brother and they didn't know her well.

Mrs. Fierro rose. Even at five feet, the woman commanded everyone's attention. "Look, life is complicated. This is a celebration. I'm delighted to welcome Chloe to our family. Ryan deserves great happiness after all he's been through…and I'd better hear some more excitement from the rest of you. We'll find a way to keep them with us here in Boston." She eyed Luca. "And we'll buy a bigger table. But regardless, she'll be the mother of our next generation, and I suggest you all remember that."

Oh no. This wouldn't do at all. Chloe had to tell them she couldn't have Ryan's children. She opened her mouth to speak, but Ryan squeezed her thigh. She looked to him, to see if he was trying to get her attention. Apparently he was, because he gave her a quick and subtle headshake.

"But…" she whispered.

"Not now," he said.

"What's wrong?" Mrs. Fierro asked.

Everyone focused their attention on the couple.

"Nothing," Ryan said.

Chloe felt her cheeks heat. She didn't usually blush, but when she did there was no missing it. Her very fair skin would turn bright pink and sometimes mottled. It wasn't a good look.

"I can't." There. She'd said it. She glanced at Ryan and he was frowning. Well, too bad. She wasn't going to mislead his family. If they didn't like the truth, there wasn't much she could do about it.

"What do you mean, dear?" Mrs. Fierro asked.

"I can't have children. I'm sorry." Chloe stiffened her posture and lifted her chin. "If you want your ring back, I completely understand. But I'm not giving your son back."

Ryan smiled and gave her hand a quick reassuring pat.

"Did you know about this, son?" Mr. Fierro asked.

"Yes, I did. She told me weeks ago. I don't care. I love Chloe." He glanced around the table at the others and finally focused on Miguel and Sandra. "There are plenty of others here who can bring the next generation into the world."

At that, Sandra blushed. Miguel looked at her briefly and they smiled at each other. "Actually," Miguel said, "Sandra and I have an announcement too."

Mrs. Fierro's eyes widened and Chloe could almost see her holding her breath.

"We're pregnant," Sandra finally blurted out.

Mrs. Fierro squealed and rushed over to her daughter-in-law, practically squishing the life out of her.

"So, you're pregnant, Miguel?" one of the younger brothers asked. "How did you manage that trick?"

"Shut up, Dante." Miguel was grinning.

Chloe was thinking the same thing. She was glad someone else made the smart-ass remark. Letting out a sigh of relief, she was grateful to have the focus shift to the other couple.

Chapter 19

"ARE YOU SURE THERE'S NO GETTING OUT OF THIS?" Ryan asked, holding Chloe's hand as they rushed across the dark street.

"Nope. I had to sit through your family's reactions when you told them, now you need to be there for me when I tell mine." She flashed him a smile. "And don't complain. You'll have it easy. My family is tiny compared to yours."

"But they don't know what I am."

"They will."

"Are you sure that's wise?"

"I can't not tell them. They'll think you're a ghost—or worse. A liar. Besides, me brother—well, he's the prince. He needs to know everythin'."

Ryan shook his head. "I still can't believe you're a real princess. I just meant it as an insult at first. Then as an endearment."

She laughed. "And how silly do you feel about that now?"

"Pretty silly," he admitted. "But the nickname stands. It fits you."

"That it does. I can't deny it."

When they reached the B and B, Chloe's hand shook.

He supposed she couldn't help being nervous, but he couldn't figure out why. This was her brother they were going to talk to. The same brother who had loved and looked out for her for a thousand years.

Maybe that was why. If he didn't like the idea of Chloe marrying a phoenix, he could prevent it. Well, not legally, but he could forbid it as her king. Ryan didn't think that would happen, but still…

She pushed open the outer door and knocked on the inner one.

"Don't you have a key?"

She nodded. "I do, but for some feckin' reason, I don't feel like this is the time to use it."

Ryan scratched his head. "Are you sure you're ready for this? Maybe you need more time."

"It's not a matter of time. I'll be nervous no matter when we speak to them."

"Why?" He couldn't help catching her case of nerves. "Are you unsure about me? About us?"

"Not a t'all." She rose onto her tiptoes and kissed him.

When the door opened, Rory exclaimed, "So that's why you knocked. You were too busy kissin' to use your key." Then his eyes rounded. "Chloe. What the feck?"

Chloe, still grasping Ryan's hand, pushed passed Rory. "We need to tell you somethin', Brother. Mind if we all get a cup of tea first?"

Rory stepped back, looking surprised. "Is tea goin' to be enough fer this talk? I see a ghost. Mayhaps whiskey would be more helpful?"

Chloe sighed. "Ye're not seein' a ghost, but now that you mention it, the other kind of spirits would be most welcome. I hope what we have to tell you is welcome news."

Rory still looked confused. "All right. Is it formal news?" He gestured to the living room. "Or sittin' around the kitchen island news?"

Chloe looked to Ryan and shrugged. "We told his family in their dinin' room."

Rory folded his arms. "Ah. So we're gettin' this news secondhand?"

"Not a'tall. It's just happened and we didn't have a chance to decide who and where—"

Rory grabbed her left hand and stared at the diamond ring there. "Is that what I think it is?"

Chloe's smile started small and spread into a wide grin.

"Apparently it's front hall news... Amber!" Rory called upstairs over his shoulder and quickly ushered the couple into the living room.

A second later, Amber popped out of the hall closet. "What's wrong?"

"Nothin', luv. I didn't mean to alarm you," Rory said.

Amber's eyes widened. "Ryan!"

"Everybody take a seat," Chloe said. "I'll pour whiskeys all around."

"Um. I think I have something better," Amber said. "Does this occasion happen to call for champagne?"

"That would be perfect," Chloe said.

Everyone strolled into the living room except Amber. She disappeared into the closet again.

Chloe needed to tell her dragon brother and his muse girlfriend about Ryan's paranormal status, but considering the man survived his own funeral, the explanation wouldn't be too hard to swallow. Speaking of swallowing, she needed a big gulp of that champagne.

At last Amber reappeared with the chilled bottle and handed it to Rory.

Rory worked the cork to the end of the bottle neck, opening the bottle with a satisfying *pop*. Amber took two champagne glasses from behind the small bar and strode over to the couple.

"Have a seat, you two. It looks like we're in for one of your long Irish storytelling sessions."

As her glass was filled, Chloe snorted. "'Tis indeed a long story, but I'm just learnin' most of it meself."

Ryan smiled at her, but waited for everyone to have their champagne at the ready before speaking.

Rory held his glass aloft. "I'd make a toast meself, but I don't know what I'm toastin' to yet. Would one of you please tell us what miracle we're celebratin'?"

Chloe laughed. "Take your pick, Brother."

Ryan rose. "I'll start. To my beautiful bride-to-be." He lifted his glass in Chloe's direction.

"Sláinte," everyone said as they took their first sips.

Chloe rose and blinked up at Ryan. "There's more, of course."

"And we're gettin' older but no wiser here," Rory joked.

Chloe sighed. "To my fiancé being a phoenix and able to rise from the dead."

Rory's and Amber's brows shot up for a moment. Then they glanced at each other, shrugged, and said, "Cheers!"

Ryan had just finished telling the whole story of his family history, the legends that hinted at a firebird called a phoenix, and his miraculous recovery, when someone knocked on the B and B's door.

Rory rose and addressed Amber. "Are you expectin' anyone, luv?"

"Nope. Wait here. I'll go." She strode to the front door, and Chloe saw her smile before she got there.

A moment later, Mother Nature walked regally into the living room and faced the couple on the couch. She was wearing jeans and a sweater. If not for her long white hair and gold sandals, she may have looked like any young woman walking around the city in early spring.

Chloe shot to her feet. "Goddess! It's nice to see you again." She was about to grab Ryan's arm and yank him to his feet, but he rose without her having to, thank goodness. "I—uh, I don't know if you two have met..." she continued.

"We have not," Mother Nature said. "Not formally, anyway." She extended her hand toward Ryan. "I am Gaia. Also known as Mother Nature or *The* Goddess."

He took her right hand and shook it reverently. "Goddess, it's an honor."

"What a nice man," the goddess said. Then she narrowed her eyes at him and whispered, furiously, "My radar went off. You told them about yourself, didn't you?"

He hesitated for only a moment. "I had to. Chloe and I are engaged to be married. Husbands and wives shouldn't have such huge secrets from each other—and if possible, from their families."

The goddess glanced at Amber and Rory. "Are you the only other...um, creatures here?"

"Yes, Gaia," Amber said. "And he knows about us too. Chloe has quite a story for you if you have time..."

Gaia dropped Ryan's hand. "I never have enough time. You know that."

She turned her stare on Chloe. "Just give me the highlights, girlie."

Chloe cringed at the patronizing label. "I'm not a girlie. I'm a firefighter. And if I don't allow the men at my firehouse to call me that, I shouldn't let you get away with it either." She tipped up her chin defiantly.

When Mother Nature's eyes rounded and she rose a few inches off the floor, Chloe coughed and added, "Meanin' no disrespect to you, *Goddess*."

Gaia's expression softened and she floated back to the floor. Then she tilted her head and started tapping her lip as she circled Chloe.

"Um, Gaia? Is there something wrong?"

"Hmmm? Uh, no. Something is kind of right, actually."

Chloe was relieved but confused at the same time. Should she ask the all-powerful one to explain herself, or would she share her thoughts whenever she was ready?

At last, Mother Nature halted, facing the men in the room. "I know you're celebrating, but I'd like to borrow the *females* for a few minutes."

Rory inclined his head. "As you wish, Goddess. There is a comfortable sitting area on the second floor. Perhaps you could all have tea…"

Mother Nature swiped the whiskey decanter off the bar. "Or something stronger." She strode to the stairs. "*Ladies,* follow me."

⁓⁓⁓

Mother Nature's proposal caught Chloe completely off guard. "You want me to be the what?"

Gaia leaned back against the padded banquet and crossed her arms. "The modern muse of assertiveness. Imagine how you could help battered women…or men. I've been wanting someone like you for quite a while."

"Someone like me? What do you mean?"

"Someone who can assess a dangerous situation quickly and stand up to a bully, while encouraging the victim to do or say what he or she has to—especially if children are involved."

"What makes you think I'd be good at that?"

Mother Nature let out a long sigh. "I think I just answered that question."

"But I'm a firefighter, not a police officer. Wouldn't it be better to have a female cop in that position?"

Mother Nature leaned her elbow on the breakfast table and rested her chin in her cupped hand. "You're all I've got, girlie."

Chloe bristled but spoke in an even tone. "I asked you not to call me that."

Mother Nature pointed at her. "There. That's what I'm talking about. If you can stand up to me, you can be assertive with anyone. I think you'd make an excellent role model for men and women who never learned to respect their sovereignty and demand their safety."

She couldn't really think of another reason why she couldn't do this—other than that she didn't *want* to! Firefighters were required to assist the public regardless of the circumstances they found when they showed up. People had been known to call the fire department instead of involving the police in all sorts of trouble.

She tried one last attempt to assert her own right to refuse. "Mother Nature, I must respectfully decline."

The Goddess of All waved her hand dismissively. "I knew you'd say that. You'll tell me you're too busy. You want to concentrate on fighting fires with your handsome fiancé. You want to go back to Ireland and rebuild your castle…"

"Wait. What?"

"Oh dear. Did I spill the beans?"

Amber cleared her throat. "Goddess. I know you like to have your modern muses nearby in Boston, but couldn't she operate from anywhere?"

Chloe rose. "Wait just a minute. First of all, who said I wanted this job? And how did you know I was thinking of returning to—" Suddenly an idea dawned on Chloe.

Mother Nature exchanged a smile with Amber.

In her stunned silence she realized Ryan could come with her to Ballyhoo. They could restore the castle together. She had enjoyed working on the B and B and he'd have the sea view he'd always wanted. Best of all, he wouldn't have to alter the face she fell in love with.

"I—I need to think about this. And more importantly, I need to discuss this with my fiancé."

Mother Nature nodded once. "I'll give you a few days, but no more. Tell Amber when you make your decision and I'll meet you back here."

Chloe took a deep breath and before she had a chance to let it out, Gaia was gone. She blinked. "Does the goddess do that often?"

"Do what? Disappear?"

"Yeah. Let's start with that."

Amber patted her hand. "You'll get used to it."

Chloe folded her arms. "Or *not*. I still have a choice, don't I?"

"Of course you do. Everyone has free will. She planned it that way."

"It seems like she could easily do away with that and make the world an ideal place."

Amber's expression became somber and she folded her hands in her lap. "That's just it. She wants us to do it for ourselves. She watches what's going on and knows human beings are hurting each other—on many levels. But she still hopes we'll figure that out and correct it on our own."

Chloe held her forehead. "Me head hurts."

"I'll get you an aspirin." Then Amber's eyes twinkled. "Imagine never having a headache again...unless you want one."

"Huh? Why would I want one?"

"Exactly." Then Amber disappeared into thin air.

"Shite," Chloe muttered.

When Amber returned with two tablets and a glass of water, Chloe had to ask. "So, you never get sick? Unless for some foolish reason you want to?"

"That's right. As a modern muse you would be a minor goddess. You'd be able to do everything I can do."

Chloe couldn't help being intrigued. "Including instant air travel without a plane?"

"Yes. Including that."

"Would I ever be able to stick the landing without wobbling back and forth?"

Amber laughed. "There will be a lot to get used to, but she'll assign you to another muse who can teach you everything you need to know. Remember Euterpe?"

"Your friend who loved listenin' to our folk songs?"

"Yup. She was my muse trainer."

"No wonder you were so irritated when she preferred our company to yours."

Rory yelled up the stairs. "When are you lasses comin' back down? We're waitin' patiently for our toast."

Chloe chuckled. "I'm tempted to act the idjit and bring him a piece of toast."

Amber grinned and produced a plate with two pieces of dry toast and a pat of butter on the side.

"Aw, you're makin' this decision harder and harder."

Chapter 20

RYAN WATCHED RORY LAUGH WHEN HE WAS PRESENTED with the plate of toast. Brother and sister had a wonderful way of expressing affection through teasing. He'd hate to take Chloe from her family, but if they were to stay together without his getting plastic surgery, they would have to move far away.

She glanced at him. "You seem...I don't know...serious, all of a sudden."

He took her aside and whispered, "There are still details we have to discuss. I was just hoping this celebration wasn't premature."

"Premature!" Rory cried.

"Crap. You dragons have superior hearing, don't you?"

"Never mind that," Rory said. "What's premature about toasting an engagement? Did you propose to me sister or didn't you?"

"I did. And I meant it. We just have a few complications to work through."

Chloe nodded solemnly. "He's right. There's the small matter of his face."

Rory rose and examined Ryan up close. "What's wrong with his face?"

Ryan leaned away. "Nothing, thanks. Just that it's the same one I had before I died."

"Ah. And you're afraid of scarin' people...like you

did when you came here tonight. It sure looked as if Chloe had brought a ghost with her."

"Exactly. You took it a lot better than most people would."

Rory nodded. "I imagine a lot of people would faint or run screamin' from you."

"Yeah." Ryan scratched the back of his neck. "I'm afraid you're right. My family has had to deal with this before, but usually the person just moves away and starts over."

"Is that what you're plannin' to do?" Rory's brow wrinkled and he held his sister's gaze. "Move away and take me sister with you?"

"I...don't know. That's one possibility."

Rory sat back down in his chair as Ryan and Chloe took their seats on the couch. "Are there other options?" he asked.

"Yeah. The family mentioned my getting plastic surgery to look like a cousin who fights wildfires in Arizona. He wants to do something else now—maybe in South America. Then I could take over his identity and get a job here—not in the same firehouse, though. It would be too easy to slip up and say something a stranger wouldn't know. But I might be able to get a job in one of the nearby suburbs."

Rory whistled long and low. "That's drastic. Even in Ireland, dragons have faked their deaths or moved around and reinvented themselves when their longevity attracts attention. We're only a small handful, but we've been doin' it for centuries. And the whole country is only the size of your state of Indiana."

Ryan gazed at his feet. "It's true that America is

bigger, but it's harder to disappear here. Everyone leaves a paper trail. Not to mention firefighters have their fingerprints on file and it would be easy to grab a bit of DNA from their gear."

"I'm beginning to see the problem." Rory rubbed his chin and looked to be deep in thought. He opened his mouth to say something, then closed it and shook his head. He opened his mouth again, then did the same thing and sighed.

"It's not up to you to think of an answer to this dilemma. Chloe and I will find a way to solve this." He took her hand and gave it a squeeze. "Together."

"I have some things to talk to you about too," Chloe said. "Mother Nature just dropped a bit of a bombshell on me."

Amber smiled. "I was hoping you'd share that with both of them."

"It's only right that I do. Rory is the crown prince and Ryan is to be my mate."

Both men gave Chloe their full attention.

"It seems that Mother Nature wants more modern muses, and she has offered me a job." She took a deep breath. "She wants me to be the muse of assertiveness. Now don't get all excited. I'm not keen on that job…"

Neither of them interrupted as she hastened on.

"She usually wants her muses in Boston, but Amber said there's no reason I couldn't do the job from anywhere in the world."

"But you said you don't really *want* the job," Amber reminded her.

"Too right. It sounds bloody awful." She faced Ryan

and took both of his hands. "It might solve a problem for both of us if we were to move to Ballyhoo. Before I knew you were still alive, I was considerin' going home. We have cousins with designs on our ancestral castle. Without Rory there, Shannon is vulnerable."

"Why? Is she helpless?"

Chloe and Rory exchanged a sad look. Rory spoke up. "Me youngest sister is softhearted, and her husband is human. All they'd have to do is hold him hostage and she'd do anythin' they asked."

"*If* the clans reunited, Conlan would be next in line," Chloe explained. "And that's a big if. But according to his next youngest brother Aiden, he said he'd abdicate if I wanted to marry one of 'em and become queen—or rather the crown princess unless we discover our elders are deceased."

Ryan shot to his feet. "Marry your cousin? That's illegal."

Rory shrugged. "If you go back far enough, there are plenty of instances of cousins marryin' each other to keep or unite royal bloodlines."

"But none of them have proposed…" Ryan glanced at the other three in the room as they looked at the ceiling, the floor, or anywhere except at him. "*Have they?*"

"Aiden has," Chloe said. "I turned him down."

"I should hope so," Ryan said. "This isn't the middle ages, and he's still your cousin."

"He is. And a feckin' nasty one too. I wouldn't marry him if he were the last dragon on earth."

Ryan relaxed somewhat, then stiffened again. "But you could have children with him."

She sighed. "And that's what he wants me to do.

He'd keep me barefoot and pregnant, livin' in a crumblin' castle. I can't think of anythin' I'd rather do less."

A stony silence followed, broken by the doorbell.

"I'll get it," Amber said.

From the other room, all three paranormals heard her mutter under her breath, "Speak of the devil…"

—~~~—

"Aiden! What brings you here?" Amber let the Ulster cousin into the foyer.

He used his Irish charm, making a comment about her wonderful hospitality and how he couldn't stay away.

Chloe groaned and shot to her feet. She jogged to the entryway, hoping to stop Amber from welcoming him too far inside.

"Chloe, me darlin'. You're lookin' well."

"What do you want, Aiden?" She knew she was being rude, but she didn't care. He'd better not be trying to talk her into the stupid marriage idea again.

"Is that any way to welcome a man who's crossed an ocean to see you?"

"If you came to see me, specifically, I'll have to disappoint you. I was just going out."

She sensed, rather than felt, Ryan coming up behind her.

"Ah, so this must be the boyfriend," Aiden said. He stuck out his hand, and Ryan stepped around Chloe to shake it.

"Ryan," he said. "And I take it you're Chloe's *cousin?*" he said, emphasizing the relation.

"I am. And proud of it too."

Chloe cleared her throat. "Forgive me for not making introductions. Aiden Arish, this is my *fiancé*, Ryan Fierro."

Aiden's eyes rounded. "Fiancé? But *we're* to be married, luv."

"Whatever gave you that feckin' stupid idea? You asked, and I said no."

"Ah," he laughed. "You can't fool me, luv. Many women say no with their mouths, but yes with their eyes and hearts."

She stepped so close to him they were nose to nose. "Read my eyes. I said no and I meant no. If you ask me again, I'll say no until the lambs return."

Aiden took a step back and frowned. Then he quickly pasted a smile on his face. "Hee-hee. Me brothers said you'd play hard to get."

"Not 'hard to get,' you stubborn fool. Not getable. At. All."

By this time Rory was standing beside his sister. Smoke was wafting up toward the ceiling and it was hard to say which dragon it was coming from. The crown prince inserted himself between the two cousins who were squaring off.

"None of that, now. I won't have you brawlin' in me house."

"We won't be resortin' to that," Aiden said. "I just need to borrow your sister for a wee bit, and I'm sure I can reason with her."

Ryan wrapped a protective hand around Chloe's waist and practically clamped her to his side.

Rory burst out laughing. "To be sure, you'd try. But I know me sister better than you do. Trust me. She gave you her answer and it will not change."

"How can you take her side?" Aiden roared. "You're the head of our clan. You can order her to marry for the sake of the…for the sake of our…". He glanced at Ryan, obviously wondering how much to say without violating Mother Nature's number one rule.

"I know she can only have children with another dragon," Ryan said.

Aiden's dark eyebrows almost hit his widow's peak. "He knows?" Then he turned his righteous anger on Chloe. "You told a human? And you-know-who didn't smite you—or send you back to Iceland? Or something?"

Chloe tipped her nose in the air. "Who says me fiancé is human?"

Aiden covered his mouth and mumbled through his fingers, "Oh, shite. What the hell is he?"

"He's someone who loves Chloe," Ryan said. "And she loves me. If you truly care about her, you'll want only her happiness."

Aiden turned his back on that logic and addressed Rory. "But what about duty? What about the preservation of our species?"

"Hang duty," Chloe shouted. "It's my life and I plan to do what I like, *not what's expected of me.*"

Rory tipped his head toward her. "And there you have it, Cousin."

"You're going to let *her* make this important decision? What kind of prince are you?"

Rory's rare openmouthed grin showed his fangs. "I'm the kind who wants peace in me kingdom. Now, if you cannot give me that, I suggest you find another place to stay."

"Mayhaps I will."

Chloe relaxed for the first time since her cousin's arrival. She looked up at Ryan and he smiled at her. She wrapped her arms around his waist and snuggled into his chest. He let go of his death grip on her and stroked her back with his warm fingers.

Aiden was about to leave when the doorbell rang again.

"Excuse me," Amber said. She strode to the door and gasped in happy surprise. "Candy Marie? What are you doing here?"

"Can't a former neighbor and coworker come to visit?"

"Of course!" Amber glared at the family group as if to say, "Behave."

Chloe was fine now. As long as her brother had her back, and Ryan had the rest of her, she could ignore Aiden and his antics.

Candy stepped into the foyer right into Aiden's personal space. The two of them stared at each other as if struck dumb. Then they smiled as if recognizing a long-lost friend.

Candy recovered first. "I—um…didn't realize you had company."

"Oh," Amber said. "This is Aiden Arish, Rory's and Chloe's first cousin from Northern Ireland. I *think* he was just leaving."

Aiden took Candy's fingers and placed a kiss on the back of her hand. "Or I could stay and get to know your lovely friend—if you don't mind, that is."

Candy grinned. "I don't mind a bit."

The sparks of mutual attraction were practically pinging off the walls.

"Stay, Aiden," Chloe said. "Ryan and I need to… um…"

"Go to my place," Ryan said helpfully.

"Yes. That," Chloe agreed.

Amber and Rory smiled at each other. "I'll get your coats."

"No need," Chloe said. "We can get them. You pay attention to your guests. I insist."

Amber kissed Chloe on both cheeks and Rory shook Ryan's hand. "Good to see you both. We'll have you over for dinner soon."

She couldn't help glancing over her shoulder at the love-struck couple being welcomed into the living room. Aiden had his hand on the small of Candy's back. She hoped her cousin would soon know what true love was like. Maybe someday they'd be able to laugh about how absurd this evening could have been.

─────

On their walk toward the South End, Ryan realized he needed Chloe all to himself for a while. Not that he'd thought for a second her brother might order her to marry her cousin…well, maybe a second, but that was all.

"Are you up for a little experiment?" he asked her.

She slowed her pace and leaned back to see around his hoodie and take a good look at his face. "What kind of experiment?"

"The good kind." He smiled, not only to put her at ease, but also in hopes that they might accomplish a couple of important goals.

"I'm listenin'."

"Well, instead of passing this lovely big hotel here, what if we just go inside and get a room?" He nodded toward the fancy place next to the civic center—right across from their fire station.

"We might be able to afford a broom closet."

Ryan laughed. "Don't worry about the expense. I have an idea to make the experience worth it."

"Oh? Do tell…" She smiled and waggled her eyebrows.

"I want you to practice coming quietly."

Her face fell. "Oh. I'm sorry. I didn't realize—"

He squeezed her hand. "Hold that thought. First, I want you to know, I love your screams. It's like applause to me."

Her face colored and she looked at her feet.

Before she could take that in any way other than a compliment, he forged on. "I just want to be sure we can visit your sister's cottage, my parents' guest room, or your brother's B and B without having to stay celibate the whole time."

She continued to watch her feet, but her cheeks bunched up like she was smiling—or grimacing.

At last she looked up and answered him. "That's supposin' I can succeed. Mayhaps you'll simply have to take your own pleasure and leave me wantin' a bit."

"I never want to leave you wanting." He leaned over and kissed her hair.

She snuggled closer. "I guess the sayin' 'practice makes perfect' might apply here. So gettin' a little practice might be worth doin' in the long run. But aren't you supposed to stay out of sight in case you're recognized?"

He frowned. "Yeah. I doubt anyone we know will be staying at the hotel."

"Darlin', your face was all over the news for days. Just goin' out for a stroll is dangerous. At least it's dark out now, but come tomorrow mornin'…" She let out a long sigh. "As much fun as practicin' sounds, the panic

your reappearance would create might be worse than
my screamin'."

"Damn," he muttered.

She glanced at him impishly. "We can go to my
place. Everyone there already knows I'm in no danger
when I scream in ecstasy."

He immediately turned her around and began walking toward her place as she laughed.

⎯⎯⎯⎯

They barely made it to her room before all of their
clothes had been removed and flung in different directions along the way. Chloe leaned on his chest as he held
her and tumbled backward onto the bed. They bounced
and she giggled.

When had she become a giggler? Somewhere along
the line, she'd lost that angry edge that kept people at
arms' length. Fortunately Ryan had forced his way past
her barriers long enough to see the lonely girl inside.

She hadn't felt lonely since he returned to her, and
she hoped she'd never feel that empty again. As much as
she loved her family, it wasn't the same. They were creating their own families now, and even though it didn't
look like there would be any nieces or nephews for her
to spoil, she could be completely happy with whatever
children came from Ryan's large family.

He cupped her head and kissed her deeply. She practically sighed into his mouth.

"I love you, Chloe Arish."

"And I love you, Ryan Fierro." Without any prompt-
ing, she sat up and straddled him. She took his member
in her hand and stroked the long, hard shaft as he

groaned in pleasure. She was plenty wet and wouldn't need much in the way of attention to come. Why wait when the goal was to practice the best part?

She rose up on her knees and positioned herself over his erection.

"Don't you want some foreplay?" he asked.

"Maybe later." She sank down onto his rod and moaned in joy as it filled her. She began rocking in a slow, undulating rhythm, which he easily matched.

"That would make it afterplay."

When he used the pad of his thumb to rub her clit, a jolt of sensation shot through her, surprising her with its intensity. He kept it up and before long she was bucking and moaning in joy. She quickly remembered to rein in the noise factor without losing the blissful feeling.

Her body trembled with the effort of holding in her screams. She whimpered, gasped, and eventually got herself under control. The sensation built to the breaking point and as she let go, soaring in ecstasy while moaning softly. *Oh me heavens…*

Ryan joined her with his own climax. She could tell because his movements slowed, stopped, and then his hips jerked several times. His eyes were scrunched shut and his straight white teeth gritted together.

Eventually, he opened his eyes and panted. He took one look at her face and grinned. Cupping her face in his hands, he said, "You did it!"

"Did I?"

"You couldn't hear yourself? Or *not* hear yourself?"

"Well, no. But for a time there, I felt like I left my body. I could have done anythin' at that point. I might have danced a jig and I wouldn't know it."

"Oh, you danced a jig all right." He pulled her face to his and practically crushed her lips in a hard kiss.

She chuckled and rolled off to curl up beside him. The two of them lay there for a few minutes, breathing heavily.

Eventually, he swept her blonde bangs away from her eyes and looked serious. "Did you mean what you said?"

"I don't know. I say a lot of things…" She grinned and hoped he'd elaborate.

He tapped the end of her pert nose. "And fortunately, you mean what you say most of the time. But there was something you said that concerned me. I don't want to put off asking about it."

"Okay. Ask."

"Mother Nature's offer… You said it sounded bloody awful. Why would you take a job like that? Are you even considering it? Is it because of me?"

She caressed his chest hair. "No. I'm not taking the job and you have nothin' to do with it. I honestly don't think I'd be the best fit. I'd probably fly into a rage and beat up a bully who was threatening a woman or child. What kind of example would that set when talkin' about assertive nonviolence?"

He nodded. "I can understand that. I might be tempted to do the same."

He adjusted his position so he could gaze into her eyes. "I'm relieved. I was afraid you might be getting into something you couldn't get out of. Something you'd hate and grow to resent."

"I could say the same for you."

He opened his mouth to speak, and then closed it. Apparently he wasn't ready to share what he was thinking regarding his own situation. At least, not yet.

After a short silence, he gathered her close. "Want to *practice* again? After all, they say practice makes perfect."

"Indeed. I think I can use all the practice I can get."

———◇———

The following morning, Ryan's phone rang. He was blindly patting around the bed for it until Chloe grabbed it off the nightstand and handed it to him.

He squinted at the number displayed by caller ID. "It's my parents' house," he mumbled, then sat up suddenly. "Shit. What time is it?"

Chloe glanced at the clock next to her and said, "Uh-oh. Ten a.m."

Ryan answered without the niceties. "I'm fine, Mom. Just fell asleep over at Chloe's place."

"For cryin' out loud, Ryan!" Chloe could hear his father's voice clearly. "Your mother is too upset to talk. We didn't know what had happened to you."

Then Mrs. Fierro's voice could be heard in the background saying, "He's okay?"

"Yeah, he's fine," his father muttered. "Just stayed at his girlfriend's house last night."

Mrs. Fierro took over as if she'd grabbed the phone from her husband. "A phone call would have been nice. We've been worried sick."

"I'm sorry. Chloe and I were—um, distracted."

She humphed. "I'll bet. Is she there?"

Ryan looked over at her, but didn't hand her the phone. "Yeah…"

"May I speak with her please?"

"Why? So you can yell at her too?"

"Of course not," Mrs. Fierro said. "I want to invite her to tea. I'd like to get to know my future daughter."

Daughter. Not daughter-in-law. Chloe's heart was touched. She nodded toward the phone and stuck her hand out.

Ryan frowned but handed it over.

"Mrs. Fierro?" Chloe said.

"Oh, there you are, dear. I was hoping you could find some time to come over by yourself. Now that Ryan is stuck there until dark, this might be a good day for it."

She glanced at Ryan who simply shrugged. *Okay. He's not reacting like I might be met at the door with a noose.* "Sure. What time today?"

"Why don't you come at noon? Does that give you enough time to, um—get dressed?"

Chloe laughed. "At work I can get dressed in the dark in sixty seconds."

"Wonderful. I'll see you at noon."

They said pleasant good-byes, then Chloe handed the phone back to Ryan. He apologized again for worrying them, then hung up.

Chloe rolled out of bed and grabbed her bathrobe. "Is this invitation something I should be concerned about?"

"Probably not." Ryan was gathering his clothes, which had landed in the far corners of her bedroom.

"*Probably not?* What does that mean?"

"It means I can't imagine my mother wanting to harm you. Chances are she really just wants to get to know you better."

"Oh." Chloe felt a little stupid for worrying about a five-foot-nothing older woman doing anything to her.

She could certainly take care of herself, and would probably pose more of a threat than anyone.

"I'll grab a shower," Ryan said. "Unless you want to come with me?" He gave her a wolfish grin.

"What? I didn't get enough feckin' practice last night?" She couldn't make her face match her stern words.

He roamed over to her and took her in his arms. While he was kissing her, he cupped her ass and lifted her off the floor. She wrapped her legs around him and held on as he carried her to the bathroom.

Chapter 21

"CHLOE, DEAR. I'M SO GLAD YOU COULD COME," MRS. Fierro said as she opened the door.

"Thank you for inviting me." She really had nothing to say after that, so she hoped her fiancé's mother could keep a conversation going.

"Let me take your coat."

Chloe shrugged out of her navy pea coat, noticing the item she got in Iceland two years ago was beginning to show some wear. If nothing else, she could invite Mrs. Fierro to go shopping with her. The woman seemed to have impeccable taste.

"Is Mr. Fierro at home?"

"No. He went off to visit his cronies. It's just the two of us."

That should have made Chloe a little more relaxed, but it didn't help. She was still plenty nervous.

"Let's sit in the kitchen," Mrs. Fierro said. "I have Irish breakfast tea. Is that all right?"

Okay. So this is to be a casual inquisition. "Perfect. Thank you, Mrs. Fierro."

"We'll have to do something about that," the matriarch said.

"Do something? Um, about what?"

"Well, I can't have you calling me Mrs. Fierro, but it's a little too soon to call me Mom. Call me Gabriella— for now."

"All right." She took a deep breath and watched as Mrs. Fierro—Gabriella—set a teapot on the stove to boil. Now she was tongue-tied again. Maybe instead of waiting for the inevitable questions, she should just start talking and steer the conversation. "So, you and Mr. Fierro—"

"Antonio," Gabriella corrected.

"Oh. Okay. So when you and Antonio were dating, did he tell you his family were phoenixes?"

Ryan's mother let out a merry tinkling laugh. "Oh my, no. He waited until our wedding night."

"Your weddin' night? You mean it was too late, if you changed your mind?"

Gabriella returned to her seat and placed a hand over Chloe's. "True love doesn't change its mind, sweetheart. It changes *you*."

She understood that. Chloe had changed a lot since meeting Ryan. She thought back to the prickly, surly girl she'd been in training and wondered why he'd wanted anything to do with her. She had done everything she could to push him away. Now she'd fight fang and claw to keep him with her.

"How did you take it? I mean, at first. Obviously you got over it, because here you are, several sons later."

Gabriella's smile slipped a bit and she squirmed. "I didn't quite understand for a while. I thought he was joking." Then the smile was firmly back in place. "He tends to do that, you know. Make jokes, I mean. It's one of the things I love about him."

"Yes, I noticed." Chloe relaxed and smiled. "It's quite charming, actually."

"That he is." Gabriella sighed, but at least she was

still smiling. "So, I was wondering how much Ryan has told you about how this family operates."

"Operates? You mean when someone gets hurt?"

Gabriella let out a long laugh that time. "No, Chloe. I meant how we work things out."

"Oh." *I feel like a feckin' idjit sometimes.*

Gabriella didn't wait for Chloe to recover from her embarrassment. She just forged on, which helped. "The eldest son is always in charge of the nest."

"Nest?"

"Just an expression, dear, meaning our home and family."

"Oh. No, he didn't mention any of that."

Gabriella's face fell. "I was afraid he wouldn't."

"Why? What's wrong?"

After a long inhale and exhale, Mrs. Fierro explained, "Ryan is actually our eldest. He had an accident when he was a child and came back at about the same age as our Gabe was at the time."

"Yes. He told me about that. So, it looks like he and Gabe are twins. Is that what you tell people? That they're fraternal twins?"

"Not if we can help it. We don't share details of our family at all unless we have to. The fewer prying eyes, the better."

Chloe nodded sagely. "That's been our policy as well. How much did Ryan tell you about me?"

"Not a lot. Just that you're quite old." She slapped a hand over her own mouth. "Oh! I'm sorry. I shouldn't have put it that way."

Chloe chuckled. "No need to worry. A girl can't be sensitive about age when she's been around for a millennium."

Gabriella's eyes rounded. "A millennium! Truly?"

Chloe smirked. "Give or take a few decades. My brother is the eldest, and then there's me, and the youngest is Shannon. Rory raised us, for the most part. Our parents had to leave after the family gained some unwanted attention and people began noticing how long the king and queen had been sitting on the throne."

"King and queen?" Mrs. Fierro exclaimed. "Does that make you a…"

"Princess? Yes. It's funny, but Ryan's first nickname for me was princess. Long before he knew."

"But he knows now…" Gabriella prodded.

"Yes. He's met my family. Well, what there is of it, to be sure. My parents could still be alive, so we don't know if my brother is the king or crown prince. He insists on keepin' the title prince and only among family when absolutely necessary…probably so he doesn't attract attention and have to explain our longevity too."

"But he will raise some eyebrows eventually. Phoenixes live for about five hundred years, and that's without reincarnating. Eventually, the younger generation takes over and the elders move away."

Chloe nodded. "Yes. Ryan explained that too."

"Did he also tell you he's the one expected to take over here?" Mrs. Fierro gave her a piercing stare. She didn't know what to make of that.

"He mentioned that he *was*, until his accident."

Gabriella folded her arms and said, "Humph. So he didn't share the plans being made to protect himself and the family?"

Chloe grew uncomfortably hot and loosened the scarf

around her neck. "He mentioned somethin' about plastic surgery and takin' on a cousin's identity."

The matriarch relaxed a bit. "Good. I'm glad I'm not the one who had to break it to you."

"Break what to me? That the man I love will look like someone else for the rest of his life?"

Gabriella chewed her lower lip. "I was afraid of that reaction. I knew you were taking it all too calmly."

"Oh? I haven't decided how I feel yet. There might be an alternative to discuss first."

Gabriella's forehead knit. "An alternative? Like what?"

"Like Ryan and I can go to my home in Ballyhoo where nobody knows him. He won't have to do anythin' drastic to his face and if he wants to fight fires, we can both be part of the volunteer fire department. Mayhaps we can even improve it."

"But where would you live?" Gabriella asked.

"We can restore the castle. I helped me brother remodel his Beacon Street brownstone and enjoyed doing it. You probably know that all Ryan wanted the whole time he was in Afghanistan was a sea view. The castle will certainly have one. It's built into the cliffs."

"He said that?"

"He kept a picture from a magazine in his wallet. It was from some Boston architectural or real estate magazine."

"Really…" Gabriella looked off in the distance as if she were trying to process some startling new information.

"I know you all want Ryan to stay here and be head of the family, but he said he'd have to do that from the suburbs anyway. He couldn't risk messing up and anyone finding out who he really was."

Gabriella held up one hand as if she couldn't take in

any more information. Chloe was about to ask why one of the other six brothers couldn't take the job, but she didn't want to upset the woman further.

"I'm sorry, Chloe. I'm afraid it's too late. Decisions have been made."

Chloe shot to her feet. "Made by who—or is it whom? Oh, hell…Does Ryan know?"

Gabriella's lips thinned. "I've said too much."

Chloe marched to the closet where her coat was. Her *possible* future mother-in-law followed her.

"Where are you going?"

"I'm going to confront my fiancé."

"No, darling, no. I don't want to stir up trouble between you and Ryan. He has a duty. It isn't his fault."

Chloe squared off with the Fierro matriarch. "Yeah? Well I have a duty too, and I just told my family to shove it."

She grabbed her coat and shrugged into it. Mrs. Fierro didn't say anything else as she stormed out of the house.

———

Ryan was surprised to see Chloe back so soon…and so angry. She slammed the door and faced him with her hands on her hips.

"Did you know?"

He squinted. "Know what?" *What is she talking about?*

"Your family has already decided your fate. According to your mother, the feckin' plastic surgery idea and your livin' in the suburbs is the only answer. Why can't one of your brothers take over? You have enough of them."

Ryan rose and strolled over to her slowly. "Did she say anything about appointments being scheduled?"

"No. But she said it was decided. That it was your duty. Like you had no say in the matter."

Ryan couldn't say anything to reassure Chloe. If the heads of the Boston and Arizona families had locked down the decision, there was little he could do...other than fly away, and he wouldn't resort to such cowardice.

"Well?" she demanded.

He wrenched his attention back to the woman he wanted by his side for the rest of his life and wondered if she'd asked a specific question. "Well what?"

"Can't one of your brothers take over? What if you weren't available?"

He was about to speak but she held a hand up, halting his thought, and continued what she was saying. "I'm asking a hypothetical question."

Ryan scratched his head and started to pace. "There's nothing saying Jayce couldn't do it. He's the one born right after me. My father might not think he has the personality for it, but Miguel would welcome the job. Plus he's married. Jayce doesn't seem ready to settle down anytime soon—although I have seen him with Diana more than once."

"Does the head of the family have to be married?"

"It's preferred." Ryan remembered how his family had encouraged him to push forward with Melanie, even when he was having doubts. It was *much* preferred. They took it as a sign of maturity, and maturity was what a good leader needed.

But Jayce seemed to be getting along with Diana quite well. A ray of hope began to peek out of the darkness, but he was afraid to let Chloe see it just yet.

"What would happen if we were *not* to marry?" She was already working the ring off her finger.

"No, Chloe. Don't do that."

"Why not? If you have to be married to take over as head of the family and let your parents retire to Florida—or wherever it is your older birds fly off to— let's wait until they come to their feckin' senses."

"It's not like that. It's...complicated."

She strode right up to him and challenged him with nothing more than the look in her eyes. He'd seen his mother twist his father's wing with nothing more than "the look."

He sighed. "I'll have to wait until after dark and meet with my father."

"Why wait? Invite him here."

"Right now?"

"Why not? Your mother said he was just visitin' his mates. I could let you two have the apartment and make myself scarce in the paranormal club across the hall."

Ryan mulled that over. Trying to discuss a change of plans would be difficult under any circumstances, but maybe here—away from his home—would be a good idea. The possible interruptions would be cut to almost nothing. And being away from *his* nest might be enough to put his father off balance and force him to think out of the box.

"I'll call him. Why don't you go to the club now, and I'll call you when I have something more I can tell you."

"Fine. But if he refuses, do me a favor?"

Ryan inhaled deeply. "What's that?"

"Consider defying the order. I know it's not your nature. You followed orders in the military and you do it at work all the time. But I think he may have to see how strongly you feel." Then she straightened her shoulders. "And I'd like to see that too."

She spun on her heel and marched out the door.

He didn't try to stop her. He needed a few minutes to get his own mind straight before he called his father. He'd never considered outright refusal. To do so would be unprecedented. He might be exiled. He could be giving up his whole family and everything he'd ever known for one woman. How sure was he of her love?

He wandered around her apartment. There weren't a lot of personal items. He guessed she'd given up most of those to come to America. He examined the few things she did have though.

Books. Her bookshelves were nearly full. He perused the titles and found many written about America and prominent Americans. However there were also titles by beloved Irish novelists like James Joyce and Oscar Wilde. From that he gathered she embraced change but cherished her roots. There were times when she seemed a little nostalgic. Perhaps she was a bit homesick, but she never complained. Never compared the countries.

The Irish flag stretched across the wall over her bed, and he'd always thought it was just a decorative touch, placed where a headboard ought to be. Now he realized it may have been more.

When she'd mentioned a solution that would serve them both, she talked of going "home" to Ballyhoo. She spoke lovingly of her desire to restore their ancient castle, but not to rule over it as *Queen Chloe*—a title she could have for the asking. Instead, she'd mentioned improving the village's volunteer fire department.

She was the kind of truly noble woman he wanted in his life. She'd had to fight for her place among the brotherhood, and before long she had their hearts and their loyalty. She would be a fine asset in *any* family.

He had never thought about all she'd be giving up by joining his.

He dug his phone out of his back pocket and dialed his father's number. Oddly enough, his father wasn't number one on his speed dial. Chloe was. And number two was the station.

His family might say he had his priorities screwed up, but he knew…they were exactly the way they should be, and he didn't want to change them.

Chapter 22

"CHLOE! WHAT BRINGS YOU HERE?" DRAKE LAID down his pool cue. He seemed to be the only one at the club at the moment.

"What? I can't visit the club I belong to...and live across the hall from?"

"Of course you can. In fact, I'm glad to see you. I heard you had a helluva time at the Harrison Hall fire."

"No one injured. I call that a win."

Drake nodded. "I do too. You made sure a mother and child got out. And apparently no one knew they were there."

She shrugged. "It's all part of the job."

A second later, they weren't alone any more. Mother Nature appeared on the other side of the pool table.

"Speaking of jobs..." the all-powerful one said, eyeing Chloe.

"I'm not takin' the job you offered, Goddess, but I had a thought I'd like to share with you."

Gaia frowned at first, then her expression softened. "Ah! The muse of fire safety. I can see why you'd think of that."

"Jaysus, can't anyone surprise you?"

She shrugged one shoulder. "Not really. So, shall we discuss this here—since you're both firefighting dragons? Or would you prefer a little more privacy?"

Chloe glanced at Drake and thought he might be able

to understand and even support her cause. "I can say what I'd like to right here."

"Would you like me to leave?" Drake asked.

"No," both women said at once.

Chloe straightened her back and said, "I'd like to propose a modern muse position be created for fire safety because so much about heating and cooking has changed since ancient times. For instance, we now have oil burners, stoves, and ovens using either electricity or gas, all of which can cause huge fires. Even matches are a relatively modern invention."

Mother Nature wandered around the room, tapping her lower lip. "Go on…"

Chloe took a deep breath. "As I understand it, all Bliss has to do is lean over someone's shoulder and whisper, 'Maybe you shouldn't send that email…' or in Amber's case, 'stay calm and contact the air traffic control tower.'"

Gaia halted. "That's putting it a little too simply."

"I know. There are plenty of things I'd need to learn about how it's done, but even if I only knew that children were playing with matches, I could whisper in their parent's ear to check on the kids and see what they're up to…"

One corner of Gaia's lip rose. "So, it sounds like you're volunteering for the job."

"Uh…no. I didn't say that." She quickly looked to Drake and whispered, "Did I?"

He smirked. "She has a way of getting people to volunteer…but it's probably not too late to back out if you want to."

Mother Nature just cocked her head, as if waiting for Chloe to make up her mind.

"I—um…I need to speak to my fiancé about it, and—"

"Didn't you already do that?"

"Well, we started to, but then we got, um…distracted." Chloe bit her lower lip and her face heated.

Drake laughed. "Give her a break, Goddess. After all, she's just experiencing the natural urges you gave her in the first place."

"Oh snap, dragon…" Mother Nature snapped her fingers, laughed at her own joke, and returned her attention to Chloe. "I'll give you one more day. The idea is a good one, but this is your last opportunity to serve me and the modern world."

"Wait! I have a question."

Gaia rolled her eyes and sighed. "Of course you do. What is it?"

"Well, you usually reward your muses with some sort of dream come true…I've heard."

"Ah! Here it comes. What's in it for you, fire-girl?"

"I was hoping you could make it so I could have children with my fiancé. It seems to be very important to his family."

Gaia stumbled back a step. "Your fiancé, the *phoenix*?"

"Well, yes. I know we're not exactly the same species, but couldn't you make it possible?"

"Possible? How? You want me to create a mutation, just to smooth the way with your in-laws? Look, girlie, there's no such thing as a dragnix or a phoegan—and I don't want to make one. Got it?"

Chloe dropped her gaze. "I understand. I was just hoping…"

"Forget it. Not gonna happen."

"As a goddess, would I be able to change my fiancé's

face without surgery so he can visit Boston when he wants to? And then change it back?"

"Yes. Now I'm going to leave before I begin to think you only wanted the job to get the perks."

"No. I truly want to help. There are advances in fire safety being developed all the time. I could encourage inventors not to give up. Fire extinguishers are good, but they could be better…"

Drake put a hand on her shoulder and shook his head. When she turned back Gaia was gone.

"Damn it! I wanted to explain…"

"She already knows. She wouldn't have offered you any job, never mind two, if she didn't think you were worth it."

Chloe's posture sagged. Now she was *really* confused. She wandered over to a nearby chair and slumped onto it. Drake followed and pulled another chair close to hers. He didn't say anything. Just waited for her to talk if she wanted to.

"How did Bliss wind up doing this? And how come she can have children with you?"

Drake cleared his throat. "It wasn't—well…let me start from the beginning. Bliss was offered the job of Muse of the Internet…"

Chloe's jaw dropped. "The whole Internet?"

"Yup. That's when she flatly refused. She knew it would be too much."

"Like I know trying to make the world a safe and assertive place is worthwhile, but much more difficult than Gaia realizes."

"Exactly." Drake did a double take. "Is that what she offered you at first?"

"Yeah." Chloe chuckled. "Can you imagine me being all calm and assertive with a bully twice or three times the size of some poor picked-on person? I'd call him a feckin' arsehole and flatten him. Somehow I don't think that's what she had in mind."

Drake laughed. "Gaia has her heart in the right place, but she doesn't understand how diverse human nature is—even though she created it."

Chloe picked some lint off her jeans. "So, you never said how you were able to have children..."

"Oh, right. Well, ours is an only child. We'll never have another as far as I know. When Bliss refused the job, and I realized I'd lose her in fifty or sixty years, I offered up my immortality."

"You what? You mean, you aren't fireproof?"

"No. Well, I wasn't—for a while. I was made human. I had no special skills and had to fight fires knowing I was in mortal danger. I found a whole new respect for my fellow firefighters who put their lives on the line every single day.

"I tried being careful, as much for Bliss as for myself and my brothers, but when I came home with second degree burns because I had fallen through a floor and couldn't shift or fly... Well, Bliss had a change of heart."

"So, she got in touch with Mother Nature and..." Chloe prompted.

"She offered to compromise with her. She'd become the muse of email for our immortality. She was already pregnant at the time and Gaia assured her that nothing negative would happen to our baby if she took the job right away."

The door to the club opened slowly. Chloe had more questions, but they would have to wait.

Drake rose and strode to the door. When he opened it wider, Ryan and his father stood on the other side.

"Fierro!" Drake said and stuck out his hand to Ryan. Then he nodded to Ryan's father and said, "Captain Fierro." They shook hands in turn.

By this time, Chloe was on her feet. "It's okay, Drake. They can come in."

He raised his brows in question but stood back, allowing the phoenixes—only he didn't know they were phoenixes—entry.

Mr. Fierro senior wandered around the club, admiring the wall of books, the kitchen that had been converted to a bar, running his fingers along the wooden edge of the pool table. Ryan eyed Drake.

Whispering to Chloe, he asked, "Is Drake a…"

"Dragon," Chloe answered in a normal voice.

Drake raised his hand as if to wave.

"And Ryan and Mister—I mean, Captain Fierro are phoenixes," she said to Drake.

He straightened and stared at them for a moment. "I, uh… Sorry. I didn't mean to look so shocked. I've just never known any phoenixes. Didn't even realize they existed except in legend."

Mr. Fierro smirked. "Legends come from *somewhere,* son." He swept his gaze around the room. "But this place should be legendary, and I've never heard of it."

"It's relatively new," Drake said. "There was a bar on Charles Street where we used to congregate. Paranormals, that is. Gaia didn't like it. She thought it was too dangerous for us to be together in a public place." He snorted. "Like maybe the werewolves would shift and get into a brawl with the vamps or something."

As he was laughing, Chloe noticed Mr. Fierro's eyes widening. So were Ryan's, for that matter. Maybe they didn't know these other "legends" were as real as they were.

"Uh…werewolves?" Ryan asked.

Chloe nodded. She didn't really know any personally, so she couldn't tell them a lot. Drake realized his mistake and cleared his throat. "I, uh…guess you didn't know there are a lot of paranormals in this city."

Captain Fierro cocked his head and said, "Do tell."

Drake bit his lower lip, then took a breath. "The bar was an experiment. A vampire owned it and when he made friends with a werewolf, he decided to try to make a place where the different paranormals could gather in safety. He believed we'd all get along if we just took the time to get to know each other better. We face a lot of the same challenges."

Mr. Fierro was staring at Chloe. She just shrugged at him.

"Well, that's the history lesson for the day. I guess I should get going…" Drake said.

Then lightning flashed and Gaia stood in the middle of the room. She was wearing a one-shoulder, white toga belted with a green vine. Her hair was long, loose, and white too. Her unlined face made it impossible to pick an age to assign to her looks.

"Yeah, now that you've spilled the beans, dragon, just pick up your pool cue and leave."

"But it isn't mine," Drake said.

Mother Nature pointed to the door. "Yes it is. Now get out. I have some things to clear up, thanks to your loose tongue."

"Sorry, Gaia. I thought they knew."

"They do now."

Drake left quickly and Mother Nature circled the three remaining creatures. Two phoenixes and one dragon. Presumably, she'd never met the Fierros and vice versa.

"Chloe," she said, "would you please make the introductions?"

Her formality made Chloe nervous. Not only did she remember her name and use it, but she'd asked her specifically to do introductions. *Was this a test?*

Chloe cleared her throat. "Mother Nature, this is Captain Fierro and his son, Ryan Fierro. They either were or are working for the Boston Fire Department, keeping the city you love safe."

Then she turned to the men. "Mr. Fierro, Ryan, this is Mother Nature, also known as Gaia or Goddess. She ah…she sort of takes care of the whole planet."

Gaia reared back and glared at Chloe. "Sort of?"

"I'm sorry. She does! She *does* take care of the whole planet."

Captain Fierro mumbled something under his breath.

Gaia strode over to him. "Well, you're still standing on it, aren't you?" She poked him in the chest. "Which all creatures seem to take for granted, by the way. Even you firefighters. You know what can happen when people are careless or hateful. Yet, you never stop to think about why the whole place hasn't burned to a crisp yet."

Chloe opened her mouth to defend them, but Mother Nature held up one hand and spoke over her.

"Yeah, that's right. I make sure you never get too close to the sun—or too far away. That enough rain falls, but not too much. And still you complain. Oh, boo hoo. It's ninety degrees in the middle of summer. Or, oh no. It's zero in the winter… Cry me a river, people. Oh, wait. That's my job."

Chloe wanted to put a stop to her rant, but she didn't know how without pissing off the powerful goddess. At last, Captain Fierro sputtered and burst out laughing.

Gaia squinted at him in confusion. "What?"

Antonio Fierro, now doubled over, slapped his own knee. "I don't know how you pulled off that lightning bit with your dramatic entrance, but clearly you're not—"

As he spoke, she rose up off the floor and grew larger than life. Then she leaned over him and he shut up. She cocked one eyebrow and he took a step back.

Ryan moved to Chloe's side and wrapped a protective arm around her.

"Um, Mr. Fierro. The Goddess of All doesn't show herself to just anyone. In fact, she rarely interacts with any of us unless there's a driving need. I imagine it would be wise to see why she's here."

Gaia shrank to her usual size and smiled at Chloe as her feet touched the floor. "Thank you, little dragon. Now, as much as I'd like to stay and chat, there is only enough time to say what I need to say and then I'm off to keep a tornado from getting so large it takes out a whole slew of states instead of a few towns."

Mr. Fierro felt around for a chair and sat down hard.

Gaia sighed. "That's better. All right. It has come to

my attention that your family has been doing things a certain way for centuries and for the most part, it has kept you all safe and sound."

Mr. Fierro nodded.

"Well, that may have worked for most of you, but it's not working for these two." She pointed to Ryan and Chloe with her thumb. "I understand you want this one…" she patted Ryan on the head, "to take over as head of the family, even though you'll have to mess up my beautiful design."

"Beg pardon?"

"His face. His spirit. That's the result of many generations of your strongest ancestors. And *you* want to interfere with all of that just for some man-made tradition? Sorry. No. I can't allow that."

"Can't allow? That's not your decision."

Mother Nature rolled her eyes and let out a long sigh. At last she strolled over to him. "You still don't get it. *Everything* is my decision. Whether you live or die is my decision. And you seem to have forgotten, I gave your family a number of options. How many sons do you have again?"

"Seven," he answered proudly.

"And not one of the other six can take over for you?"

"It's tradition that the firstborn—"

"Oh, shut up about tradition. I have no patience for made-up rules. I understand they have their place, but it's not like you need to follow them when plain old common sense says you shouldn't."

Gaia continued. "In this case, you did one thing right. Your son Ryan died and you kept the human population from discovering his paranormal ability to rise from the ashes. As far as they know, nobody comes back from that, and that's what I want them to think."

Mr. Fierro seemed to relax a bit. "We try not to call attention to our abilities, because we know humans would envy us and want to study us, or hate us and want to end us. We'd never be left in peace again."

"That's absolutely correct. See? You're not hopelessly stupid."

He bristled. "We're not stupid at all!"

"Then I suggest you listen to what these two have come up with. They have some good ideas. Meanwhile, you can look at the rest of the young men around your dinner table and find a suitable replacement for yourself. I know you and your wife want to move to a warmer climate and avoid suspicion when your longevity comes into question. Might I suggest the Amazon rain forest?"

"Why there?"

"Less scrutiny. You'll find a few others who want anonymity hiding out there. And maybe you can stand in front of the bulldozers that keep trying to take down my beautiful trees."

Ryan and his father shared a meaningful look.

"Oh! And if you ever expose your paranormal abilities or this club to a human, I'll find you, wherever you are, and…and…" She waved in frustration. "I'm all out of threats, but I'll think of something bad." She nodded once, as if satisfied. "Well, my work here is done. I'd say 'until we meet again,' but I hope we never will." And with that, she disappeared.

Mr. Fierro glanced between Ryan and Chloe. At last he took a deep breath and let it out in a whoosh. "I hate to say it, but she's right."

"About what?" they asked simultaneously.

"About letting you two move to Ireland. I do have several sons."

"Ya think?" Chloe slapped her hand over her mouth.

Mr. Fierro laughed. "Don't worry, 'little dragon.' I love an honest quip." He turned to Ryan. "I'll call an emergency family meeting. Come home tonight and we'll tell the others."

"Chloe should come too," Ryan said.

She sighed. "I may have my own emergency family meeting. Since I go back to work tomorrow, I'd like to do it tonight."

"Fair enough." Ryan gave her a long, languorous kiss, ignoring his father when he cleared his throat.

At last, they broke apart and grinned at each other.

"I might as well not even be in the room," Mr. Fierro said. "See you tonight, Ryan."

Chapter 23

"Well, that's the last one," Amber said when she and Eagan came out of the closet. Literally. "We really need to get a different front door with a peephole instead of a big pane of glass."

They joined the rest of the Arish family in the B and B's living room. Shannon sat on Finn's lap on the sofa. On one side of them sat Chloe, and on the other, Aiden. They were staring in opposite directions, ignoring each other.

Rory took one comfortable armchair and Conlan took the other. Eagan and Amber pulled straight-back chairs away from the wall and over to the group.

"Good. Now we can get started," Rory said.

Everyone remained quiet while he welcomed the family to his home and asked Chloe to make her announcement.

She squirmed slightly, unaccustomed to being in the spotlight, and then came right out with it. "I'm getting married and moving back to Ireland."

Amid congratulations and everyone hugging Chloe, Aiden piped up. "Where in Ireland?"

She faced him squarely. "Ballyhoo, of course. We'll be rehabbing the castle."

"We?" he asked. "You and the firefighter?"

She bristled. "I'm a firefighter too, you know."

"Yeah, yeah. Don't go all feminist on me. I'm just wonderin' where you're goin' to live while this rehabbin' is goin' on? It's not like the castle has running water, heat, or electricity."

"Not yet," she said and grinned, because she knew something he didn't.

"You intend to install those things in a castle from the fourth century? What about the structural integrity? And the historical significance—"

"Shut it, Aiden," she barked. "Don't be causin' trouble just because I chose my heart instead of my duty. Our crown prince is fine with it."

Rory cleared his throat. "About that…"

She snapped her gaze to her brother. "What?"

"Oh…not your decision, luv," Rory said. "You're fine. It's about my bein' crown prince. I hereby abdicate my position, since an absentee ruler makes no sense. I choose to make my life here in Boston with my darlin' fiancée Amber."

Aiden and Eagan gasped and turned their eyes toward Conlan.

Conlan held up his hand to halt their assumption. "I will not be takin' over. I have more important things to do, and the Erin Arishes won the castle fair and square many centuries ago."

Eagan's eyes rounded. "What could possibly be more important than taking over as ruler?"

"A little matter of finding a way to continue the species."

Aiden glared at Chloe. "We *had* a way."

"We never had a way, Aiden." Chloe rose and paced. "Look. There are certain truths that should be stated." She held up one finger. "First, close relatives should not reproduce. Their offspring could be idjits." Holding up two fingers, she said, "Second, the royal lineage passes down through the family from eldest to youngest, be they male or female. The two eldest have abdicated their claim. That leaves me next. Since I intend to actually live in Ballyhoo and restore our childhood home, I will accept the title of crown princess—in name only."

Rory cleared his throat. "I don't recall hearin' anythin' about our parents in the last eight hundred years." His expression became somber. "They came for a visit dressed as beggars. I've since wondered if it wasn't a disguise. Since everyone who could possibly recognize them has long since died and they could have returned at any time, I think we can safely assume they've met their demise."

Conlan solemnly added, "Quite right, Cousin. I have thought so as well."

Aiden moved to his side quickly and whispered in his ear. Since dragons have such sensitive hearing, Chloe caught the gist of it anyway. What she heard surprised her.

Conlan rose and said, "Long live Queen Chloe!" He dropped to one knee and reverently placed his fist over his heart. His brothers did the same. Rory followed suit.

Shannon giggled but slipped off Finn's lap and onto her knees. "Long live me queen sister. May she remember where she came from and never get a big head."

Chloe couldn't help smirking. "All right, all right. I can see how it's goin' to be. Get off your feckin' knees. Let's all return to our seats and speak as equal adults."

As soon as everyone was reseated, she said, "There's one other thing I should let you all know. I have decided to accept Gaia's offered position of muse of fire safety."

Aiden's jaw dropped. "You mean to tell us, you're not only a queen now but a goddess as well?"

Chloe shrugged. "Minor goddess…and the queen thing was your idea."

"Actually, it was Rory's—"

"The jig's up, Cousin," Rory said. "And the others should know. It was Aiden who came to me with the suggestion that we declare our parents dead and make Chloe queen when I formally abdicated tonight."

Chloe turned her surprised gaze on Aiden. "Is that true, Cousin?"

He nodded. "I want you to know that I said nothin' until *after* I knew you were lost to me and goin' to marry the firefighter—I mean the *other* firefighter."

Her smile grew as did her respect for Aiden. He didn't seem to hold a grudge.

"So what does the muse position entail?" he asked.

"I will encourage people to protect themselves from fires, encourage inventers to come up with new and better ways to help them do that, and look after firefighters everywhere."

"That sounds like a tall order," Conlan said.

"'Tis. But not as tall an order as yours. Am I to understand you mean to find another female dragon? How do you expect to do that?"

Conlan smiled. "I'm goin' on a grand adventure. Eagan and Aiden can manage the whiskey-makin' business. I know there's another dragon out there. I can *feel* it."

"Um…I might not return to Ulster right away," Aiden said.

"Why not?" Eagan and Conlan asked simultaneously.

"There's this friend of Amber's I'd like to get to know better."

Amber clapped her hands. "I knew it! I saw the chemistry between you and Candy Marie."

"We took bets on you," Rory added.

"Did you now?"

"Is she a flight attendant too?" Conlan asked.

"Yes," Amber said with a grin. "So she can visit Aiden wherever he is."

Aiden's eyes lit up. "So you think she'd be willin' to fly all the way to Northern Ireland just to see me?"

Amber laughed. "I'd say you could count on it."

Aiden grinned and leaned back in his chair.

"So, Chloe, how long do you think it will take to restore the castle?" Eagan asked.

"A while. There's no rush. Ryan will work with the volunteer fire department in Ballyhoo, updating and improving their methods, while I attend to my muse duties. When we have free time, we'll restore the castle, together."

Aiden scratched his head. "It sounds like you won't have much free time at all."

She glanced at Amber. "Oh, you may be surprised. We have a few tricks up our sleeves as far as time management is concerned."

"It sounds as if your duties have already begun."

"Not yet, but my training will begin soon. Amber will be teaching me whatever I need to know."

Eagan chuckled. "Like how to fly people from the other side of the ocean and land in closets?"

Rory laughed. "The closet is just because disappearin' and reappearin' in full view of a front door, which has a glass inset, is against Mother Nature's rules. I intend to replace that door with a solid one."

"I'll help," Finn offered.

"Thank you, Finn. Now that Chloe is so busy, I'll take you up on that."

"I could help after my four-day shift is over," Chloe said.

"I wouldn't dream of askin' your highness to do manual labor," Rory said with a wink. "You might break a nail."

She frowned. "I might break one on your head, if you tease me like that, Rory Arish."

"Ah, it's good to know that rulin' isn't goin' to change you a bit."

Everyone laughed.

Ryan stood on the emerald-green grass looking out to sea. Chloe strolled up beside him and slipped her arm around his waist. He welcomed her warmth. The breeze off the ocean was a bit chilly, even in May.

"I'd like to bury the power lines if we can," Ryan said. "That way it wouldn't block Shannon and Finn's view, plus the cables should hold more securely against winter weather."

"Winters aren't nearly as bad here as they are in Boston. I can't believe how much snow fell and how heavy it was." She shuddered. "We were lucky there weren't more roof collapses."

He kissed her hair. "They really knew how to build solid roofs in the past."

She chuckled. "Yeah. If one sprung a leak, they just

slapped another roof over it. You should have seen all the layers Rory and I uncovered when we looked at buildin' a roof deck on top of his B and B."

"Hey. Maybe we could…"

"If you say build a deck on top of the turret, I'll have to talk you out of it. I'd like to keep the integrity of the castle on the outside. You can make it as modern as you like on the inside."

He gave her a side hug. "I was going to suggest a patio on the grass, but your idea of modernizing the inside is welcome news."

"Oh. You don't want rock walls and dirt floors?"

"Not so much." He wandered toward the site of the future staircase, taking her with him. "I can see floor-to-ceiling tempered glass windows. Wide wood floors. Sheetrock with modern, but sophisticated wall treatments… Modern plumbing will be a trick, but one I'm willing to puzzle out."

Suddenly they weren't alone.

Gaia stood on his other side. "My muse hasn't picked out her reward yet. Perhaps I can help you with that."

Chloe faced her. "My reward will be toilets?"

Mother Nature shrugged. "Unless you don't want them. After all, your ancestors were used to peeing in cold porcelain bowls which they kept under the beds—"

Chloe gagged. "Ah, no, Goddess. You have the right of it. I became used to indoor plumbin' decades ago and would welcome your help bringin' it into the castle."

"Good. It would be a shame to mar the beautiful facade with whatever waste you had to toss out the windows."

"What facade?" Ryan asked. "I imagine working on

the inside will be tricky enough. I can't ask anyone to put themselves in danger by working on the outside walls."

Gaia rolled her eyes. With a wave of her hand, she created a beautiful stone stairway that led to an oval patio below. "Go ahead. Take a look over the side."

Ryan gaped at Chloe. "Should we trust it will hold us?" he whispered.

Gaia's back stiffened. "If you think I'd allow you to set foot on a structure that might collapse and send you falling to your deaths, you don't have a very high opinion of me."

"It's not that, Goddess. I just imagine you haven't had a lot of building experience."

She snorted. "How you humans try to restrict me with your own limitations! I can do anything you can do, only instantly and better."

"Sorry, Goddess," he said and bowed. "You're absolutely right."

Chloe elbowed him and whispered, "Those are smart words. Keep talking that way."

"I can hear you *think*, little dragon. Never mind whisper."

She aimed her smile at Mother Nature. "I know. I was teasin' my husband."

"Oh. I may never get the hang of this 'teasing' you speak of."

"Mayhaps that's a good thing, Gaia," Chloe said.

Mother Nature nodded. "Yes. And getting back to your reward for taking the modern muse job, I think I can do better than providing bathrooms for your joint project."

Ryan and Chloe focused their attention on her.

Gaia waved her hand and a huge pile of lumber

appeared. "I believe you wanted wide solid hard-wood floors?"

Ryan breathed deeply, "Shit. Yeah, I did."

She waved at another spot on the grass and a pile of sheetrock appeared. "And walls…" Then suddenly a structure popped up between the two piles of supplies. "Inside you'll find tools, glass panels, fixtures…basically everything you'll need down to the finish nails and caulking."

"I'll be damned," Ryan mumbled.

"No, you won't." Mother Nature said. "I don't do that to people. Oh, by the way…" A man appeared before them. "Here's an architect to help you design your dream."

The man scratched his head and mumbled something about not realizing he'd had that much to drink.

"Will you need laborers, or do you two want to build the whole thing yourselves?" Gaia asked.

Chloe squeezed Ryan's hand. "I think we want to be involved as much as possible, but we could use one completed bedroom and bath."

One side of Ryan's lip curved up. "I can think of six strapping young men who'd be willing to help." He turned toward the architect. "We'll need to build a few guest rooms for family visits."

"Mayhaps ten or so?" Chloe added. "We've cousins as well."

"True."

The architect whipped out his pencil and a pad of paper and started jotting down notes. "Maybe a few guest suites, with their own baths?"

"To be sure." Chloe looked to Gaia. "How many baths did you provide for?"

Mother Nature rolled her eyes. Suddenly the storage shed doubled in size. "Eleven," she said with a smug smile. "Let me know when you get to the furnishings. It sounds like you'll need a huge dining table. I think the one from Camelot might be about the right size."

"Camelot?" The architect gasped. "I thought that place was a legend."

Ryan, Chloe, and Gaia all answered at once. "Legends have to come from somewhere…"

Keep reading for an excerpt of

HOW TO DATE A
DRAGON

from Ashlyn Chase's Flirting with Fangs series!

Chapter 1

"I'M NEVER ATTENDING A DESTINATION WEDDING again."

Bliss Russo dragged her garment bag and carry-on up the ramp to her Boston apartment building. Her purse had fallen off her shoulder ten minutes ago and dangled from her wrist. She needed the other hand to hold her cell phone to her ear so she could bitch to her friend Claudia.

"Oh, poor you. Someone made you go to Hawaii." Claudia chuckled. "The bastards."

"Seriously... do you know how long the flight is? Or I should say flights. First there's the leg from Boston to L.A., then L.A. to Honolulu, and finally Honolulu to Maui. Two days later, I go from Maui to Honolulu. Then Honolulu to L.A. Then L.A. to Boston. Plus I had to follow Hawaiian wedding tradition—at least what the bride's parents assured us was the tradition—and party all night. I haven't slept for days."

"You're exaggerating."

"No, I'm not. Unless you count the five-minute nap I took at LAX. I was so exhausted, I woke up on the chair next to me when the guy I had apparently fallen asleep on got up and left."

"Sorry. Okay, you're right. It was a lousy, miserable thing to make you do. So where are you now?"

"Almost home. In fact, I'll probably lose you in

the elevator. Give me a few days to sleep and I'll call you back."

"Call by Thursday if you can, and let me know if you want to go out Saturday night."

Bliss jostled the door open, and one of the residents held it while she maneuvered her luggage through. "I shouldn't. I worked a little harder and got a few days ahead so I could go to this damn wedding in the first place, but I really can't afford to take any more time off. The competition will crush me."

"That's what you get for landing in the finals of your dream reality show. What is it? America's Next Great Greeting Card Designer?"

"It's not called America's Next… oh, forget it. I'm at the elevator now and I'm too tired to care. I'll call you."

"Okay, sugar. Sweet dreams."

"Thanks." Bliss hung up and dropped her phone into the bowels of her purse. She yanked and stuffed her luggage into the tiny elevator, which she rode to the second floor. Eventually, she dragged everything to her door, rattled the key in her lock, and brought it all into her bedroom. Passing out on top of her bed fully dressed seemed like the only good idea she was capable of having, so she donned a sleep mask, did a face-plant, and stayed that way.

Hours later—or maybe days—Bliss awoke to a deafening blare. Still disoriented, she had no idea what the hell the noise was or, for that matter, if it was night or day. She tore off the sleep mask and still couldn't tell what was going on. But what was that smell?

*Oh. My. God. Smoke! That ear-piercing screech is
the friggin' fire alarm.*

Bliss tried to remember what to do. *Oh yeah, crouch
down low and get the fuck out of Dodge.* Thank the good
Lord she lived on the second floor, because she couldn't
use the stupid elevator.

Bliss remembered just in time to put her hand to the
door before opening it. It didn't feel as though there were
an inferno on the other side. Staying low, she opened the
door. The smoke was so thick she could barely see. She
held her breath and charged toward the end of the hall.

Suddenly, her head hit something firm and she fell
backward. "Oomph." The sharp intake of breath resulted
in a coughing fit.

Looking up to see what she had hit, she realized she
had just head-butted a firefighter's ass.

He swiveled and mumbled through his mask.
"Really? I'm here to save you, and you spank me?"

Despite her earlier panic, Bliss felt a whole lot safer
and started to giggle. *Oh no. My computer!* "Wait, I
have to go back…"

"No. You need to get out of here, now." The firefighter
lifted her like she weighed nothing—an amazing feat in
itself—then carried her the wrong way down the rest of
the hallway, through the fire door, and down the stairs.

"Wait!" She grasped him around the neck and tried to
see his face through watering eyes.

His mask, helmet, and shield covered almost his
whole head, but she caught a glimpse of gold eyes and a
shock of hair, wheat-colored with yellow streaks, angled
across his forehead. She thought it odd that the city
would let firefighters dye their hair like rock musicians.

As soon as they'd made it to the street, she could see better and noticed his eyes were actually green and almond shaped. She must have imagined the gold color. He set her down near the waiting ambulance and pulled off his mask.

What a hottie! But I don't have time for that now. She staggered slightly as she tried to head back toward the door.

He grabbed her arm to steady her. "Hey," he shouted to one of the paramedics. "Give her some oxygen."

"No, I'm fine. I don't need any medical attention." *Thanks to the gorgeous hunk with the weird hair.*

"Please… let them check you out."

"I'd rather let *you* check me out." She covered her mouth and grinned. "Sorry. It must be the smoke inhalation.

He laughed. "Seriously? First you grab my ass, and now you're hitting on me?"

"I didn't 'grab your ass.' For your information, I ran face-first into your… behind."

"Oh. Well, pardon me for being in the way."

His smile almost stopped her heart—or was it the lack of oxygen? Regardless, she *had to* rip herself away from him and get her computer out of the building before it melted. No matter how hard she pulled, he didn't budge.

"You need to go back in there for my computer. Apartment twenty-five, halfway down the hall."

He took off his gloves. "Look, I'm sorry, miss, but if I went back in there now, my chief would have my hide."

"But my whole life is on that computer. I'm in the finale of a huge TV competition."

He didn't seem impressed, so she tried again.

"It's my greeting card business and all my newest designs are there. This show would pay for a whole ad campaign and give me fifty grand if I win." Realizing she sounded like a babbling idiot, she pressed on. "I've worked so hard to make it this far. If I lose my work, I'll never catch up. I'll wind up presenting a half-assed portfolio, and not only can I forget about winning, but it could ruin me!"

———

Drake couldn't believe what he was hearing. His weakness might be beautiful brunettes, but did she honestly expect him to risk his life for an object that could be replaced? Could she not see smoke pouring out of the building? Sure, he could probably manage it, being fireproof and all, but after the chewing out he got the last time…

"Don't you keep a backup file online?"

"No. I don't trust the Internet," she said with the saddest expression in her beautiful brown eyes. "There are too many hackers out there, and this greeting card competition is outrageously competitive. Pleeeease!"

All this hoopla for a piece of paper that reads, "Roses are red. Violets are blue?" The brunette didn't appear to be insane, no matter how stupid this reality show sounded. There were crazier things on TV.

His chief had already warned Drake about risking his neck and told him to knock off taking stupid chances. He'd lucked out the last time. The mayor, a big dog lover, heard that Drake had gone back into a two-alarm blaze to rescue a greyhound. Then Mr. Mayor made the chief disregard any thought of suspending Drake by giving him a medal. But that sort of luck wouldn't hold, especially if this insubordination was about an inanimate object.

Drake reached out and physically turned the woman around so she could see the inferno behind her. The feel of her soft, warm skin sent an unexpected jolt of awareness through him.

Her hands flew to cover her mouth, and the same sad, desperate sound all fire victims made as they witnessed the destruction and loss of something precious eked out. The tears forming in her eyes did him in.

If he weren't fireproof, running back into that building would toast him like a marshmallow, but being a dragon, he knew he could do it.

"Ah, hell." Before anyone could stop him, he dashed in the side entrance. He could always say he thought he heard a call for help.

"Stop. Oh crap," was what he really heard. Apparently the brunette had changed her mind, but he was committed now.

Second floor, halfway down the hall, he repeated to himself until he found it. She had left her door open. Fortunate for him, not so much for her apartment. Smoke and flames were everywhere. He felt the familiar tingle just under his skin that signaled an impending shift. *Fan-fucking-tastic*. Skin became scales. Fingers became claws. His neck elongated, and out popped his tail, creating an unsightly bulge in the back of his loose coveralls. His wings were cramped and folded up under his jacket, but it couldn't be helped.

His sight was greatly improved in his alternate form,

and he spotted the Mac on her glass tabletop. The flames hadn't reached it yet, so he did his best to grab it with his eagle-like talons and carry it against his chest.

Lumbering down the hall, he wondered where, and if, he'd be able to shift back before anyone saw him. *Maybe it's cooler in the basement—but what if I get trapped down there?*

Instead of heading down another level, he opened the emergency door just enough to toss the laptop onto the grass outside. The outside air was so much cooler that he thought he might be able to shift back right there.

Concentrating on his human form, he inhaled the fresh air and sensed his head and body shrinking and compacting. He glanced down and saw his human hands again. His back felt enormously better without squished wings digging into it.

Ah...I made it undetected.

Or had he? The brunette was standing a few feet away, wide-eyed and open mouthed—hugging her computer.

Acknowledgments

Major thanks go to Susan Vallera, a Massachusetts firefighter, who let me interview her, gave me a tour of the fire station, and made me a cup of real firefighter coffee. (It wasn't that bad…with lots of cream.)

Also to another Massachusetts firefighter, Tom Madigan, who beta reads all my firefighting scenes and wipes the potential egg off my face.

Thanks, of course, to my wonderful critique partner, Mia Marlowe, a.k.a. Lexie Eddings, who keeps improving my first drafts, and to my editor, Cat Clyne. She "gets" my sense of humor and has one of her own — thank goodness! When many travels derailed my writing, she gave me a deadline extension and just said, "Make it exactly how you want it." She's awesome.

Big love to my agent, Nicole. Without her in my corner I'd be a lot less successful with contracts and such. By the way, she just landed me a five-book contract to tell the Fierro brothers' stories! Stay tuned for news of this new series!

About the Author

Ashlyn Chase describes herself as an Almond Joy bar: a little nutty, a little flaky, but basically sweet, wanting only to give her readers a satisfying experience.

She holds a degree in behavioral sciences, worked as a psychiatric RN for fifteen years, and spent a few more years working for the American Red Cross. She credits her sense of humor to her former careers since comedy helped preserve whatever was left of her sanity. She is a multi-published, award-winning author of humorous erotic and paranormal romances, represented by the Seymour Agency.

Ashlyn lives in beautiful New Hampshire with her true-life hero husband who looks like Hugh Jackman with a salt-and-pepper dye job, and they're owned by a spoiled brat cat.

Ashlyn loves to hear from readers!

Visit www.ashlynchase.com to sign up for her newsletter. She's also on Facebook (AuthorAshlynChase), Twitter (@GoddessAsh), Yahoo groups (ashlyns newbestfriends), and you can ask her to sign your ebook at www.authorgraph.com.

Billionaire in Wolf's Clothing

by Terry Spear

USA Today Bestselling Author

—∿∿—

He wants answers…

Real estate mogul werewolf Rafe Denali didn't get where he is in life by being a pushover. When sexy she-wolf Jade Ashton nearly drowns in the surf outside his beach house, he knows better than to bring her into his home and his heart. But there's something about her that brings out his strongest instincts.

Rafe has good reason to be suspicious. Jade Ashton and her baby son are pawns in an evil wolf's fatal plan. How can Jade betray the gorgeous man who rescued her? But if she doesn't, her baby will die, and her own life hangs in the balance.

To get to the truth, Rafe is going to have to gain Jade's trust. If he can do that, he just might be her last—and best—hope…

—∿∿—

Praise for Terry Spear:

"Terry Spear has a gift for bringing her *lupus garous* to life and winning the hearts of readers." —*Paranormal Haven*

For more Terry Spear, visit:

www.sourcebooks.com

Undiscovered

Amoveo Rising

by Sara Humphreys

Award-winning author Sara Humphreys expands the world of the Amoveo Legend with dragon shapeshifters!

—◆◆◆—

In a world where shapeshifters and humans live uneasily side by side, and where dragons haven't been seen in over five hundred years, shapeshifter Rena McHale from the Fox Clan dreams every night of a gorgeous dragon shifter. Zander Lorens's Dragon Clan powers have been cursed and he's been aimlessly roaming the planet for weary centuries. When he finally meets Rena, he knows that she is what he's been searching for all this time…

—◆◆◆—

Praise for Sara Humphreys:

"Spellbinding… This fast-paced, jam-packed thrill ride will delight paranormal romance fans." —*Publishers Weekly* for *Undone*

"Humphreys' stories get better with each book! The world that she has created is so fascinating, and the characters so engaging, that each new book is like catching up with old friends." —*RT Book Reviews*, 4.5 Stars, Top Pick for *Unclaimed*

For more Sara Humphreys, visit:

www.sourcebooks.com

A Promise of Fire

The Kingmaker Chronicles

by Amanda Bouchet

Kingdoms will rise and fall for her...

Catalia "Cat" Fisa lives disguised as a soothsayer in a traveling circus. She is perfectly content avoiding the danger and destiny the Gods—and her homicidal mother—have saddled her with. That is, until Griffin, an ambitious warlord from the magic-deprived south, fixes her with his steely gaze and upsets her illusion of safety forever.

But not if she can help it

Griffin knows Cat is the Kingmaker, the woman who divines the truth through lies. He wants her as a powerful weapon for his newly conquered realm—until he realizes he wants her for much more than her magic. Cat fights him at every turn, but Griffin's fairness, loyalty, and smoldering advances make him hard to resist and leave her wondering if life really does have to be short, and lived alone.

"Fantasy romance at its finest! Fall in love with these delicious characters." —Darynda Jones, *New York Times* bestselling author

For more Amanda Bouchet, visit:

www.sourcebooks.com